INNER DEMONS

Gloria Oliver

DEDICATION

To all the awesome folks responsible for the show
"Supernatural." My very first obsession.

CONTENTS

Also by Gloria Oliver

Novels:
Cross-eyed Dragon Troubles (YA Fantasy)
In the Service of Samurai (YA Fantasy))
Inner Demons (Urban Fantasy)
Jewel of the Gods (Fantasy)
The Price of Mercy (Fantasy)
Vassal of El (Fantasy)
Willing Sacrifice (YA Fantasy)

Coming in 2019:
Alien Redemption (SF)

Novelettes:
Charity and Sacrifice

Has short stories in the following Anthologies:
Tales From a Lone Star
A Lone Star in the Sky
Ladies of Trade Town
A Time To … Volume 2
Ripple Effect
The Four Bubbas of the Apocalypse
Houston: We've Got Bubbas
The Best of the Bubbas of the Apocalypse
Flush Fiction

ACKNOWLEDGMENTS

To the folks at Mundania Press – thank you for having faith. It was sad to see you go.   You will not be forgotten.

CHAPTER ONE

"Getting a little excited, are we?" I couldn't keep the grin out of my voice as I kicked off my shoes and dug my toes into the carpet and stretched. Getting home in the evenings was one of the best perks of the day. Switching the phone to my other hand, I picked up my low heeled pumps and stepped into the bedroom.

"Yes. No? Mostly I'm totally stressing out! Richie is useless at this stuff. He's got no idea that Peach, Taffeta Peach, and Candy Peach aren't in *any* way the same color." Debbie sighed from the other end of the line. "Honestly, he could try a little harder. We'll only get married once."

I didn't have any idea what the differences between those colors were either but figured it wasn't the time to say so. I tucked the shoes away in the closet and grabbed a pair of gray sweat pants and an old Beatles t-shirt, feeling the day slide off my shoulders as I changed. "You've known he's been color impaired for years, love won't change that. Or have you forgotten his color choices for the college mixer two years ago?" Drifting to the kitchen, I pulled down my favorite cup, chipped handle and all, and filled it with water and stuck it in the microwave to heat.

A stifled giggle came from the other end of the line. "What a disaster! That won't ever be happening again on my watch."

"I should hope not." Grinning, I brought out my tea colander and opened the cabinet to pick the flavor of the evening. Blueberry Cheesecake Tea seemed just the thing.

"We're still on for this weekend, right?" A slight note of insecurity bled through.

I worked hard not to smile. Though I usually wasn't much into fashion or agonizing over what cake flavoring would please most people, I'd do almost anything for Debbie. "Of course, looking forward to it."

"I love you, Tam."

"I love you, too. But don't tell Richie, he'll get jealous."

Debbie laughed. "It's a secret. Pick you up at nine."

I hung up just as the microwave dinged. Pulling out the mug, I put it on a tray with everything else needed, and went to the living room, looking forward to stretching out on my gray couch and sipping my tea.

I'd just set the tray down when I noticed an odd smell…like rotten eggs. I half turned, then…

A pair of headlights was coming right for me.

I froze, my breath catching at my throat, my brain refusing to accept the impossible change.

The car swerved at the last moment, and time slowed around me as a flush of adrenaline hit my system. The blare of a pressed horn crashed into my ears.

The dark blue Oldsmobile missed me by mere inches, the glow of streetlights reflecting from its sides. Humid wind whipped over me, trying to drag me along in the car's wake. The stench from the exhaust coiled about me, and I spun around to watch the trailing red tail lights.

"Lunatic!" An arm shot out the window, the middle finger held up as an extra commentary on the near miss.

The car never even slowed.

This was real.

Other pairs of headlights bore down my way. Fear spiked through me, yelling at me to get the hell out of there. I tripped when I took my first panicked step, the shoes on my feet feeling strange and awkward. I glanced down and saw I was wearing white boots with six-inch heels. Worse, I was also wearing a dark sequined dress that only covered a small part of my upper thighs.

I wasn't a prude, but I had taste, dammit, and this get up just wasn't me. I stumbled toward the sidewalk to my right, only too aware of the traffic heading toward me.

I almost collapsed once I made it, the high heels messing with my center of gravity. A Shell gas station and a combination KFC/Taco Bell sat in front of me. The location didn't look familiar, though, at the moment, nothing did.

How did I get here?

Panic nibbled at the back of my mind, confusion clouding everything.

I slowly turned where I stood and spotted a freeway with an overpass on my right. Across the blacktop street was a bank and several grassy lots set back from the curb. The street sign said Beechnut Street. That rang a bell—could I still be in Houston? Just thinking it gave me hope. At the moment, though, it wouldn't have surprised me to find out I was on another planet entirely.

Chilled, I rubbed my arms, even as a bead of sweat ran down my neck. A small purse on a long chain strap smacked against my thigh. I brought it close, never having seen it before, and opened it. Wads of loose cash lay inside, as well as a tube of lipstick and a set of keys hanging off a skull keychain. There was no driver's license or other type of ID. No cell phone, either. I couldn't tell if the purse was even actually mine. Yet the shape of one of the keys looked familiar. I was pretty sure it belonged to my apartment.

It looked like I had cash, what I hoped was my key,

and I was possibly in my city. This meant I could get back home to things I knew.

Home—yes, getting home sounded excellent right now.

Taking a deep breath, I felt slightly more in control. Yes, home, I needed to get myself home. That was a plan, something to aim for. I half walked, half waddled toward the KFC/Taco Bell, hoping to find a pay phone or beg to borrow someone's cell. I'd never worn such tall heels. They tried to sink into the grass as I cut across the strip to the parking lot. As I neared the bank of glass windows advertising value meals and combo platters, I spotted my reflection and came to a complete stop.

The image that mirrored my movements was and wasn't me. I had screaming platinum blonde hair. Straight and startling in its color, it dropped down to my shoulders. It couldn't be real. No matter how many straighteners I used on my hair, it'd never been that cooperative. A shaking hand with platinum, luminescent nail polish rose up to touch the hair. After a quick inspection, I realized it was a wig. Though I wasn't considered that dark-skinned, especially when compared to the rest of my family, out here, my face and eyes seemed to suck out the light, especially with my face being framed by the platinum hairpiece, my eyes shaded with glittering eye shadow and lips with matching lipstick. The black and way too short sequined dress showed stripes of startling white and matched the tall-heeled white boots that rose up to my knees. I wasn't sure if I looked more like a hooker out of a cheap 60's cop show, an extra out of an old Soul Train rerun, or some exotic alien in a B-movie showing on the Syfy Channel. Either way, it wasn't me.

I swayed where I stood, the surreal feeling of it all

making me dizzy. I leaned against the glass door, no longer trusting my legs. How did I come to be dressed like this or be at this place? I liked to have fun as much as anyone, but I wasn't a raving party girl. Some might even call me boring since my idea of a good time typically consisted of staying at home dressed in my sweats, curled up on the couch with a good book. So why?

Darkness prickled at the edges of my vision, so I scrunched down and placed my head between my knees while trying to force my breathing to slow, sure I was close to hyperventilating. The accountant in me whispered that all numbers added up, even if you didn't have every bit of data. All you had to do was find them. What came in always had to balance what came out, even though it might not look like it. I just needed to hold it together long enough to find all the pieces—then everything would make sense. Everything.

But to do that, I needed to keep it together—I needed to stick to my plan of getting home. My breathing slowed, and that in turn brought down the hammering in my heart.

Feeling slightly calmer, I gingerly stood up.

The night air pressed in around me, hot and sticky with humidity, not the usual norm for April. But with Texas, you just never knew. The odd thought, however, helped ground me.

I reached out for the handle on the glass door and then went inside to try to borrow a phone and get back to things I knew.

CHAPTER TWO

The pimple-faced kid behind the counter ogled me as I came up trying to keep my balance on the boots' high heels. You'd think he'd never seen a psychedelically dressed black woman before. The thought made me giggle, which only served to scare me. I was losing it.

"What's the street address here?"

"Uh, 9836 Beechnut."

Then the hard part. "And the city?"

That got me a raised brow. "Houston, of course."

The wave of relief at hearing I was still in my home city made me weak at the knees. "Do you have a pay phone?"

Instead of answering he pointed back toward the bathrooms. He was no longer ogling but stared at me to determine if I was about to cause trouble.

"Thanks." I put as much heartfelt gratitude as I could to try to ease his suspicions, already having had more than my fill of weirdness for one night. "I'll have a medium Coke, please."

The ten I put on the counter seemed to alleviate his worries more than my smile had. As long as he gave me some change for the phone, I didn't care.

I took the empty cup and my money and made the call. The cab showed up less than twenty minutes later.

The Yellow Cab added to my sense of ease, the bright cars a familiar part of the Houston landscape. The driver didn't bat an eye at my 'loud' appearance, for which I was grateful. I gave him my address, and we got underway.

My eyes stung as we came within sight of my apartment complex. I'd never been so happy to see anything in my life. I paid the driver and then just stood at the security gate staring at the white clubhouse with its dark red Spanish tiled roof. I managed to make it to the clunky keypad without falling on my face and slipped inside the complex.

My steps echoed eerily into the dark as I followed the sidewalk amidst the manicured trees and lawn toward building 4C. My eager steps slowed as I got close. Growing dread bubbled up past my previous elation.

I came to a stop five steps from my apartment door.

My last memories, before finding myself on that dark street alone, were of the apartment. So whatever had happened to me had started here. There was nothing to say it couldn't happen again.

My arms and legs broke out in goosebumps.

The red door with its silver 102 below the peephole, the tiled entryway covered by the dark wood underside of the stairs leading to the apartment above—it had always been a welcomed sight. Yet for reasons I couldn't name, it now seemed alien and menacing. I shifted from one foot to the other, rubbing my arms with my hands while staring at it, feeling cold though the night was warm.

I'd never been one to back down, though—not with the pushers trying to hook us on drugs in middle school, not with the racists that harassed me in high school, or even the few prejudiced college students or teachers at Rice. I hadn't run from any of that then, and I wouldn't start doing it now. Nothing was going to stop me from going into my own apartment. There might be answers there.

Yet those last few steps ended up being harder to manage than anything I'd done before. Dread and fear mingled inside me, throwing warnings at me, yelling at me not to do this, that I'd be sorry, and I didn't understand why. My throat clogged up tight.

Concentrating on keeping my breathing steady, I took the last step to the door. The spot between my shoulder blades twinged. I glanced behind me, but there was no one there. I reached for the key in the small handbag and felt my fear double as I saw the skull keychain again. It wasn't me, it wasn't mine. My hand shook as I inserted the key into the lock and turned it.

The euphoria because it worked lasted less than a moment, for an open door meant I could go inside. It was the last thing I really wanted to do.

I pushed the door open but didn't go in. The twinge between my shoulders grew painful. The interior of the apartment was dark. Taking a deep breath and holding it, I reached past the threshold and flicked on the interior hall light.

I exhaled with one long breath of relief as the light showed me nothing but the familiar. The space before me was still the same white, gray, and red tile of the foyer, the plush gray carpet filling the hall. I could even see the edge of my comfy couch just where it should be. Chiding myself for my bizarre apprehension, I took a tentative step inside.

Nothing changed. Everything looked exactly as it should.

I closed the door behind me and locked it.

Never taking my gaze off the hallway before me, I unzipped the uncomfortable boots and took them off. I held onto one of them, twisted around with the spiked heel in front in case I needed an impromptu weapon. Though I knew this was home and everything seemed fine, that heavy sense of dread was still clamped tight to my chest. I inched forward, listening for anything untoward.

My hand went around the corner and switched on the kitchen lights. Brightness flooded the room and bled out into the living room over the open counter.

I spotted a red flowing lava lamp on the coffee table. A shiver ran down my back. I didn't own a lava lamp. Had someone broken in here while I'd been gone? Steering away from the thought, I quickly moved around the room and switched on every light then surveyed the place again. The twinge grew into a yank between my shoulders as I noticed other little changes.

Food stains on my gray couch. Water rings on my polished coffee table. Dust on the picture frames and floor corners.

Dust…

I'd only been gone for a few hours…why would there be dust? I shied away from the question, sure I wouldn't like the answer and instead moved from room to room turning on more and more lights.

At my bedroom, I swayed at the doorway, my chest so tight I couldn't breathe. The room was nothing like I'd left it. Gone were the off-white, comforting, textured walls. Instead, it was currently painted in blood red with a black crackle overlay. A metallic black four-poster bed with red satin sheets and comforter had replaced my maple sleigh style bed. A huge flat screen TV took up a chunk of one wall where I'd had several oil landscapes. Video recording equipment sat beneath it, as well as standing lights. New shelving on the walls held more lava lamps of different colors and an assortment of accouterments that only belonged in X-rated or gothic films.

I stepped back, shaking my head in denial. This

couldn't be my apartment. That wasn't my room.

Turning around, I gazed at my home office. Before I could think about what I was doing, I stepped inside, the familiarity of the room making it that much easier to ignore the other.

The computer was on, a screen saver of running half naked nuns flashing on the screen. I leaped forward and hit the mouse to make it go away. Popups for AIM messages were all over the screen. The login was for someone called ChocolateLover. I scanned a few of them thinking they might hold a clue. I quickly regretted it.

Requests for sex talks. Queries as to when ChocolateLover would be on tonight. Demands she give in to their fantasies. Some even offered money or goods if she'd only meet with them in person.

Grabbing the mouse, I frantically closed all the rest of the boxes, having had enough. Then I moved the cursor down to the corner for the system date. My eyes grew wider and wider until I thought they'd pop out of my head. The computer said it was Friday, July 23rd.

I let go of the mouse as if it'd bit me. No, it was April, April 15th! It couldn't possibly be July. This was all a joke. A sick twisted joke.

I grabbed the mouse again and double-clicked the icon to pull up my browser. I clicked the Favorites folder and then the link to the US Time website. The screen pulled up showing the time, day, and date—July 23rd.

No… No…

My knees quivered. Then I fell down to the carpet, my hands shaking, my brain numb.

This couldn't be happening. This couldn't be right!

Someone had to know what was going on. Someone had to be able to help me. Debbie! The thought of my best friend gave me a jolt and I could think straight again.

Debbie would have some idea, some clue.

Despite the tiny voice in the back of my head saying that was unlikely, it was still something to cling to. I rose shakily to my feet and stumbled back out to the kitchen. I hadn't seen a trace of my iPhone, but I'd kept the landline after setting up DSL so I could use that instead.

The phone had changed from a non-descript cordless to a giant set of red lips. Trying not to think about it, I picked up the top.

I punched in Debbie's number, heart racing, ideas popping up one after the other as to what might have happened and being dismissed just as quickly. Lost Time. I'd heard the term but couldn't remember if it related to aliens or mental conditions or what. Aliens, that was an even more remote possibility. This wasn't the X-Files. Aliens made great TV but didn't hold up to reality. Split personalities though, schizophrenia, those were real things, documented, studied. But I wasn't mental. I would have noticed something before this, wouldn't I?

The phone started ringing on the other end and I forced my thoughts to still. I held my breath as the other end picked up. Tears prickled the corner of my eyes as I heard the familiar voice.

"Hello?" She sounded hesitant, and that's when I realized I'd never called her from the landline before. My name didn't show on her cell phone, only the number.

"Debbie, thank God. I'm so glad to hear your voice!"

There was only silence from the other end. It'd been three months, (oh god, three months!) maybe she didn't recognize my voice? "Debbie?"

"Who is this?" The question was hard, cold. I didn't understand it.

"It's Tamara. Listen, something weird is going—"

The phone went dead. She'd hung up on me… I

pulled the phone from my ear and stared at it, dread chomping at me from the inside.

I redialed. The phone rang three times then went to voicemail. I didn't leave a message, just disconnected and tried again. Why wouldn't she pick up? My sense of dread jumped up a couple of more notches. By the third time, I was desperate. "Debbie, please! I don't understand. I need your help! Something weird is going on. My apartment, my clothes, the time. Look, I, I don't get any of this, but if I, if I somehow did something to offend you… I can come over if you don't want to talk on the phone. You're my best friend, and I really need your help."

I hung up and stared at the phone, willing her to call me back. But as the minutes ticked away, the certainty that she wouldn't grew inside me. Yet why would I think that?

The lip phone shrilled out, making me jump though I'd hoped for a call.

Caller ID on the answering machine flashed Debbie's number. I felt a shot of hope. It didn't last long.

"*If?* You say *if* you did something to offend me?" Her breathing was fast and heavy. "Don't you dare get within a hundred feet of my house! If I see you, I'll shoot you dead!"

She was mad, more than mad, furious. I'd known Debbie since we hooked up as lab partners in college. As all friends do, we'd had some fights on occasion but never had she sounded so full of rage. "Debbie, I…I don't understand. What happened?"

There was a harsh laugh on the other end of the line. It was full of bitterness, and thorns, and wasn't anything I'd ever heard from her before. "Okay, I'll play." Another bark of a laugh. "Richie. You remember Richie, my fiancé, don't you, bitch?"

It wasn't anger. It was hate, pure unadulterated hate and it was aimed at me. I almost dropped the phone at the realization. How long had this been building inside her? How long had she been waiting for an opportunity to vent her rage? "Y-yes?"

"And June first, June first rings a bell, doesn't it?"

Oh no, I'd missed the wedding. Debbie had talked of nothing for months except being a June bride. I was supposed to be her maid of honor. Was that where all of this was coming from? Deep from inside me a whisper said 'no.' I was cold all over. "Yes."

"And I bet you remember the night you went to see him, too. The one where you got him drunk. And gave him pills. Where you had sex with him?" Again the bitter laugh rang in my ears. Numbness crawled up my arm and spread all over me. I'd done what?

"How you then brought him to my house at three in the morning and left him on my doorstep naked and bombed out of his mind for me to find? Is any of that ringing any *bells* for you?"

No, it wasn't. But what was worse was the fact I didn't doubt her in the least. As if I already knew it was true. Which made no sense at all. I would have never done something like this to her, never. Yet seemingly I had.

Disgust and horror swelled up my throat. "Debbie, I…"

"Just die, *bitch*, and never, ever call me again!"

The line went dead, but I barely noticed. I slid to the floor, the phone falling from my hand.

CHAPTER THREE

I don't know how long I just sat there and stared at nothing, the unhooked phone bleating at me in protest. But at some point, I crawled to the doorway and used the doorjamb to drag myself back up onto shaking legs.

Stumbling into the bathroom, I closed and locked the door as if the flimsy prefab could hold the awful world at bay.

I stripped, kicking the alien clothes and thong underwear into a corner, throwing the platinum wig after them. Avoiding my reflection, I turned on the shower and climbed inside while it was warming up. Goosebumps flared over my skin. Reaching for the soap, I cringed as I saw that had changed as well. Rather than the simple soap dish and hooked bottles for shampoo and conditioner, there was a shelved contrivance. My bar of Oil of Olay was gone, replaced by some brand I didn't recognize and which smelled of musk. There were at least six brands of hair products as well as small flasks of oils and perfumes. A vibrator sat at attention in the corner of the highest shelf.

Turning away, I stepped under the stream of water, a shiver wracking through me. My home, my whole life, had been violated. But why? How? If only I could understand what was happening.

I scrubbed my face, my hair, every last inch of me. I kept staring at the drain thinking I would see something coming off of me, something to explain why everything had changed, but there was nothing.

Shivering as the water eventually turned cold, I shut off the shower and stepped out. I flinched as I reached for a towel, only now noticing their blood red color. Pushing myself, I took it anyway and used it rather than drip everywhere. Wrapped in it, I stared only at the carpet as I returned back to that awful bedroom to search for some clothes.

Opening drawer after drawer I just grew more and more disgusted. I'd always believed in having certain lacy items in reserve for special dates, but what I found bordered on the ridiculous, and so many of them looked to have been used as regular wear: thongs with the barest strings, crotchless panties, edible underwear, bras so sheer they left nothing to the imagination. There were even a few items I possessed no idea what they were or how anyone would wear them. I tore through the drawers' contents, dumping the things on the floor as I grew more and more desperate to find something, anything close to normal.

Fighting back tears, I turned to the closet, already sure my search there would fare no better but refusing to give up. On one side I was surprised to find all my work jackets, slacks, skirts and blouses intact. Yet all my casual wear was gone, replaced by other things. As I shied away from leather items and slick black and white plastic get-ups, I noticed a box half hidden in the back. Not daring to hope, I pounced on it. The word 'useless' had been written on the side in my handwriting. I'd never seen it before.

Opening it flooded me with instant comfort. I'd found my non-work clothes—some of them, anyway. At the moment that didn't matter, I was just thrilled to find something I knew without a doubt belonged to me, the 'me' I'd known all my life, not whatever or whoever I'd been for the last three months.

Because that really was the only explanation, wasn't it? That I'd been someone else. Despite the fact it still made no sense whatsoever.

But I couldn't deal with that, not at the moment. It was hard enough just swallowing the fact I'd somehow lost three months of my life. The likelihood I might be insane would have to wait.

After dragging out the box from the closet, I put things back where they belonged, kicking or throwing the other stuff toward the tiny trashcan in the corner. Some Hanes for Her and my flannel pajamas worked beautiful magic on my frightened soul. Going to the hall closet, I grabbed one of the extra blankets I kept there and headed for the living room. No way was I spending the night in that metallic four-poster bed.

I wanted, needed normalcy, and of the few rooms I'd braved looking at so far, the living room was the least changed, or unchanged enough I could pretend the rest of it away—for a while.

So I snuggled into the blanket on the couch, leaving all the lights on and stared at the mottled ceiling and wished for sleep to come so I could escape all this.

It was a long time coming…

CHAPTER FOUR

I sat up on the couch, breathing hard, panic bolting through my system. Something dreadful had happened, something beyond horrible. It jiggled in the back of my mind, but I couldn't quite grasp it. The answers were there, I knew they were, yet I didn't want to see them. I didn't want to know. Like everything else that had happened since I woke up on that dark road, it made no sense whatsoever.

All I knew was that something had been here—something terrible. And it scared me more than anything had my entire life.

I stood up, trying to look everywhere at once and almost falling over the coffee table in my hurry. My heart beat so hard I wasn't sure I wasn't having a heart attack. There was a metallic taste on my tongue.

Sitting on the coffee table, I hugged myself, trying to calm down. There was no one here. Everything was as I'd left it last night. The door was closed and bolted, the lights were all still on. Yet despite the evidence, it took me a long time to convince myself.

I hated feeling like this. Was this what people meant by a panic attack? I was a grown woman, not a child. There were explanations for everything. I could handle this. Repeating this over and over, my pulse started to slow until I felt more like myself.

Stumbling into the kitchen for something to drink, I saw it was a little after seven in the morning. I couldn't quite remember but I thought it'd been close to midnight when I made it home last night. So I'd only suffered less than eight hours with this weirdness I found myself in.

I pulled away from the thought and grabbed an empty glass instead. Opening the refrigerator, I got another shock. Packs of Budweiser, large bottles of Pilsner lager, take out bins and pizza boxes randomly piled inside, some of them not even closed properly and looking as if they were growing life forms. Trying not to gag, I slammed the door shut and filled my glass from the tap instead.

It's as if a total stranger had been living here. As if I'd moved away and someone took my place. Maybe I had a split personality? Weren't there signs for that kind of thing? My hand shook as I brought the glass to my dry lips and I guzzled the contents down.

Just the normal activity was soothing. Not everything would be affected. There'd be things that wouldn't have changed. I clung to that, clung to it desperately—hating the whispering voice deep down saying nothing would ever be as it was ever again.

I rinsed the glass out of habit and put it on the strainer to dry. Normalcy, I needed more of that. I needed grounding before I could delve deeper into this mess. So I made some for myself. I cleaned out the fridge, pitching everything I wasn't familiar with and then taking inventory of the rest. My diet Dr. Peppers were gone. Most of the salad dressings were too. Almost as if someone had done what I was doing now, cleaning out the fridge and reclaiming it as their own.

Checking the freezer, I saw that hadn't gone unscathed as well. All the low cal and high end frozen dinners were gone, replaced by frozen pizzas, Hot Pockets, White Castle burgers, and other frozen fast food. Those got dumped into the trash as well. I'd had enough of cheap frozen food as a child to last me a lifetime.

A fresh box of baking soda and some elbow grease and Fantastic got rid of the spilled food and odors. I'd be able to house actual real food in there again.

With a satisfied sigh, I closed the refrigerator door. One down and a whole lot more to go, but at least I knew I could reclaim my place. I would do it, too, piece by piece.

Until whatever happened before happened to me again and ruined it...

My nails bit into my palm as my hands curled into fists. Not if I could help it. This was my life and I would keep it. The biggest problem was how?

To answer the how I'd have to figure out the what. Though the mere thought of it made me uncomfortable, I didn't see how I had any real choice. So after another shower and a hunt for something wearable (an old pair of jeans and a red t-shirt from the 'useless' box), I sat down in front of the computer again.

Taking a deep breath, I typed 'split personality' into the Yahoo search engine. I clicked on the first link that wasn't an ad, and it sent me to Wikipedia. I skipped the explanation at the top looking for a list of symptoms: multiple mannerisms, unexplainable headaches, distortion or loss of time, other present disorders, depersonalization, derealization, depression, flashbacks. The list went on. As I stared at it, I could dismiss most of the items, but there were a few that stood out like neon signs: severe memory loss, unexplainable phobias, panic and anxiety attacks. Yet would only having a few of these be enough to say that's what was wrong with me? How had I gotten this way if I was?

I scrolled down to the section on causes and read through it quickly, my stomach in knots. All they had were theories. The most popular was the fact that it tied back to childhood trauma. At twenty-nine I was a little old for that. Besides, I didn't remember any trauma from my childhood aside from the usual ones all kids from the low end of the income scale typically went through. No way had I blocked something from back then. I refused to believe I was that weak! And what would have triggered it to go off now anyway? Life had been moving on as usual.

This fit but didn't.

I went to a few more sites, but they all pretty much said the same thing. There weren't that many options on treatment—psychotherapy, drugs, counseling. But I shouldn't need these things. There'd been nothing wrong with me!

Still, I needed help. I needed guidance. Something, anything. So who, where? Debbie was out, there was no way the hatred she radiated last night was faked. I was lucky she didn't come here and just shoot me. Especially, if I'd done the things she said I had. Could I blame her?

The rest of my friends I wasn't that close to, at least not close enough to bring up something like this.

That left family…

I was pretty sure I could convince Momma to keep this between us, but that would entail being able to get her alone for more than five minutes in the first place. She'd be sympathetic, and she'd help, but I so hated to bother her. She and Poppa had worked multiple jobs just to take care of us and the deadbeats of our extended family who preyed on their kindness. If not for their efforts and support I wouldn't have been able to go to college and do more than expected. I was sure my troubles weren't what they'd sweated and worked all those years for.

Movies and TV made their efforts sound common, clichéd even, but that wasn't the case. The farther down the rungs you started out in, the harder it was to climb your way up. It was only because of them, Jamal and I started higher than most in our neighborhood. I wasn't ever going to forget that.

Whatever was going on, we'd stick together as a family. They would help me make it through.

CHAPTER FIVE

I was actually surprised to find my car in the parking lot. Having come to myself so far from home, though still in the city, I'd been afraid the car had been left out there somewhere. Catching a break was nice. I would be quite happy for them to keep on coming.

So I was even more relieved when I found my wallet with my work security ID in the glove box. Not so exciting was the assorted package of condoms tucked inside there as well. There was a rank smell in the car I'd been trying to ignore. One look toward the back seat was all I needed to make me drive up to one of the dumpsters in the apartment complex and clean out the crushed beer cans, empty wrappers, and other slimy things I barely glanced at before throwing out, picking them up by the corners. It grossed me out so much I re-parked back in my space and rushed inside to wash my hands. I'd need to get my poor Prius cleaned, fumigated, detoxed, and even then I wasn't sure it'd be enough.

If somehow I did have a split personality, she was out of here. There would be no co-existence, no way. Too much was too much.

As I came back out, I spotted my upstairs neighbor on her balcony. I gave her a tentative wave as she glared down at me, her arms crossed over her chest. She didn't return my wave. If anything her glare grew more intense. Someone else I'd not gotten on the good side of while I was 'gone.' I slinked away into my car and drove off.

I got on the I-10 and crossed downtown to get on US

59 to head north to the Fifth Ward.

The closer I got to my parents' house the more nervous I felt. Yet the feeling was nothing compared to the dread I'd felt going home to my apartment the night before.

The Fifth Ward was an extension of the first black neighborhood in Houston in the Fourth Ward. The Southern Pacific Railroad shops from the 1890s had been a boon to the area at the time, bringing in skilled workers. It was the building of the very highway I was on that tore the neighborhood apart and brought it into decline—the ugly side of progress.

Collingsworth took me to Otis Street, which led me home.

The old neighborhood was like another world onto itself. The homes changed from brick and stucco to mostly wood, one story houses. The majority of windows were barred and the doorways gated. Older cars reigned, some rusting some not, making my gold Prius stick out like a sore thumb. Porches sagged, some roofs were missing shingles, but almost every one of the yards was neat, the flowerbeds tended, the sidewalks swept. Regardless of their income bracket, there was a lot of pride here—a grim determination to make the best of what they had. I knew some neighborhoods where they didn't feel the same. They were so dilapidated a strong wind could sweep them away to nothing.

Once I'd gotten out of the Fifth Ward, I'd offered to help my parents move and live elsewhere. Between the toxic waste issues and Chinese slum lords that had been moving into the area, I'd wanted them gone from here before things got worse. They'd summarily refused. Home was home. They'd been there most of their lives and planned to die there. They and their neighbors fighting in their own quiet way to salvage all they could.

I pulled up to the familiar red house with the white trim and just stared at the place I'd grown up in. The tons of hours my brother and I spent on the extra wide porch, the mosquito netting patched and frayed in places but keeping us safe from both mosquitoes and prying eyes. The attic—our winter fortress when it was too cold to be on the porch, and also our safe haven when we got sick of family. The paint on the house looked a little worse for wear. Probably time for me to offer to get some paint and spend a long weekend at the house. Maybe after I got a better grip on things. Yet the need for such a mundane thing was a sharp ache inside.

Getting out of the car, I was suddenly looking forward to going inside, to being surrounded by the smell of wood oil and lavender that always hung about in the air. To sit on the lumpy couch nestled in one of Momma's Afghans. Tears prickled the corner of my eyes. I couldn't believe how I could have ever hesitated in coming. Everything I needed to get through this was here.

The front door opened and I felt my heart jump in my chest. But rather than from excitement, it was that sense of dread again as if a part of me knew something I didn't. My Aunt Monique came out, closing the house door behind her and standing behind the iron rod screen door cutting off the porch. She had a floral print dress, her nails in their usual glaring pink. Her small lips were pursed as she watched me come up the walk. She made no move to unlock the screen door.

"You have a lot of nerve."

"Excuse me?" Not a good beginning. Not good at all. My heart started pounding hard as if I were standing before a cliff looking down, sure someone would push me off at any moment.

Arms came up to cross beneath her bosom, the expression on her visage more resistant than any gate. "Showing your face around here after the things you've done. We don't allow trash in our neighborhood."

I ignored what she said though inside it felt like I'd been stabbed. "I need to talk to Momma. Please, Aunt Monique. I need her help."

She snorted, her head bobbing in a circular motion telling me just what she thought of that, which was not much. "Should have thought of that before you come round here looking like a whore and talking trash. After everything your family has done for you. The worst thing they ever did was wasting their lives on one such as you."

I could feel my cheeks flushing though I had no idea what she was talking about. "That wasn't me! I…I'm not well."

"Really?" A sarcastic brow went to high mast. "Drugs I bet. Always thought there was something wrong with you. So high and mighty and full of ideas. Never did know your place."

This coming from a deadbeat aunt who preyed on her sister's kindness to keep her solvent. "Think what you like. You always have. But let me talk to Momma."

She leaned back her nose raised in the air. "Your momma doesn't want to talk to you. And neither does your poppa."

My heart skipped a beat. No, that wasn't possible. They would never turn from me. "Liar!"

The half smirk I got for that was all acid. "I'm not the one who practically spit in their faces and called them Black Trash and looked down my nose at them. I'm not the one boasting about her internet 'services' and going into details about nasty exploits. I'm not the one slapping them in the face with the fact they wasted their lives to make yours better so you could throw it all away."

"That wasn't *me*!" I kicked at the screen door as if somehow it could drive the truth into her thick head. Probably not my best move.

"Whatever you say, Chocolate Lover." She flicked her hand up palm out, rudely dismissing me, then turned away to go back into the house.

"Please! I'm begging you. Listen to me! I don't remember the last three months of my life. Please! I need help. *I need help*."

She slammed the door after going inside, not once looking back.

I couldn't believe it. I just stood there wondering how this had happened to my life. Even with Monique pressing them, how could they have disowned me like this? Didn't they care? Didn't they want to know if there was a reason for all the unpleasantness?

I stared at the screen door in a daze, my chest so tight I thought it would collapse in on itself. It occurred to me I could scream, I could rant and rave, but that would only make me look like the uncivilized loon who'd used my body for three months. Besides, I would not beg. Williams' didn't *beg*. I might not have my sanity, but I still had my pride.

Turning away from the house, I wiped at my eyes, my vision suddenly blurry. The fact that my hand came away wet meant nothing, nothing at all.

I was on my own.

CHAPTER SIX

I got back in my car and somehow made it back home. Home, the place where the 'event' had happened. Where my life had gone off the deep end, and I had no understanding as to why. It was a place that didn't even feel my own anymore. As I came up the walk, the fear from my first night pushed at me again. I wasn't sure, no matter how much effort I put into setting it back as it used to be, whether my apartment would ever truly feel like home ever again.

But I was going to give it my best shot.

Finding a drawer full of take-out places, I chose one at random and dialed the phone number.

"Blossom Palace. May I help you?"

"Hi. Yes, I'd like to place an order."

"It's you…"

I ignored that and rattled off what I wanted off the menu. The heavy breathing pouring into my ear as I talked tried to rob me of my appetite but I pushed on anyway. I guess my other me had called there often. I shuddered as I hung up the phone. Running for my office, I grabbed an envelope and put money in it and sealed it, then clipped it to the outside of my door. I had no intention of meeting anyone she'd forged relationships with while I was gone.

When the doorbell rang, I waited a good five minutes before braving the door open to retrieve the delivered food. I gobbled the Pad Thai and coconut soup down as if I hadn't eaten in days. It scared me a little just how hungry I felt the moment I smelled the exotic aromas drift up from the packages. Almost as if my body had shut down in some way until it felt safe enough to make its needs known.

Once I finished, I found a pair of dishwashing gloves and went through the apartment, taking everything that wasn't mine and piling it in one corner of my office. It surprised me how much stuff she'd collected over such a short time. She'd probably cleaned out my bank account or maxed my credit cards while she was at it.

The thought sent me to my computer. The automatic payments for the Chase card had gone through. Nothing looked to have bounced. Then I saw my balance. It was over fifty-three thousand dollars. The room spun round and round for a second. Fifty-three thousand dollars?! What had she done? How could she have accumulated this kind of money in just three months?

I stared numbly at the computer until a timeout warning popped up on the screen for the bank site. Getting rid of it, I logged out and closed the browser. Every time I turned around I stumbled over some new horror I'd perpetrated while I wasn't myself. Yet I still didn't have the vaguest clue what had happened to drive me there.

There were several icons on the desktop that hadn't been there before. One was of a pair of red, pouting lips. The name associated with it was Chocolate Lover. Whatever it was, wherever it led, it would be bad. I had no doubt of it whatsoever. So I was shocked as I found myself moving the mouse and double-clicking on it.

The browser came back up and loaded a website—www.chocolatelover. com. A black screen with the same pursed lips as the icon, except much larger, loomed before me. Again without my express agreement, I clicked on the graphic. A box popped up requesting a login and password. There was also a new user link. I clicked that. An age warning flashed for a couple of seconds then asked for acknowledgment. Next was a page of links with graphics of figure outlines with the name of the section in letters in the middle: Stills, Videos, RP videos, SM videos, Other, and Gift Shop. As I stared, trying to figure out which might be the safest to click on, pounding music poured from my speakers. It was full of drums and animal cries. At least I hoped that's what they were.

I clicked on Stills.

A flashing message at the top of the next page claimed that for higher resolutions photos and no watermarks a secure server had been prepared to take care of my purchases. Each would come with a free autograph from Chocolate Lover herself.

Thumbnails loaded onto the page, grouped under headers: lace, leather, rope, nighties, el natural, and more. Acid sloshed around in my stomach, making me regret having eaten. Though they were small, I instantly recognized who was in them. It was me.

I owned my own porn site.

And my family knew. My face burned as I realized they'd probably been here. They'd probably seen the pictures, maybe even clicked on the videos. They knew my flesh was available on the internet for anyone to see as I posed and did who knew what.

I barely made it to the bathroom before my half-digested food struggled forcibly up my throat and out.

CHAPTER SEVEN

Rinsing my mouth at the sink, my throat throbbed with pain, my stomach continuing to twitch in painful hitches. It took three doses of Scope to finally get the rancid taste out of my mouth. I wished I could scrub the memory of those pictures out of my mind as easily. All of this was just insane. But I would put a stop to it. Had to, if I was going to live with myself. That horrible site would be the first thing on the list.

The rest of the day was spent trying to locate providers and accounts, deleting content, canceling services, whatever I could find that had been made or contracted into during my absence.

I found her video editing software. Her raw feeds. I accidentally clicked on one when trying to get rid of it. My changed bedroom flared to life, the bed dead center on the screen. A woman sauntered in from off camera. Wearing a see-through teddy, she draped herself on the bed. I could barely breathe as the fact registered that it was me. Not a look-alike, not someone pretending, but me. Yet the expression on my face wasn't one I was familiar with. I couldn't tell if it was acting or real, but the look was one of insatiable hunger and need sprinkled with wickedness. One very much aware of the audience out on the web who would be seeing this.

Shaking, I shut it down before it could go any farther. I didn't have to see it; I didn't *want* to see it. That wasn't me!

My stomach churned in warning. I closed my eyes and

took deep, slow breaths to calm myself. I didn't want a replay of what had happened before. Repeating over and over that I was back, that I was still here and in control helped.

As soon as I felt steady enough, I went back to deleting files, making sure to be more careful so nothing else would open by accident. I'd seen more than enough already and didn't care to do so again.

Eventually, everything was gone, but I found I wasn't feeling better. I had to face facts. I could destroy everything that had been bought or made while I was 'gone' but it in no way guaranteed it wouldn't happen again. Until I knew what had caused it or what was wrong with me, I could lose everything again at a moment's notice. The thought of that chilled me to my core.

I'd have to go in and see someone, a psychiatrist, and get treatment. If there was a treatment for this type of thing. I really had no idea. Since I didn't seem to quite fit the definition for a split personality, someone who knew better would have to tell me what I had.

But who to see? It wasn't like I'd ever needed the services of a psychiatrist before. Then I remembered one of the side services in the company's insurance plan. I couldn't remember whether it was for a specific psychiatry practice, just a general 800 helpline, or what. But it would give me a place to start. Plus it was supposed to be completely confidential.

The bottom drawer of my desk at home was where I kept copies of my company information. But when I opened it, I saw all my folders were gone. Instead, there was a bottle of whiskey, a bottle of scotch, a bottle of vodka, and a giant box of assorted condoms in their place. All my files were gone.

I slammed the drawer shut for a moment, seeing red.

How many more surprises were in store for me? Would this never end? A swell of hatred so deep flashed through me and left me shaking. If I did have another personality inside me, I swore right then and there I wouldn't rest until she was dead.

Once I calmed down, I got my keys and went outside. Originals of the documents I wanted would be at my desk in the office. My security card was still in the Prius' glove box so it wouldn't be a problem getting in. Accounting didn't always cater to just eight to five, so I had twenty-four-hour seven-day access. For once I was very glad of it.

The sun was just starting to go down, making it sometime after seven. I caught my reflection in the rearview mirror and didn't recognize myself. I'd forgotten to put on any makeup or lipstick with all the chaos, but I didn't normally use much anyway, so that wasn't it. Mostly it was the tired, hanging face and frightened, almost dull eyes staring back at me I didn't know. I felt so much older than I had less than a day ago. And I was sure it wasn't over yet.

Taking a deep breath, trying hard to pull myself together, I drove off. A stop through a Starbuck's drive-thru got me some much-needed caffeine and calories with a steaming Chai Latte. I nibbled on a piece of lemon pound cake as well, mindful of the crumbs, despite the fact I wasn't hungry. The energy was needed whether I felt like eating it or not.

I drove down the 610 service road and spotted my office building. The seven-story glass and white concrete monolith stood the same as always, familiar and comfortable. I'd been with Swendon, Inc. for over seven years, one of several small companies owned by Patrick Swendon. A handful of his 'babies' were housed here. We didn't see the owner often, and though the eighty plus year-old man didn't look like much in his white boat shoes and shuffling gait, his eyes were clear and sharp. He missed little. Plus checking up on his ventures and making people hop when he showed up unexpectedly was definitely one of his few delights. You could see it in the added twinkle in his gaze, especially if he found something he wanted explained. In the rare occasions we needed an influx of cash, the hoops we had to go through to get it would drive many an accountant mad. But it was the price we had to pay, whether any real explanations and new accounting sheets were necessary, it was just his way.

I enjoyed the challenge though. By this time I knew Swendon well enough to know mostly what to expect beforehand. Keeping the books as squeaky clean as possible meant there were no faults to find. I was happy there and comfortable. As I slipped into the turn lane though, I found my pulse speeding up. This other me had touched everything else in my life and soured it, why should work be any different? It stopped me cold.

Could I handle that? Could I manage going in there and seeing how my office had changed? Did I even have a job anymore? I held tight onto the steering wheel, suddenly afraid to drive into the parking garage in the back.

It was the weekend though. No one should be there. If my key card didn't work, then I'd know the answer immediately and not have to live through the embarrassment of facing any of my coworkers when I found out I'd been fired. Besides, I wasn't going to let fear rule me.

The fact that I wasn't able to trust myself to stay 'me' was scarier than anything I'd ever faced before, but that didn't mean I would allow it to define me. I was going to take my life back and keep it, and no one better get in my way!

Pumped full of false courage, I drove into the parking garage and took the first spot I came across. Slipping out of the car, I headed for the employee entrance in the back of the building. I swiped my key card, and the telltale light turned green. I was more relieved by that little light than I could ever say.

I slipped inside before it could change its mind. The elevator took me to the fourth floor.

The doors opened on a dark floor except for every fifth light. Walking through the gloom, I looked around me, feeling the unchanged visage of the office flow over me, calming me, reassuring me. I needed all the help I could get as I came closer and closer to my office door.

When I opened it, it was almost anticlimactic. My office looked exactly as it always did—the piles of neatly stacked paper, the small potted plant on my desk, the picture of my family on one of the built-in bookshelves. It seemed too good to be true. The other me so far had made sure to mar every other aspect of my life, why should it be any different here?

I turned on my computer. While it booted up, I searched for my copy of the insurance papers. The folders in my drawer were intact. New items from work seemed to have been added just like I would have done. It confused me, but I didn't have the energy to think about it.

In the insurance booklet, I found an 800 number for generic mental assistance but also a website with psychiatrists and other mental health care professionals. More than once, in big, bold letters, it assured the reader of both anonymity and confidentiality. Two items I very much wanted if at all possible. I would copy the pages I needed and take them home.

With the computer up, I checked my company email. Traffic seemed about the same as usual. Documents had been moved into their appropriate folders depending on the subject, responses sounded cordial and thorough like I usually did them. It creeped me out. It was as if I'd never been gone at all. Yet, with all I'd seen up to this point, it didn't make sense.

Curious at the seeming anomaly, I logged into the time management system. According to its records, I'd not missed a day since I stopped being myself. Stranger still, I'd been coming in on the weekends—every weekend. What was that about?

I checked the time card for the week where my memories stopped. April 15th had been a Thursday. And there was my time for the 16th. I'd even come in at seven. It only served to confuse me more.

Scrolling to this week, I saw that Friday I'd left early. The first time I'd left early in my entire missing block of time. Had the other me known I was coming back? Was where I found myself on my return some kind of joke on her part? My head started to pound.

I logged out of everything and picked up the insurance papers and headed toward the copier down the hall. As I waited for the machine to come out of power save mode, I noticed a light was on in Jim Prentice's office, though his door was closed.

My boss avoided the office like the plague on the weekends. He'd rather stay till midnight on a Friday than have to come in on Saturday or Sunday even for an hour. Curiosity waved a hand I had to fight to put down, wondering why he was here. It would be easy enough to just go over there and knock, but I didn't dare. That jiggling feeling that I wouldn't like what I found was front and center. So with more effort than it should have taken, I turned away and concentrated on making my copies.

With no one in the office, the machine must have made more noise than I realized, because next thing I knew, Jim's office door yanked open and when I looked he stood centered in the doorway covered by shadows.

CHAPTER EIGHT

Several awkward seconds ticked by as I just stood there. I tried for a smile, telling myself everything was alright. "Hey, Jim."

"Williams."

My throat tightened, stomach doing flip-flops. Since when did Jim call me by my last name? I looked away from him, suddenly not wanting to have anything to do with him or whatever it was my other self had obviously done. Was there no one in my life she hadn't screwed over? How was I ever going to fix all this? "I'm, I'm just copying some insurance information I needed. I'll be out of your way in a minute."

"I know it was you."

The words ran an icy finger up my back. I couldn't bring myself to look at him, dreading what he might say next. When had I turned into such a coward? "Jim, whatever it is you think I've done, it wasn't me."

Though it may have been done with my body, it hadn't been me. But how to tell him that without sounding like a total lunatic?

"You're the only one I've ever confided in about Karla. It could be no one but you." He took a step toward me, partially out of the gloom. There were dark circles beneath his eyes, razor stubble on his cheeks. His clothes looked slept in, his graying hair mussed. I'd never seen him looking so unlike himself.

Heart pounding hard, I tried to think of something to say. "I would never knowingly betray your trust, Jim. You know that! I didn't think it was right, and I didn't want to be involved, but that doesn't mean I told anyone about it. Your problems with Rachel back then put you in a bad spot, and you made a bad choice, but it's not my place to judge or to tell. It's your private business."

Two years ago his marriage was suffering, looking like it might crash and burn. The two of them could barely stand to be in the same room together but were still trying to find a way to make it work for their children. Rachel didn't give him certain favors during the mess, and frustrated, angry, and stressed, Jim had succumbed when someone else offered him physical comfort.

A change in jobs for Rachel, some couple's counseling, and a three-week vacation without the kids had gone a long way to fix things between them, to let them rediscover why they'd gotten together in the first place. Jim had ended the affair once things started coming together again and never told his wife about it. He'd only confided in me at the time because I'd noticed he was keeping extra clothes at the office and I'd heard Jim tell Rachel more than once that he'd be working late when in actuality he ended up leaving on time.

I'd always dreaded being put on the spot while the affair lasted, but luckily Rachel back then had liked it when he came home late and never much questioned it.

The hard look on his face didn't relax. "Then why am I being blackmailed?"

"You're being what?" It shocked me. I don't know why, but it did. Blackmail was something that happened in books or TV, not in regular life.

His expression crumbled for a second then grew tough again. "I'm not the only one having trouble. The whole office has slowly been going insane the last few months. Crazy rumors about the company being up on the block putting everyone on edge, stupid mistakes being made on procedure with fingers being pointed everywhere, misplaced reports. Like the company is under some kind of curse." He snorted then ran a hand over his tired looking face. "Heck and that's not even throwing in the punctured tires, the graffiti, the spiked coffee, and a hundred other little things…"

I rubbed my free hand against the fabric of my jeans and stared at the floor. Yes, she'd left nothing untouched, had she? Despite none of it being my doing, I could feel the guilt piling up on me trying to weigh me down.

"But you know what? I don't think any of it has ever affected you…" The accusing tone pounded down on me like a hammer.

Could I possibly hate myself so much I would come up with a personality to totally wreck every aspect of my life? But why? I may not be the best person out there, but I tried to be decent, to be good. How truly sick was I?

"Jim, I don't know! I have absolutely no recollection of the past three months. I woke up Friday night in the middle of the road with no idea how I got there." I grabbed the sheets off the copier and waved them at him, my embarrassment at admitting my problem raking through me. "It's why I came here today to get a copy of these. So I can try to get someone to tell me what's going on."

It was as if saying the words out loud broke the damn I'd subconsciously built to try to hold everything back with. I felt tears welling in my eyes, my nose trying to clog up, and I cursed myself for it. Keeping my mask intact was what had gotten me through so many other hardships before. Looked like even I had my limits. I didn't have the faintest idea of how to deal with all this.

In a way, I also felt relieved, relieved to finally be able

to open up about this to someone I felt somewhat close to. A different point of view, someone who might help me get through this.

"Wow, you actually think I'm going to fall for that?"

If he'd slapped me I couldn't have been more shocked. "Wha…?"

"I don't know what the hell's happened to you, but I'm not falling for this load of crap. It's as stupid as 'it was all a dream' shit they like to pull on TV every once in a while when they want a do-over."

"But I'm telling you the truth!"

He gave me a look dripping with disgust. "Are you listening to yourself, Williams? I know you. You've been suffering no memory loss. You've been here every day, same old same old. Why the heck you decided you hate us all and have been doing all this stuff behind our backs I've no idea, and honestly, I don't care. But I'm warning you if I find any shred of proof you're out of here. You get me? And no more payments. You want to tell Rachel some crap you can't even confirm as true, you go right ahead. I've had enough of this shit."

He turned his back on me with a dismissive gesture and headed back toward his office.

Seven years. I'd known this man for seven years. We'd joked together, spent late nights at work together, discussed books, movies, TV. He was a friend. And just like everyone else seemed to be doing, he was willing to write me off without even listening to me. And he'd had the least of the horrors pushed on him. He might as well have taken a letter opener and stabbed me in the chest with it. "I'm not lying, *you son of a bitch*!"

I slapped my hand over my mouth, amazed the words had come from me. Yet at the same time, I was glad. Anger at the barrage of unfairness that had been dumped on me by everyone I knew flamed at the edges.

Turning around, I stomped back to my office to ditch the original insurance papers back into the drawer before he decided to do or say anything else. Then I took the back stairs and left the building, my whole body shaking.

CHAPTER NINE

I drove randomly for a while, not wanting to face my apartment, not wanting to think, not wanting to do anything. When I got tired of that, I stopped at a random grocery store and went shopping.

Though my preference would have been the Super Walmart near home, I was loath to go anywhere I usually frequented. As messed up as everything had become, I no longer dared believe any piece of my life had gone untouched. And I'd had about all I could take for one day.

Having delayed it as much as I could, I paid for my gains and went home, the sun falling to hide behind the horizon.

Though lit up brightly, that same sense of trepidation I felt before when approaching my door flared up almost as strong as the first time, as if the time of day made a difference. I hated the feeling. Loathed it. This was my home! *Mine.* This wasn't what coming here was supposed to make me feel.

Yet despite all this, it made my hand shake no less when I put the key in the lock or moved to turn the doorknob. The yawning darkness within made my heart stammer wildly until I could reach in and turn on the light.

As if entering a minefield, I cautiously slipped inside.

By the time I locked the door, slid the chain, and made my way to the kitchen, turning on all the lights as I went, I was breathing hard, exhausted. Even then my gaze roamed all around me making sure I'd not missed checking anything.

Grabbing a cup from the cupboard, I filled it with water from the tap then shoved it into the microwave to heat up. My stomach grumbled, but I ignored it for the present, quickly putting the groceries away.

When the microwave dinged, I took the cup out and added a Chamomile tea bag from the new package I'd purchased. During my forays earlier, I'd learned my entire stash of different flavored teas had been gotten rid of and replaced by various brands and kinds of cocoa. My other self had been a chocolate lover in more ways than one.

I grabbed my tea, a package of Fig Newtons and headed for the couch. Not the most healthy or nutritious of meals, but I'd earned it. Comfort food all the way tonight, and some mindless TV for company.

Catching the tail end of a news show helped me put things into a slightly better perspective. I might have sabotaged my friends, my family, my coworkers, but I hadn't killed anyone, bombed a subway, or betrayed my country. That I knew of... My body seemed in good health, no permanent damage that I'd noticed. Aside from dread, bouts of panic, and wanting to beat the bitch's head in, I was perfectly fine.

Closing my eyes and laying back, I tried to calm down, my pulse pounding at my temples. Without meaning to, I fell asleep.

I woke up later gasping, my hands grabbing at the air. I was trapped, I couldn't get out, someone had shoved me in a black box, and it was crushing me! Flailing, I sat up and smacked my hand against the coffee table. The pain made me scrunch down. Blinking, and holding my stinging hand, I truly woke up, the lit living room making its way into my awareness.

There was more to the nightmare, glimpses of things that flittered around but I didn't try to grab them. If anything, I encouraged them all to go away, like a coward, and dug myself into the corner of the couch, touching the table, the lamp, the cushions, affirming they were all real and I was really here.

When I finally began to believe it, I glanced up at the kitchen clock and saw it was past three in the morning. I already knew those few hours were all the sleep I was going to get. I was covered in sweat, not because it was warm but from terror; terror that chilled me to my bones. No way was I going to ask for more of the same again so soon.

So I grabbed some clean clothes and went to the bathroom to take a shower, making sure to lock the door behind me.

The hot water was amazing, pounding at my tight shoulders and rigid muscles, forcing bits of me to relax. Afterward, I cooked up a lavish breakfast, French toast, cut fruit, more tea. I would need the energy, as I wanted to finish flushing the rest of the apartment of those things that weren't me, or as much of them as was possible.

Stuffed to the gills, I went to work.

During a break, I looked over the papers I'd copied from the office. Going to the website, I did a search for the list of psychiatrists which were part of the plan. I couldn't possibly set up an appointment today, with all the offices closed on Sunday, but I could be as prepared as possible for Monday morning. I sent an email to Jim, letting him know I was taking a PTO day. I was sure he wouldn't be all that disturbed by my not coming in. And before I faced everyone there, knowing that it was highly likely I'd injured them in some way or another, I wanted to be armed with the knowledge I was forging some headway into making sure it would never happen again.

I would fix all this. One way or another. I *had* to.

Which led me to think about how I might exactly go about doing that. It would all have to come from me. I would need to take the first steps. Then hope and pray people would listen to me and find it in their hearts to understand and possibly forgive. Doing things in person or over the phone was out for the moment, those hadn't worked too well so far. So I turned on Word and for a couple of hours tried putting my feelings and what little I knew onto paper. As well as what I meant to do to get help.

I reread the letter once I was finally done. It read like the desperate ravings of a lunatic, but I didn't know how to fix it. Yet maybe that's how it needed to read. Perhaps that would get across to them none of it had been on purpose, that none of it had been done with intent.

I printed out three copies and signed them. I only put a delivery address on the envelopes, knowing they would most likely go unread if they knew who they were from. Jim's I addressed to his home after scouring for it in my computer files. The one for Momma and Poppa got written up for the church she worked at on the weekends. Debbie's I addressed to her Mom's. I would mail them on Monday at the post office. Then I would wait until they called or came to see me or wrote back.

Until they called… I needed to check my answering machine. If my other self had used it, who knows what welcoming message she'd put on the thing. No way did I want them calling into that! Checking it, I saw there were no messages. But when I played the greeting, I was ever so grateful I thought to do it. This was not what I wanted anyone to hear when calling me.

The throaty voice was definitely mine. It gave me chills

listening to it, to the deepness she'd added as if she were playing at phone sex for anyone who rang. "Hi… You've reached CL. I'm not in right now, but I should be coming soon. Leave a message so we can party afterward."

I promptly erased it and changed it back to what it'd been before.

But this wasn't the only greeting message of mine people could run into. I tried to remember if I had seen my iPhone since I'd been back. That was another pitfall I needed to rectify. The charger was still in the bathroom where I kept it, so I could only assume it was still around somewhere. I dialed my number but didn't hear it ringing. When it hit voicemail, I got that same throaty voice as before. I cut it off before it could get very far. I didn't want to hear it.

In my frantic cleanup efforts, I'd found my cordless, so had placed it back where it belonged and thrown the big red lips away. I now had enough of a charge I could take it with me, and I kept redialing keeping an ear out for a ringer or something rattling if she'd set the cellphone to vibrate.

I eventually found my iPhone in the Prius, shoved between cushion seats. It didn't even faze me that she'd changed the ringer to "Back In Black." After altering that and the greeting, I checked voicemail. Thirty messages were waiting to be heard.

I told it to play the first one.

"CL, baby! Where are you? Been holding the place warm for you. Come on, call me back. I need my itch scratched. You know I like it when you—"

The delete key cut him off. I felt dirty all over again. Another shower wouldn't help though. I played the rest of the messages, only letting a word or two pass before I deleted them, to make sure none of the messages were actually for me. Every last one of them was from men, and not all the same voice. I'd need to get my number changed. Hopefully, she'd not brought any of these people home, or I might have no choice but to move as well. If what she was wearing Friday night was any indication, I didn't want to meet any of these men under any circumstances.

This was all just getting old.

I headed back inside.

CHAPTER TEN

"Yes, but is there any way I could get an appointment today, maybe tomorrow? It's really urgent." I bit my lip waiting for an answer. I'd had another bad night. Once the psychiatry offices started taking calls, I hit one wall after another. I'd run out of names on the insurance listing and was going through those not covered. I had almost reached the end of that list. Who would have ever thought there were that many people needing help out there?

"I'm sorry, ma'am. Dr. Romano is booked solid for the next two months. I could give you a call if he gets a cancellation. Or if this was some kind of emergency…"

I rubbed at my forehead feeling the tendrils of a massive stress headache. I couldn't put this off anymore. Was I really just that full of pride? This woman didn't know me. What difference did it make if I admitted to a weakness? Yet just the thought of it totally rankled. I'd made my own way, I hadn't let people's flawed assumptions or my origins stop me. Although I'd always had my family in the background for support, the only one I ever tried to rely on was myself. But I couldn't even count on me anymore, could I? "Yes, actually it is. Look, I have a gap of three months. Someone who wasn't me basically went out and destroyed everything I ever built. I need someone to help me figure out what's wrong and how to make sure it never happens again. Please, I need an appointment. *Please.*"

There was nothing from the other end for several long

agonizing moments. "Hold on, let me go talk to him for a minute, see if something can be worked out."

"Thank you."

I closed my eyes and prayed. Church, Bible study, membership get-togethers had all been very prevalent in my youth. But the fact there was cruelty in the world, the politics and prejudice I saw amidst the church's own deacons and more, I'd grown out of touch, left it behind me. I believed but had ignored Him as He seemed to ignore us. Yet if there was the vaguest chance He might be listening… I had to ask. I couldn't handle this on my own, whether I liked it or not.

"Hello, this is Dr. Romano. Who am I speaking to?"

I half jumped in my seat at the new voice. "I'm, my name is Tamara Williams. I really need your help. If there is any way you could see me today, any way at all." Grimacing, I shut up, knowing I sounded desperate.

"Pamela says you have missing time?" The smooth voice had a slight accent though I couldn't entirely place it.

"Three months' worth!" I closed my eyes again, my desperation bubbling up out of control now that I had someone who might listen. "Doctor, nothing like this has ever happened to me before. I don't, I can't have it happen again! Please help me…"

There was a long pause on the other end. "Tell you what, come over to the office at noon. I can see you during my lunch hour if that's agreeable."

The rush of relief was so profound I felt dizzy. "Yes, yes, thank you. I'll be there."

"Pamela will give you directions. You should probably show a little early to fill out paperwork."

"Thank you. I will. Thank you very much."

He put the secretary back on the phone, and I took

down the information. I already held an idea of where they were located but wanted to leave nothing to chance at this stage.

I dressed in a gray conservative suit and made sure to pull my hair back and apply what little makeup I usually wore. It'd be like going to a job interview. I could do this. Only my sanity was at stake.

Driving past the post office to mail my letters ate up some of the time before the appointment. The place proved quite easy to find, right off I-10, and I stayed in the car until half-past eleven, fidgeting the whole time. Before I got out, I took a few deep breaths and tried to relax. If I wanted him to take me seriously, going in there as a nervous wreck wouldn't help at all.

I stared at myself in the elevator's reflective doors, hitting the call button several times. The tapping of my foot echoed in the lobby until I made myself stop. Once inside the car, I shut my eyes and did some more deep breathing.

By the time the doors opened again, I felt somewhat more in control.

The hallway was clearly marked. Suite 315 welcomed me with a set of dark wood double doors with a golden plaque with the doctor's name. It was a lot fancier than I expected and once I stepped inside, it was even more so. The waiting room was large and had thick, plush carpeting colored in a soft tan with dark swirls. Spaced between large potted plants were deep, comfortable looking dark-red, leather chairs. Lacquered trunk wood coffee tables, huge oil paintings of forests, and a light scent of wood oil in the air completed the setup. It was lavish, tasteful, and had unexpected warmth to it. It also looked expensive. In my frantic hurry to get help, I'd neglected to ask for the man's rate. Luckily my other self had left me with plenty of money to make sure she wouldn't return.

A crescent desk also in natural cut wood took up the far corner, nestled next to a carved dark wooden door. Behind the desk sat a woman in her late forties, dressed as conservatively as I was, her hair streaked with gray. She looked up as I entered and gave me a high wattage smile. "Good morning. May I help you?"

"Morning. My name's Tamara Williams. I have an appointment to see Dr. Romano at noon."

The secretary's eyes widened minutely in recognition. "Ah, yes, glad you could make it. I'm Pamela." She placed a clipboard full of paperwork and a pen on the desk. "I have a new patient packet all ready for you. If you could fill these out, I can get your file started."

"Great..." I grabbed the clipboard and pen and retreated to the other side of the waiting room.

The first couple of forms were easy, the standard name, address, phone numbers, and insurance questions. There were the usual patient consent filing and release as well as information forms. I slowed down on the family and personal history ones, some of the questions things I should have expected, but which surprised me all the same: Why have you come to see us? When was the last time you felt OK, like your usual self? What made you come for help now? From there they got even more personal. Current treatments, treatment history, how I spend my free time, who with, what alcohol and how much have I been drinking, what street drugs have I been taking...

I dutifully filled out everything I could. Though questions on habits for the last month weren't something I was able to answer. To be honest, I didn't really want to know.

Returning the filled paperwork to Pamela, I also pulled out my driver's license and insurance card when she asked. She opened a side drawer on her desk to reveal a compact scanner. Within moments I had my items back.

"Dr. Romano should be done with his eleven o'clock soon, then he'll be able to see you." She leaned slightly forward and lowered her voice. "The doctor normally brown bags it, so I hope it'll be okay if he eats while you talk?"

"Not a problem. I know I'm being inconvenient. I'm just grateful he's agreed to see me at all."

Pamela nodded, sitting back. "That's good then." I got the strangest feeling she was checking me out, not in a sexual way, but like a scientist checking out a new kind of bug. I must not have fit any of her profiles for prospective clients. I wasn't sure if I should be reassured by this or not.

I grabbed a random magazine off the coffee table and sat down to wait.

CHAPTER ELEVEN

At five minutes to noon, the door next to the receptionist's desk opened. A tall, lanky kid covered in leather boots, leather pants, and a leather vest strutted from the other side. Behind him came a short, attractive, tan colored man, with the thickest and darkest black hair I'd ever seen. He wore pleated slacks, an off white shirt, and was wearing a casual jacket with patches at the elbows. I guessed his age to be around forty-five.

"Good session today, Damon. Looking forward to seeing you next week."

Now that I heard him in person, I guessed his accent might be Italian with some Bronx thrown in. Yet he could be from another planet for all I cared, as long as he could help me.

"Yeah, whatever, doc." The youth threw up a hand in a lame farewell then headed for the door out of the office. He paused a second at the door. I could feel him giving me the once over before throwing a smirk toward Romano then taking his leave. The stack of conclusions he'd just erroneously jumped to was higher than the coffee table.

Romano shook his head then turned on a smile in my direction. "Miss Williams, I'm David Romano. Good to meet you."

I got up and moved to shake his hand. I was glad to see mine was steady. "Again, thank you so much for seeing me. I know I'm a major inconvenience, but I totally appreciate it."

He waved it aside. "Don't worry about it. Come on in." He grabbed a file Pamela handed over then gestured for me to go before him.

Beyond Pamela's safeguarded door was a common room with a coffee machine, peripherals for tea, hot cocoa, even a small fridge with cold drinks. A plate of chocolate chip cookies and lemon squares sat in the corner of the table as well as small plastic plates and forks.

"Do help yourself if you'd like anything." He grabbed a cookie as if to encourage me along.

I wasn't particularly hungry but figured I might as well. Herb tea and a lemon square were quickly acquired as I made sure to avoid anything with caffeine. I was wired enough already.

We passed a large file room and a small office I figured was for whoever kept his books. Soft pastels were everywhere oozing with calm, all the paintings were of serene locations, the plants with broadleaves as if to catch patients if they fell. His office was larger than all the other rooms. A moderate mahogany desk took up a corner as if to be out of the way. There was the traditional psychiatric couch as well as a beanbag chair, a rocker, a regular loveseat with extra padding, a recliner, and one of the chairs from the waiting room as well as different styles of end tables. The scent of fresh pine leaves and cinnamon permeated the place.

"You can sit wherever you like. Make yourself comfortable." Romano headed for the desk and pulled out a brown bag from one of the drawers.

I sat down on the plush loveseat and set my cup and plate on the end table there.

He grabbed the chair matching those in the waiting room and pulled an end table around to the front with his foot then deposited his lunch, dessert, and my file. He returned to his desk to grab a fresh notepad and pen.

"Relax. Eat. I just need to look through your paperwork for a minute then we can get started."

Nodding, I made myself grab my tea and take a sip, relaxed far from what I was feeling at the moment. Romano paid rapt attention to the sheets as he leafed through them. I took a tentative bite of the lemon square.

My mouth exploded with flavor, and it shocked me. It was very, very good. I took another bite, then another, and before I knew it, the bar was gone.

I had to resist licking my fingers.

"You could go get another if you wish."

I looked up and found Romano staring at me, a slight smile on his face. My cheeks grew warn. "No, I'm fine. Thank you."

He nodded and after taking a bite out of a sandwich, picked up the pad and pen. "You had three months of missing time, is that correct?"

I took a deep breath then plunged in. "Yes. From April 15th until this past Friday."

"Anything unusual happen on the fifteenth?" Though the pen was poised to write, his dark eyes were focused on me.

"No. It'd been just another day. I was home from work and was getting ready to enjoy a quiet evening."

"Do you remember how you were feeling at the time?"

Since as far as I was concerned it'd only been a couple of days, I remembered it very well. "A little tired, and glad I was home. I was looking forward to catching up on the last few episodes of LOST."

"Fun show." Romano nodded. "And your first memory on Friday?"

I told him. From there he had me explain everything I saw and felt and then had me walk him through the last couple of days.

After a while, I quit looking at him, focusing instead on the shelves or the window to stare at the sky outside. I'd never been so glad to be black as I was that day, my coloring helping to hide my deep embarrassment as I mentioned some of Chocolate Lover's activities. I had to tell him. I didn't want any misunderstandings as to the seriousness of my situation, of how badly this other personality had messed up my life.

When I ran out of words, I waited, but he didn't say anything. I glanced in his direction, unable to help myself, and found him flipping through my paperwork again. He looked up and his gaze locked with mine. "You're sure there wasn't any kind of childhood trauma?"

"Not that I know of."

"And you're positive there's only been this one missing chunk of time?" I nodded.

Dr. Romano watched me for a moment. "I think we can definitely rule out DID, Dissociative Identity Disorder, what you'd think of as a split personality. Without the childhood trauma, it's highly unlikely. And people with an alternative personality never have just one."

He shook his head. "The next obvious choice would be a Dissociative Fugue, but you don't recall having any kind of shock or undue stress before the blackout, correct?"

I nodded again. "That's right."

"You also remained in town and remember everything from your past clearly up to the point of the blackout."

I got the feeling he was ticking off a mental list rather than asking me a question, so I kept silent.

"I think before we take this any further, we should rule several other possible causes off the list. Rather than psychological, these would be physical." He got up from the chair and moved over to his desk and opened a drawer. He pulled out a business card and wrote down some information on it from something he looked up on his computer.

That my problem might be something physical rather than mental had never occurred to me. The word 'tumor' suddenly trumpeted around in my brain.

"Mitchell is top in his field. I'd like to run some scans on you and have him take a look, to make sure of what this isn't." He handed over the card. "Then we can knuckle down and figure out what's going on."

It'd never occurred to me I might be dying. The room no longer as felt spacious as before.

"Miss Williams."

I jumped when he touched my arm, too self-absorbed to have noticed him come closer.

"I didn't mean to upset you. And I have to point out, it's too early to jump to conclusions."

Nodding, I looked away, feeling my business mask cracking. The only consolation was if I did have a tumor, I would definitely have proof for everyone I'd not been myself. The guilt they'd feel when they learned of it would be almost worth it. I barked out a laugh without meaning to. It sounded a little off-kilter even to me.

"Let me give him a call for you so I can get the ball rolling. Mitchell owes me some favors, so I'm sure I can get you in. What's your schedule like this week?"

I didn't have the faintest idea. "Anytime is fine. I'll work around it."

"Come out to the common room with me. You can have some more tea while I try to set this up. Will that work for you?"

I wanted to laugh again, but this time was able to hold it in. He was giving me that tone people reserved when walking on eggshells. Guess my mask was more than cracked. "Yes, sure. I just, I just don't want this to happen to me again. I can't allow it to happen again."

"And you won't." His dark eyes stared into mine with assurance.

He almost convinced me.

Except I knew he possessed no real idea about what was wrong.

Like a good patient, I sat in the common room and drank more tea, even nibbled on a cookie, though I didn't really taste it.

How long would I have to wait before I could take these scans Romero wanted? If his friend Mitchell was a specialist, a consultation could be months off, despite the man owing him favors. I'd dealt enough with helping Momma and Poppa set up appointments with specialists to know such waiting times weren't unusual. These people tended to be high in demand, their numbers few.

I needed to start making plans on how I'd deal with having to wait. Or not deal with it. The not knowing was the most nerve-wracking thing about all of this. If I knew what it was, then I could take steps. And I was taking steps, by being here. By asking for help. But would it be in time? Might I have another episode before I got any answers?

"Good news!" Dr. Romero gave me a half smile even as Pamela escorted someone else to the doctor's office. "Mitchell's office has made an appointment for you at the Memorial Hermann Imaging Center in Memorial City Hospital. Pamela will get you the address and a map. The appointment is for ten tomorrow morning. They'll send the scans directly to Mitchell's office. He'll give me a call once he's had a look at them."

Relief surged through me. A day, I could wait another day for answers, couldn't I? But could everyone else? "Dr. Romero, do you think perhaps I should stay at a medical facility tonight? In case of a relapse?"

He frowned down at me for a second. "Do you feel there's a likelihood of that?"

The question caught me off guard. Weirdly enough, I didn't think so. Though I had no clue what I was basing that on. The possibility of another blackout was there, but it wasn't likely. Though I trusted my instincts, the certainty of it made me more confused than ever. "No… Probably not…"

I looked up wondering what he'd make of that. His gaze searched my features for I don't know what, and seemed satisfied by what he found there.

He grinned.

"To be honest, most facilities don't have the bed space to take self-admitted patients. Unless I felt you'd hurt yourself or someone else physically, I can't really in good conscience suggest it."

I stood up and held out my hand. "I understand. Thank you, doctor."

His grip was firm. "We'll figure it all out, don't worry. I'll give you a call as soon as I hear from Mitchell."

Though I knew I'd already more than intruded into his time, I found myself loath to leave.

"Miss Williams, this way please." Unnoticed, Pamela had returned to the reception room's doorway and beckoned to me.

Nodding to Romero, not trusting myself to say anything more without totally losing it, I turned away to follow Pamela out.

CHAPTER TWELVE

Free for the rest of the day, and knowing I wouldn't be worth a lick for anything, I went to the movies. The email letting Jim be aware I would be taking another PTO for tomorrow had already been sent through the phone. For the moment I just wanted to get away from everything. This would be the easiest way to do it.

Some cheap Chinese from the food court made for a late lunch then two films back to back. I knew nothing about them, only that their times were convenient. I was amazed I'd not heard of either of them, going to the movies on the weekends being one of my regular amusements. It just drove home again how truly long I'd been gone—three months, twelve weeks, a quarter of a year—gone, taken, stolen.

Even if life sucked, the time would have still been mine, the memory of it would be there. Having it gone was like a hole punched through a wall. It left a terrible void. You knew something should be there, but it wasn't. Unlike a wall though, I wasn't sure my hole could be filled.

As I stared unseeing at the screen for a while, I was quite happy for the darkened room. Eventually, I was able to get myself under control again. Dammit, this would not *defeat* me!

The comedy finally drew me in, Robin Williams in top form. The science fiction film after it helped me lose myself even more—just like movies had always done when I was younger. Nothing like a projected story on a screen to get you to forget all the things you could do nothing about as a kid except endure—even if just for a little while.

I suppose it'd been foolish of me to think I would never need them in that capacity again; living in a fantasy world of my own making.

Emotionally wrung out, I headed back to the apartment and crashed.

It didn't last long. I was up again around three, my heart pounding so hard I was sure it would burst, the fear so thick it filled my mouth. Once more I could remember nothing, just fragments, feelings. Could a tumor do that? I had no idea.

Since I was up, I headed back into my office and looked up everything I could find on the subject on the internet. One of the primary indicators was headaches—I was pretty sure the one I had from reading all the medical jargon didn't count. Seizures—hadn't had any, but then with three months a total blank, how would I know? Mental and/or personality changes—right up my alley.

A tumor in the Frontal Lobe or front or back of the Corpus Callosum could cause memory loss, personality changes, or both. Still, you'd think if I had memory loss, I wouldn't have been able to function even with a changed personality. Wouldn't I?

Just like when Romano asked me if I thought I would have a flare up tonight, I knew I wasn't on the right track. Whatever happened to me wasn't a tumor.

But I shouldn't have any way to know that. Maybe I was in denial. Maybe it was part of my psychosis. If the brain scans showed nothing, I'd have to remember to mention these weird feelings of certainty.

Did insane people normally narc on themselves?

I rubbed at my face. It was clear I was unraveling at

the edges.

Time to get busy and push it all away.

A hot shower and the usual morning fight with my hair later, I thought I could pass for normal again. Not looking long in the mirror helped me shore up the illusion. The glance before the shower had been more than enough. I had the shell shocked look of a disaster victim: slack face, a lost look in the eyes.

I had time, so I decided to splurge and go to an IHOP not far from the imaging office. Good thing I left early as rush hour was on and it took almost twice as long to get to the restaurant as it should have. Being annoyed at the traffic had given me something else to think about, though, so probably for the first time in my life, I'd been thankful for road construction and traffic congestion. I was sure it wouldn't last.

The IHOP was packed, but I got lucky and got seated right away. Getting service was something else altogether. But it was ordinary. The irked people on the highway, those in here rushing through their food or yelling for their tickets, all commonplace, everyday, safe. Yet as I waited for my French toast and orange juice to arrive, I got the strangest feeling as I looked out at the mass of people. Any one of them could be like me. Any one of them could have their lives disrupted by another taking over, shoving them helplessly back into ignorance, until all the damage was done.

Goosebumps rushed up my arms and back. I shook my head trying to dislodge the odd thought, but it wouldn't go away. Where was all this coming from?

I left half my meal untouched, paid, and went on my way.

The Imaging Center was located at the Medical Plaza of the hospital's extensive campus. The lobby was huge.

There were at least ten other people already there waiting with plenty of room for more. I walked up to the whale of a front desk where I was handed papers to fill out. Turning those in about ten minutes later, I was then given a pager, like those used at restaurants–except this was a totally different type of reservation, for the item being served was me.

I leafed through several available magazines, barely glancing at the pictures. When the pager went off, I jumped. Cursing at the thing under my breath, and not looking around to see who might have seen me make a fool of myself, I grabbed it and returned to the front desk.

They buzzed me in.

"Hi. My name is Jackie. I'll be your tour guide for today." The blonde flashed me a quick grin at the joke then led me down the hallway. "You'll change in there, from the waist up only is fine, and just pick a locker to put your stuff in." She pointed to the left at four small rooms and then at a wall of wooden lockers, each with a number and most with a key hanging from the lock. "Please make sure to take off all your jewelry and anything else metal you might have. The key for the locker has a bracelet so you can keep it with you." She handed me a smock.

"Okay."

"When you're done, just take a seat. I'll come to get you when they're ready." She indicated a small waiting area with a coffee table full of magazines and a TV hanging from the ceiling.

"Thanks."

I did what I was told. The one size fits all red and pink smock did nothing for me, but then it had nothing to do with why I was here. That I even bothered to notice and be annoyed by it just pointed out to me how nervous I was about this. Which, since I didn't believe there was anything to find, didn't make any sense. But then a lot of things had stopped making sense since I'd come back.

The sooner this was over, the better.

The Food Network helped keep me distracted until the tech came back for me.

The room she took me to was large and beige. The MRI machine took up the center of the space, the main unit filling up from the floor to the ceiling. But what grabbed my attention and held it was the ceiling over the long bed. There was a U shaped window there, or mirror, showing the blue sky and the full limbs of trees.

"Since we're doing a thorough scan of the brain, we'll need to put your head in a rig to minimize movement. Have you ever had any problems with claustrophobia?" Jackie observed me. "We can give you a mild sedative if you think you'll need one."

I made myself look away from the odd window to pay attention to what she was saying. "No. I don't think I've ever had any problems."

"Great." She gave me a relieved smile. "Come on then, let's get you set up so we can get this done."

CHAPTER THIRTEEN

The brace to keep my head still wasn't uncomfortable, and neither was the sliding bed. Jackie left the room. A few moments later, her voice rumbled back through a set of speakers set into the machine.

"You doing all right, Tamara?"

"I'm fine."

A soft rumbling filled the room from behind me.

"I'm going to slide you in now. I'll let you know when I need you to hold your breath. Make sure to say something if you have any problems, okay?"

"You bet." I took a couple of really deep breaths. There would be nothing to this, nothing at all.

The bed jerked slightly as it moved to insert my head and part of my shoulders into the MRI machine. The hum grew around me. I stared staunchly at the top side of the round hole I was in.

"Okay, on the count of three, hold your breath. One, two, three, hold."

The humming rose in pitch. I knew right then giant magnets were manipulating the water in my body, allowing pictures to be made of the organs and processes going on inside me.

We went through the procedure several times. "Okay, one last pass and I think we'll be done." *It's no use fighting me.*

The rasping voice, the words, froze my blood with terrified recognition. My whole body tensed as if from a sharp jolt of electricity.

"You've been doing great, keep it up. Now on three. One, two, three, hold."

The feeling of being trapped, of not being able to escape, the only dregs left of the nightmares I'd been suffering from, returned tenfold. I grabbed onto the edge of the sliding bed with a death grip, to keep myself still, but also to prevent someone from shoving the rest of me into the hole. The key that dangled from its squeegee at my wrist dug into my palm.

"We're done!"

A moment later the bed slid out. My breath rushed in and out faster and faster as if some part of me were afraid I'd forgotten how to breathe. The sight of the bright blue sky and green leaves over my head gave me something to focus on, to regain my balance, the edge of my vision already filled with black. I wanted to rip the get-up from around my head and run screaming until my throat was raw. It took everything I had to keep my hands holding onto the bed so I wouldn't be tempted to carry through with the panicked impulse.

"Tamara?" I heard Jackie come into the room and half run to the bed. "What's going on?"

I took in a great gulp of air and held it, then let it go, keeping my eyes locked onto the calm view on the ceiling. "I guess I might be slightly claustrophobic after all..."

"I'm so sorry! You were doing so well."

I was happy to note her hands were unsnapping the clamps for the rig. The moment it was off me, I half jumped out of the bed almost falling on my face as my legs wavered beneath me.

Jackie reached out and grabbed me. "It's okay. It's over now. There's nothing to be worried about."

I nodded quickly, moving out of her hold. My mind knew she was right, but my heart felt differently. "I'm fine. Really."

She hovered by me as we moved out of the room back toward the changing area. By the time we made it there, I was slightly more in control.

"Would you like some water? Juice? You can sit here and watch TV for a while. Relax a bit."

"I'm, I'm okay really. I just want to change and go. Please?"

Jackie frowned at me with concern. "Are you sure?"

I scraped up a smile for her. "Honest."

She still didn't look totally convinced, but I didn't really give her much choice. "When will the scan go to the doctor?"

I opened my locker, keeping my back to her to hide my still shaking hands.

"They should be ready this afternoon. You'll hopefully get a call tomorrow or the next day."

"Awesome." I turned back around with my stuff in my arms and gave her another smile. With any luck, this one would prove more convincing than the last. I was feeling more and more in control by the moment. "Thanks again."

"Uh, sure. It was nice meeting you."

"You, too!" I headed for one of the changing rooms. I closed and locked the door, then collapsed onto the bench there. I put my face in my hands, cutting out everything.

What the heck had happened to me in there? That, that voice! I know I hadn't heard it for real. There'd been no one else there. It had the feel of a memory. Had I blacked out the past three months instead of having been shut from them?

I was sure Romano would have a field day with this. More bizarre things to mention to him next time we met.

But I couldn't stay here. Jackie would more than likely check to make sure I was gone next time she came round. Fumbling more than I should have, I got my bra and top back on. Casual had been the order of the day for something like this, and I was more than glad of it now.

Double checking I had everything, I took a deep breath to center myself, then opened the door of the changing room. A woman in a blue and gray smock was sitting in the small waiting area, drumming her fingers on the arms of the chair. Of Jackie, I saw no sign. After using the restroom to wash my face, I left.

The front desk needed nothing else from me, so I went on outside.

Halfway to my car, I knew I was in no condition to drive. My hands still weren't steady, and neither was the rest of me.

So I walked off toward the hospital proper instead. Hunting down the cafeteria and getting something to drink and a snack would give me something to do. The Memorial City Shopping Center would probably have better choices, but it was too far to walk. I entered the east tower, and as luck would have it, the City Café was on the first floor.

With a hot chocolate and raspberry filled donut in hand, I found a bench outside with some shade and sat down. Now that I was settled, I didn't quite know what to do with myself, so I just sat there and tried to stare at nothing—dreading what horrible thing might happen to me next.

"Your cocoa is getting cold."

I flinched as I looked up, so spaced I'd not been aware anyone had come around. "Excuse me?"

"Your cocoa, it's getting cold."

Cocoa? Who said that? A warm smile met my

questioning gaze. The man was tall, six foot at least. He had black hair with streaks of white. Hazel eyes and a weathered square face made the smile stand out more. He was dressed casually, jeans, worn hiking boots, a black t-shirt, a camo fisherman's vest, and a small backpack slung over one shoulder. Like some kind of ultimate outdoorsman.

The only weird thing about him was an odd scar running straight down his left cheek. It was hard to tell, but I guessed he was probably in his late thirties or early forties.

He stood casually, hands in his pockets, yet I got the strange feeling it was for my benefit rather than his actually feeling at ease. His voice was free of the southern twang that was so prevalent down here, yet it was also deep and rich, even strangely knowing.

What I didn't understand was why he was talking to me. "Did you need something?"

The smile turned embarrassed, and he glanced away for a moment. Curiouser and curiouser. Then it occurred to me he might have seen me on the internet. I jumped to my feet, spilling half the hot chocolate in question all over the sidewalk, the donut landing with a splat beside it. "I'm not her, all right! She doesn't exist. Just leave me alone!"

I backpedaled toward the building not willing to turn my back on him in case he decided to try something. The look of surprise on his face gave me a twinge of doubt, but it didn't matter. I already had more than enough to deal with.

"Wait! Please. I can help you."

I stopped. It was the last thing I expected him to say. "Help me with what, exactly?"

He kept his distance, which was good. He took his hands slowly out of his pockets as if afraid he'd spook me. He had no idea. "You have missing time, yes? Things have happened to you or those around you that you would have never done?"

How did he know that? "Who are you?"

"My name is Jensen White. I'm sorry it's taken me so long to find you."

CHAPTER FOURTEEN

I stared, dumbstruck. This man had been looking for me? He was apologizing? Had he somehow had something to do with what happened to me?

"I mean you no harm," he added gently. "I promise you I only want to help. I might even be able to give you back some or all of your lost time."

It suddenly got hard to breathe. "You, you know what happened to me?"

He stared at me with sad, knowing eyes. "I believe so, yes."

"Did you have something to do with it?" I crushed the paper cup, spilling the cooled drink all over my hand and onto the walkway.

He flinched at the accusation, his expression growing grave. "No, I did not. And if there'd been some way to spare you from it, I would have."

White stepped back to the bench and sat down at the far end, either to make himself seem less threatening to me or because he was so self-assured he thought I wouldn't leave. I tried to ignore the fact that my heart felt it was more the former than the latter.

"In all probability, it might be best not to get your memories back. The decision will be up to you, though. But with what little you do know or remember, make sure to ask yourself if you think you'll be able to handle having them back."

I stared at him, unable to move. I knew what he was

saying. If he somehow had a way, if he could bring my memories back, I would know the truth, and if the truth was what I'd seen and been told… But that wasn't *me*! I would never have done any of those things! Bitterness, frustration, anger, fear, all took a turn rolling inside me. Could I handle knowing for sure? Worse, could I handle not knowing?

"Why should I believe you can even do such a thing? Why would you even care to?"

His eyes dulled for a moment as if recollecting something. The scar on his cheek suddenly seemed more prominent than before. "Because I've been there. Because I wish there'd been someone there to help me through it."

I believed him. What he said made no real sense, but I believed him.

Yet another sign of my growing madness perhaps. "What did happen to me? Tell me."

He ran a heavily callused hand over his face then looked at me again. "It'd be best if that waited until you got your memories back. If you choose to get them back. I doubt you'll believe me otherwise."

"Try me." I took a step toward him.

He shook his head, a small, sad smile on his face. "Unfortunately it's all or nothing. There's not even any guarantee what I do will bring your memories back at all. Not everyone is strong willed enough."

That surprised me. What he said implied there were others who'd gone through this. That he'd tried to help them as well. As if this was some kind of mission for him or a calling. He could also just be stark raving mad. Yet I found myself taking another step closer.

Madman or not, would it hurt to try? It would give me something else to strike of the list of possibilities. "What do I have to do?"

He pointed to the other end of the bench. "Sit, please."

Though the suggestion wasn't unreasonable, I found myself abruptly very nervous. We were outside, in a public place, there wasn't much he could do to me here someone wouldn't see or that I couldn't call for help for. My rusty self-defense classes from college would come into play as well.

Even with all that, I still had to make myself walk forward and sit down, my insides churning, wanting me to turn away and run instead. It was similar to the dread I got when confronted by my apartment door. But these feelings weren't about Jensen, they were more about what I was about to do instead. "What now?"

"Now, I'm going to show you something." He reached inside one of the many pockets of his vest.

I felt a drop of sweat roll down the back of my neck.

A moment later, he brought out a thin vial filled with what looked like green-yellow mucus. "What is—" I bit my tongue to stop the question, not sure I truly wanted to know just yet.

White took the stopper from the end of the vial and held it out toward me.

The longer I stared at it, the wider my eyes got. There was something queerly familiar about the off greenish-yellow color. I quivered inside though I had no idea why. My fingers dug into the fabric of my jeans.

Jensen held the vial directly between us, a neutral look on his face. "Take it. Smell what's inside. Then we'll see what we shall see."

The muscles in my right arm jerked from tension as I tried to make it move and it resisted. A shrill scream inside my head insisted I didn't want to do this. That if I did, there'd be no way to take it back. "I…I'm afraid."

That I would admit such a thing to total stranger shocked me, but made it no less true.

"Unfortunately, you should be." He jerked forward, putting the vial directly beneath my nose.

The smell smacked me like a hammer, knocking my head back as if hit. The scent resembled that of burning matches, acrid and intruding like rotten eggs. It was sulfur.

And it was the key.

My eyes half rolled back into my head as a flood of hidden memories washed out over me. Being in the apartment, getting a weird feeling in the back of the neck as if I was being watched. Goosebumps rushing up my arms as I became aware of a foreign presence. Spotting the flickering shadow just at the edge of my vision. A sense of pressure suddenly engulfing me, entering me, ripping at my mind, raping my soul.

My mouth opened in a silent scream, my back arching, almost pitching me from the bench.

A malevolent intelligence had invaded me and rummaged carelessly through all that I was, then slammed me to the background, making me an unwilling passenger in my own body. The hate it spoke through my mouth, the atrocities it committed with my body, all as I sat trapped, forced to bear witness, unable to fight or stop it in any way.

That thing had told my Momma and Poppa how stupid they were for wasting their lives away trying to make a better one for their kids. How I'd found a better way to make a living, one I could have been indulging in all along.

I saw its calculation as it threw itself at Richie, how it'd plied him with liquor and slipped drugs into his drinks.

How it had punctured tires of cars at work, spread malicious rumors. It all stacked over me, plunging me farther and farther down an endless hole.

Strong arms grabbed me and pulled me sideways on the bench then held me tight. "Shshsh, it's all right, it's all right. They're only memories. Don't let them overwhelm you. This is the past. You're free. The thing is gone." White whispered this to me over and over in that deep voice of his, rocking me in his arms.

The flow finally slowed. I struggled to get above it, not to drown in it, horrified to my core.

The nightmares I couldn't remember, these were them—my memories— shoved deep inside me by that thing, where I wouldn't find them.

How the creature had teased me in its hissing cold voice, told me of its little ploys in detail before carrying them out, working me up to fight against it over and over again though it was always to no avail. Like poking a fish out of the water with a stick as it thrashed to get back with its last breath, knowing already that it would never make it and enjoying the futility of it. A creature of pure evil. And it had used and discarded me like so much garbage.

My whole body shook, sobs wracking through me at the immensity, the unbelievability of what had happened to me. I was peripherally aware of Jensen's arms around me, holding me, gently rocking me, whispering encouragements, like an anchor trying to keep me from being lost in a raging sea.

After a time, the tears stopped falling, my body and mind numb.

Then the realization trickled in that I was in a complete stranger's arms, one who had unlocked the horrors within me and of whom I knew nothing. Anger flared, and I clung to it, preferring it to the endless despair circling inside me.

I pushed away from him, though I felt weak and my limbs shook. He let me go, and I moved as far away as I could on the bench, not trusting my legs to hold me.

CHAPTER FIFTEEN

"Who *are* you?" I glared at him, focusing on him rather than delving into the things I now remembered.

"Like I said before, my name is Jensen White." He sat in a relaxed pose, his calloused hands on his knees where I could see them. "I'm an expert, of sorts, on some unique maters." As if letting down a mask he'd worn just for me, his eyes changed. Rather than warm and worried as they'd seemed moments ago, they appeared haunted, giving glimpses of deeply buried pain. "Twelve years ago, I was where you are now."

I wiped my nose on the sleeve of my top, stalling for time. Should I trust this man? Should I actually believe his life too was stolen? "What happened to me? Tell me."

He stared at me for a long moment, as if weighing how much I could take, then looked away. "You were possessed. Possessed by a demon."

My hands rose to cover my mouth as a disbelieving laugh rumbled up my throat, even as a cold fist rattled in my belly. "You're mad."

"I'm not." Then he added, "And neither are you. The memories you've recovered tell you the truth of what I'm saying."

I couldn't help but tremble at his conviction. Demons weren't real. They were creations of the superstitious, of medieval clergy wanting to manipulate the uneducated masses. They did not exist. Yet what else did I know of out there that could do as I knew had been done? I shook my head, not ready to deal with such things for the moment. "Why couldn't I remember?" I pointed at the vial, which lay on the sidewalk where it had fallen. "Why did that bring it all back?"

"Most victims never remember, not even with help," White said. "Most of the time the subverted consciousness sleeps while the demon is inside them, unable to deal with what's happening. It's actually the type of individuals they prefer and look for. They love to reap all the knowledge of their stolen bodies, yet leave them with nothing in return except the fallout of whatever chaos they leave in their wake.

"For those who are stronger willed, who will not 'sleep,' they lock away the memories, shove them down deep where they can never be found."

His gaze locked with mine. "But sometimes the memories leak, leading to strange emotions, bringing out unspecified feelings of fear, paranoia, barely remembered nightmares."

I found my breath coming a little faster. "But the vial..."

"A catalyst." He reached down to retrieve it from the ground. I shied away from it. "If the mind is strong enough, the smell of what invaded them can cause the memories to resurface. As it did with me. As it did with you."

I stared at the vial with a new intensity. "That...that belonged to it?"

He replaced the stopper at its top. "Certain activities they indulge in leave it as a residue. Some believe it a manifestation brought forth from their actual plane."

I closed my eyes then drove the heels of my hands against them. Planes of existence, demons, possession—total insanity. But inside me, the knowledge, the validity of all he said rang true. I pulled my hands away and opened my eyes. "But what did it want? Why did it do this to me?"

Jensen wouldn't meet my gaze. "There's not always a why. Most times the one they possess was just convenient at the time, nothing more. Most times..." He glanced up. "Only you can know if it was more."

"That makes no sense! How would I? How could I? I was helpless!" The admission stung.

"Yes, but you were still there. Just as it could look into your mind, to some extent, you should have been able to see into its."

Too much. This was too much! The mere thought I might have looked into that vile thing's head shook me with revulsion. I stumbled to my feet and backed away on unsteady legs. "You're crazy!"

White didn't try to go after me. Instead, he sat as before, only his gaze following, sadness radiating from him in waves. "If I could spare you any of this, I would, but I can't. The thing chose you. If by some chance it actually had a reason, if it wasn't just a random possession, it could be important. It could be something I could use against it."

I leaned against the trunk of the tree offering us its shade, my legs wobbly. The sunshine, the grass, the birds, the building beside me, everything felt surreal even as I realized several things at once. "You're hunting this thing, aren't you? You only 'helped' me because of what I might be able to tell you about it!"

White bowed his head at my accusation. "I'm hunting it; you're right on that score." He looked up, his gaze locking with mine. "Omens, demon sign led me to Houston. For over three months I've been looking for a trace of the thing, for the destruction that usually follows its kind. Yet there was none.

"It's not its usual MO. This makes me think it had a purpose. Restraint isn't something they're known for. I think if you ponder on it, you'll know it's true."

I looked away, shaken by his words.

He was implying I got off easy, and without even trying to think about it, the truth of it resonated deep inside me. I just didn't want to know how I knew. I could feel the information tickling the edge of my consciousness, the knowledge that thing wouldn't have hesitated at using my body to torture or kill anyone I knew or loved just because it could and what it would have meant to me if it actually had.

"I would have given you the option to remember, whether I thought you knew anything or not."

I had to strain to hear him as he went on.

"Though the truth is bitter and hard to take, I prefer it to not knowing. So if I'm able to give anyone else the chance to put some answers together, I'll do it. It's up to you whether you believe me or not."

Yet something else bothered me more than his motives. "How did you find me anyway? How did you know this thing was in me? How did you know it was gone?"

White stared me right in the face. "You won't believe me."

"Because accepting that a demon used me as his puppet is so much easier…?"

He coughed out a short laugh, his face clearing from its previous coiled expression. "I see your point. Not that I think it'll help." He gave me a half grin. "Sit, and I'll try to explain."

I did as he asked though I made sure to stay as far from him as the bench would allow. Although I doubted he'd try to hurt me, it made me feel as if keeping my distance also kept all the thoughts and memories I didn't want to know about away as well.

"You've heard how humans use only ten percent of their brain capacity, have you not?"

"Sure." This was definitely not starting in a direction I could have anticipated.

"Well, the statement is false. We're using just the amount we're actually supposed to."

His tone and face were serious. The hairs on the back of my neck tickled, a sense of foreboding washing over me.

"The rest of our brains aren't actually for us..."

My breath caught in my throat, the implication of what he'd just said sending chills of horror through my body. "You're joking! You actually believe we were made to be ridden by those things?"

Jensen held up his hand. "Please, let me just get this out. I already warned you that you wouldn't believe it. I'll answer what I can after I'm done."

I hunched down on my end of the bench, arms wrapped around myself, wanting and not wanting to hear the rest of his explanation.

"There are very few of these beings, or there had been very few..."

I wasn't too excited about the implications buried in that sentence either. I pressed my lips together to keep from asking about it.

"Once a demon has inhabited a person, used up more of the brain space, it seems to trigger other areas of the brain to function. A side effect of the possession, a consolation gift, you might say." His expression clearly said it in no way compensated for the trouble.

"They express differently in each individual. Some are never aware of how they received the power, only that they have it. Abilities and strength levels vary. Mine is the gift to see auras. The auras of those touched, as we've been, has a unique flare not found in those who have not."

I shuddered, hating the thought of not only having been violated and my life turned upside down, but also of having been marked in some way as well—like a brand on cattle.

"I didn't know if part of the reason there'd been no activity was because it'd not remained here long, or like I suggested previously, that it had a reason for being here. So I've been driving around the city, hoping to spot whom he'd taken. Today I finally found you."

He'd been looking for a needle in a haystack? I shook my head, not able to reconcile myself with that. He might have never found me. He must be mad or truly dedicated. Or both.

"I saw your aura on the highway and was able to follow you here. Then I waited, hoping for a chance to talk to you."

My head throbbed. "I… I need time to absorb all this."

His expression turned grave. "I understand, but I'm not sure we have it."

CHAPTER SIXTEEN

My headache spiked, my pulse jumping into a higher trot. "What is *that* supposed to mean?"

Again I got that odd embarrassed look from him. Like a little boy, innocent almost, though he was much older. "I told you my name. Will you tell me yours?"

The headache thumped along at an eye-squinting pace. "Tamara." No way was I giving him my last name.

It didn't seem to bother him.

"Tamara, I need to find this thing. Try to stop it if I can. It's got a head start of possibly weeks if not months on me. You're the last one to have seen it, to know what it was up to. I hate to ask, but I've no choice. If you can give me this one thing, I promise to get out of your life the instant we're done."

He was back to wanting me to look into my memories, to see if I knew why the creature had possessed me in the first place. I felt very cold. "I...I don't know if I can. Or if I want to..."

"Don't sell yourself short. You're strong, very strong. You can win through this." His conviction confused me. He didn't know me. Did he? "It just takes time to assimilate it all, to make sense of things. But what you need to always remember, to cling to, is the fact you did none of those things. Something else did them, not you."

He gave me a tight smile, his eyes full of emotion as if he knew exactly how I felt and how little such truth helped in the long run. Strangely, it did make me feel slightly better. I wasn't alone in this anymore.

"Tamara, the thing that attacked you is not the only one. There are others. More than have been seen in ages. Something is starting, something that could end up being very bad for everyone. I know it's a lot to ask. But I need your help. I need to know what it knew. Will you help me?"

I could only stare at him. Stare at his open face and realize he wouldn't press me if I said no. Yet he'd done me a favor, in a way. I knew the truth now. I wouldn't have to spend weeks, months, years, vainly searching for a reason for my missing time, waking each day in terror whenever I dared close my eyes due to things I could feel but not remember. Giving me the certainty all the awful things done to those I loved these past few months hadn't been done by my hand, even if with my body.

"I'll…try…"

"Then close your eyes and think only about what we need to find. Let the memories wash over you, but don't cling to them. Remember, all of that is past."

I did as he asked, though my skin crawled with the knowledge of what I was about to attempt, then tried to find the information White wanted. They were only memories, but thinking of them still felt dirty, too immediate, invasive. I rifled through what I could find as quickly as possible, not trying to look at any of it too closely. Yet the horror, helplessness, and fear of the past flooded through me regardless, as if I was reliving pieces of what happened before. Stubbornly I kept at it, my head pounding with violence until I couldn't take anymore.

I opened my eyes with a painful gasp, the grass, the trees, the very sky spinning.

White was suddenly at my side, his hands keeping me from pitching from the bench to the concrete walkway.

"Are you alright?"

I nodded, not totally trusting myself to speak. I wiped my hands on my jeans over and over as if that could get rid of the oily feeling of the evil thing's thoughts. "You're…you were right. I was not…random…"

His expectation was like a fire beside me, yet he let me go and sat back before he only asked quietly, "What was it trying to do?"

I took a deep breath, trying to still my pounding heart. "It was waiting. Waiting for a pair of brothers."

"To kill them?"

"No." I shook my head, regretting the movement as it set the world to spinning again. "It was to watch and wait. And if it saw them, it was to go to Oklahoma." My hands bunched to fists on my thighs. "It was forbidden from drawing attention to itself and wasn't supposed to leave any clues as to its passing." I barked a humorless laugh. "Guess it didn't really do a good job of that."

"Did it know why the brothers needed to be found?" White's brows were bunched together as if my information wasn't what he'd expected.

"No. It wasn't told why." I tried to force myself to relax, every muscle taut. "I don't think it was too happy about any of it."

White stood up and started pacing. "Did it see them? Did it find those it was waiting for?"

I shivered, the creature's glee only too palpable at the event. "Yes. They went in one afternoon to a storage place next to where I work." My office window gave a clear view of the main entrance and parking lot to the storage complex. I'd been picked for possession only because of my office view. Bile rose in my throat.

This foul creature, this demon, while waiting, had distorted my life solely out of boredom. It used me then discarded me, purely because it could. As if somehow I were less than nothing. As an American, my ancestors had fought to gain their freedom from England. As a black woman, my race had struggled to prove itself the white man's equal and for the most part succeeded, though it'd taken generations. And some alien *thing* thought it could belittle me like this?

A burning sensation welled inside me. I knew it well. I'd fought against it ever since I came to understand how some perceived me and those like me, the judgments made based solely on the color of my skin, of my sex, things I had no control over. Oh yes, I knew the emotion well, but this time it came with something more, something which needed satisfying.

White stopped in front of me. "Did the demon know their names? Can you describe what they look like?"

I held up my hand, forestalling his questions. "You said you're hunting this thing, right? That something is coming, and you want to try to stop it?"

"Yes...that's right." His brows drew together again, this time with rising concern.

It had used me and discarded me, crushing my memories of all it had done, attaching itself to another unsuspecting victim who happened to be going in the direction it wished to go. As if people were nothing but *things*. Dispensable. Subhuman. The heat inside me grew to a burning pyre. "I'm coming with you."

"What?"

"You heard me." The words came out with bared steel, though I'd not meant them to. My body shook with fury. "I'm coming with you. Whatever this thing is working toward, I don't want it to have it. I want it to regret ever having used me." The bitterness in my voice surprised me, but I didn't care. This thing had toyed with me. Crippled my life. Used my body in unimaginable ways. Left a path of emotional destruction behind it, I might never be able to repair.

"Tamara, no, think about this." Jensen tried to catch my gaze in his. "It didn't kill anyone using you, am I right? You can rebuild what you had. You can get your old life back. Don't you want that?"

I stood up and took several steps away, my back to him. "What would be the point?" I snapped back around, my face and body feeling hot. "Don't you see? Maybe I could salvage something from all this. Maybe I could rebuild my relationship with my parents, maybe even my friends. But they will *never* trust me again. Suspicion would always be lurking in the back of their minds that I might go crazy. It's not like I can tell them the truth of what happened, can I? How would I prove it? But let's pretend I worked harder than I ever have in my entire life and by some miracle regained my family's love, the trust of my friends…"

I shook my head, the fire inside raging higher and higher. "What I cannot stand is the thought of going through all that effort, all that anguish to recover just a little of what I've lost and then having to live with the fact that *at any moment*, at some creature's whim, it could all be stolen from me again! And there would be absolutely nothing I could do to stop it!"

I trembled with fury. "Before I can go through all that effort, I want to make sure I can keep what I get back. I want that thing destroyed. And I want to be there when it is and laugh in its face as it ceases to exist!"

I realized all at once what the heat rolling inside me really was—it wasn't righteous anger, it was vastly more than that—it was loathing, total, *undiluted hate*. And I despised the thing that much more for making me feel it.

"Tamara, no, I didn't help you to—"

"You said it yourself, I was never supposed to remember. What do you think it will do if it ever realizes I have? You think it's going to leave me alone? Especially since I wasn't 'random'?"

The cold truth of what I said slowly dawned on his face. Of the part, he'd played in it.

"Take me with you." I wasn't sure I could handle rejection, but no matter what he decided, I knew my path, even if I had to go at it ignorant and alone. The evil bastard would pay!

Jensen stared at me, pain, understanding, and possibly even relief shining in his eyes. "May God forgive me, but yes, yes, I will."

CHAPTER SEVENTEEN

I felt feverish as we exchanged numbers and I gave him my address then drove home. I'd been loath to let him out of my sight, the possibility he was only playing along until he could ditch me, prevalent, but he was insistent. He would meet me at my apartment later after getting his things. I was supposed to pack and tie up what I could of my life before hitting the road with him.

If I wasn't insane before, surely I was now. No, I wasn't going to change my mind about going, but I really had no idea what I was getting into. The fact it made no difference had to mean I wasn't well.

White might just be giving me space to change my mind, but it wasn't going to happen.

Walking toward the apartment was almost as hard as on that first night except for totally different reasons. Bits of memory played through my mind of the hundreds of times I'd gone up the walk, my body's strings pulled by a puppet master. Flipping the bird at my upstairs neighbor. Accidentally dropping things and moving provocatively to pick them up, knowing men were watching nearby. Flirting with all the delivery men and women.

My home felt more alien to me than it ever had before.

I closed the door behind me with a sigh. More memories bubbled up, though most of these were harmless. The thing's critique of my taste in furniture. Purposely staining the couch knowing how it would irritate me. Berating my taste in foods. Small petty things.

I couldn't shut the outflow. It was as if now that they'd been uncovered, my memories wanted to be sure to be remembered. There was so much of it I could do without, however.

Head still pounding, I sat down on the couch to rest a moment. Next thing I knew my headache was better and several hours had passed. I'd inadvertently fallen asleep but felt better than I had since all this started.

I checked my cellphone and home phone, but no one had called. It was just as well. The enormity of my leave-taking started weighing on me as I made a quick list of things I needed to take care of, though my resolve never wavered. My hatred for that thing was raw and hot and not going anywhere. Not doing anything about it was out of the question.

With four months left on my current lease, I got online and set up automatic payments to cover them with online banking. With the money in the account, it was easy to pay off what little remained of the balance on my car. I canceled my home internet and cable but paid up enough for them to run till the end of the month as well as the other utilities not covered by the complex. Then I exported my contacts list and after making a free mail account at Google, emailed the file there. I'd change the settings on my laptop to receive Google mail on a later date, the internet covered by 3G and AT&T. The time I had now was for cleaning up and shutting down. Set up could come later.

A very brief note to Momma came next. I explained I needed to leave town to work on my 'problem'; that I'd received a diagnosis and was going to work 100% on getting better. I let her know my rent was paid through the end of the lease and if I wasn't back by then, would she please do whatever she wanted with my things and I would make other arrangements once I returned for a place to live. In all honesty, the apartment was no longer home to me. I doubted I'd be able to stand being in the place ever again, especially with the flood of memories of what the demon had done trickling up wherever I went.

Placing my spare key for the apartment and my car in the envelope, I addressed it to the church as I had the previous letter. Then came a short resignation letter for work citing the same reasons I had for Momma. This thing I had to do might be over quickly, but my workplace was another location I doubted I'd be able to go back to again. Although I shied away from the memories, I knew the thing had done a lot of evil there. All indirect damage, yet I would remember every lie, every rumor, every plan, the ugly reactions my coworkers had had on each other due to the nasty things I'd done, the relationships destroyed with me as its instrument. They weren't something I wanted to be reminded of by seeing my coworkers every day. To know that the closeness we'd all developed as a working unit was cracked forever and would most likely never be the same. I wouldn't have been surprised to learn several of them were looking for other employment already.

I hesitated a moment before sealing the envelope. I wasn't a coward. I wasn't just running away. Was I? Suddenly I wasn't so sure, but it made no difference in the end. Better to cut off all ties than leave them hanging wondering what had happened to me. Without me around as a constant reminder, maybe they'd be able to work past it, maybe forget about it, be happy again. Without me…

Something splashed onto my hand. I realized belatedly it was a tear. I swiped at my eyes to make myself stop, not wanting, not needing to go there. I was made of stronger stuff than this! Yet something else to add to that hated bastard's list of grievances.

Putting the letters on the kitchen counter, I then headed toward the bedroom. I stared at the floor as I moved down the hallway and totally closed my eyes as I came to the entrance to the room. While I'd removed the camera equipment and the 'toys,' the bed was still there. I wanted nothing to trigger the memories of what had gone on here. So I followed the wall blindly until I could make it to the closet and closed the door. I found my small suitcase in the back and stuffed what I could in it before moving blindly to the dresser for everything else.

A couple of bumped shins later, I was out of there and headed for the bathroom. Stupidly, I didn't suspect anything as I went in, assuming it would be a safe room. I was wrong.

The moment I saw the shower I stumbled as rabid memories flowed over me. The videos it'd made with my body hadn't been restricted to the bedroom. My breathing grew ragged as I tried to keep them back, even as my nether regions reacted with a flash of heat. I grabbed my travel bag from the drawer by the sink and staggered out of there. Whatever else I might need I'd pick up on the road.

My cell hadn't rung. No one came calling at the door. As I sat on the couch waiting for White, I began to wonder if his agreement had been a ruse—an easy way to ditch me. He was the one with the experience. The one who seemed to have a grasp on what the heck was going on, not me. Aside from the face of two men and an address in Oklahoma, I had nothing to go on. I didn't even have the faintest idea how to safeguard myself against that thing if it decided to come at me again, *if* by some miracle I was able to find it.

Fluttering cold panic and then raging hot anger washed over me in crashing waves.

He'd given me his number. Was that even real? I pulled out my iPhone and opened the contact listing but couldn't bring myself to hit the call button. If he'd deserted me, too, I wasn't sure I'd be able to handle it. There'd be no proof then about possession and demons except what I knew, and without Jensen, could I trust my own knowledge of events? For all I knew, I could have made him up as well.

I'd never felt so utterly alone.

CHAPTER EIGHTEEN

The doorbell rang. I jumped to my feet, almost falling over the coffee table as my heart slammed around in my chest.

I forced my mind blank, not daring to hope, not daring to think. Keys in my hand in the chance I might need a weapon, I hurried to look through the peephole of the front door.

It was Jensen White.

After taking a deep breath to calm myself, I opened the door.

"I wasn't sure you were coming." I hoped he didn't notice the accusing tone in my voice. I'd not been able to help myself.

He sheepishly looked away, a bit of color staining his face. "It did cross my mind, but I'd already told you yes. Though if you've come to reconsider your decision…"

I shook my head. "Not happening. I'm going."

He nodded as if having expected nothing else. "Guess you'll want this then. Took a little longer to make than I expected." He held out his hand and inside it was a small, carved, wooden cross on a leather cord. "It's made from Acacia wood grown in holy water and has been blessed. It will help protect you."

A cross.

Would this really protect me from demons or was it more like a placebo? But then again, if demons existed, why couldn't everything else.

"Please, take it."

I hadn't worn one since I was a teenager. Not since I realized God didn't take a direct interest in the world. That most of its misery was due to the very beings he was supposed to have created.

Taking it, I didn't immediately put it on. The cross felt cool in my hand, its shape not the typical straight planks but symmetrically curved. Roses had been carved on the ends. The wood had been stained in a brown darker than my skin. It was simple yet beautiful. He had made this?

On the back was a line of carved runes like nothing I'd ever seen before. Was this a spell or a prayer of some sort? I blinked several times, my eyes itching. As long as the cross actually worked, I realized I didn't care. I put it on. "Thank you."

I glanced up to find his deep hazel eyes studying me intently.

That's when I realized I'd been blocking the doorway this whole time, keeping him outside. "Won't you come in?"

"Thanks."

I got out of his way then made sure to lock the door before following him into the living room.

"Nice place."

I shrugged. It wasn't anymore as far as I was concerned. But I said nothing knowing he was just trying to be polite. I found that my patience for such things had pretty much evaporated. "I'm packed, and I've put things in order as much as I can. I'm ready to leave whenever you are." He turned to look at me, his face filled with surprise.

My brows drew together. "You still want to talk me out of this, don't you?"

"No, I just want to make sure you really want to do this." He sat down, still looking at me. "There are no guarantees in what I do. It's constant travel, heading to a thousand dead ends. Sometimes I get to places too late to help, only able to bear witness to the devastation left behind and attempt to put back some of the pieces. There is no fanfare, no riches. A lot of it is guesswork, looking for patterns, following tips."

He edged forward. "You still have a chance to live your life. And while I'd love the company, I don't want you making this choice lightly. You could one day regret it."

It was strange, I felt angry and yet weirdly touched by his words at the same time. I knew what I wanted, what I had no choice but to do. The fact he would save me from it if he could was kind of him but also useless. I knew my course. "Trust me, I'm doing what I want, what I have to do. I'll have no regrets. Anything is better than trying to pretend nothing happened— because nothing in my life will ever be the same again."

His face filled with a flash of deep sadness and torment, which got quickly tucked away. He was a fool if he blamed himself for this. He'd opened my eyes, he'd shown me the truth. I would have gone nuts living with the horrid nightmares, fearing things I could make no sense of, living in the ashes of my life never knowing how it'd all gone so very wrong. "I'm in this for the long haul."

He lowered his head as if bowing to the inevitable. "I see."

"We need to head toward Durant. The meeting place, if it found them, was supposed to be the Choctaw Hotel and Casino on Central Expressway."

Jensen looked up. "Did it try to find out anything about the two men? Question the storage people about them?"

I closed my eyes for a second, shuddering as I made

myself rifle through the thing's past actions again. "No. It didn't even bother to follow them, though it was tempted to. It had been ordered not to." I wondered why. Would the two men have known what it was if it'd gotten too close? Using something like Jensen's aura readings? Perhaps they'd been possessed before and had taken steps.

"That should be our first move." He rose to his feet. "But first we need to get a likeness of them done, so we know what we're looking for. I've arranged for us to meet someone tonight to have sketches made."

The coil of heat that had made its bed inside me since I learned the truth of what had happened, flared. "You do understand that thing is riding someone else right now, don't you? That the moment it left me it started destroying someone else's life? And you want to go get drawings made?"

Jensen's lip twitched, a flash of guilt marring his face which was then replaced by sadness. It was like dousing a fire with ice water. He knew. Of course he knew. Yet he'd still made the decision to play it this way—and not lightly.

"Fine. Forget I said anything." Gathering my suitcase, laptop bag and letters, I struggled to keep my anger in check and said nothing else before heading toward the door and leaving him to follow after me.

Once we were both outside, I shut the door, avoiding taking a last look inside. Everything I'd worked so hard for. All the struggles, all the victories, the life I'd built for myself despite my beginnings were encapsulated here. Turning the key in the lock gave it an odd sense of finality. The Tamara Williams who used to live here didn't exist anymore.

Jensen reached out to take my bag, but I pulled it away. I'd always carried my own weight and would need to do so now more than ever.

"My car's over here."

He led me to a dust-covered charcoal gray Ford Taurus. It looked like it'd seen better days and was easily forgettable—definitely not a current model.

White popped the trunk, and I slipped my luggage inside. There were a couple of duffels in the very back next to a strange looking wheeled trunk with a combination lock. It looked heavy. But there was more to it than that. It made my eyes itch, even more than the cross had—it was a bizarre sensation. "What is that thing?"

Jensen's brow rose at my choice of words. "Holds tools of the trade. I'll take it out and show it to you later."

"Sure…"

He opened the passenger side door for me, and I got in. The interior was immaculate, a lighter gray than the outside. The passenger seat looked almost new while the driver's side was patched in several places as if long hours had been spent behind the wheel. A simple wooden crucifix along with a Star of David hung from the rearview mirror.

Jensen started the car. I could feel the power rumble through the engine before turning into a smooth purr. I didn't know much about cars, but it made my Prius seem totally tame in comparison.

A light sense of relief filtered through me as we left my apartment complex's parking lot. With any luck, the unwanted memories of what the demon had done inside my home wouldn't plague me anymore. But I wasn't counting on it.

CHAPTER NINETEEN

Jensen was pensive and quiet as he drove down the streets of Houston. Although, if I'd understood correctly, he'd been here only around three months, he seemed to know the roads pretty well. He even found a nearby post office to drop off my letters before continuing to wherever it was we were going to get his drawings made.

The sun dipped low in the horizon, the colors past the city skyline turning orange and pink. I fidgeted in my seat, still trying to reconcile myself that going after the demon directly had to wait.

After a short while, White turned into the darkening parking lot of the St. Anne's Catholic Church. It shocked me. Though I possessed no previous idea of where we were going, I wouldn't have expected it to be here. It was a nice looking building, its façade imbued with an old world feel. A five storied bell tower rose from the side and was open in the four directions of the compass.

The church appeared to be part of a larger campus, a private school by the looks of it. Its white buildings and red-tiled roofs gave them a Spanish feel.

We parked and got out, Jensen heading toward the entrance to the church.

I'd been born and raised a Southern Baptist—same God, same savior, mostly the same bible, and different rules and ways of looking at certain things. Aside from movies, I'd never set foot inside a Catholic Church before.

It was beautiful. A long hall running side to side

greeted us as we came in, three sets of doors opening into the main room, while others appeared to lead to other side rooms. The main room was filled with columns and pew after shinning pew with bars to kneel on. Red bound books sat in the open boxes built onto the back of the seat in front of it.

Jensen stopped to dip his fingers in a vessel of water by the doors and knelt at the first pew toward the life-sized figure of Jesus hanging on the cross above the pristine altar on the far end of the room. Stained glass windows of saints, angels, and more stared at us as we made our way down the red-carpeted walkway between the pews. The smell of wood oil and incense tickled my nose as I followed Jensen's lead.

What a contrast to the church I'd grown up attending as a kid. The little white building with its covered porch and double doors would have easily fit into this building. Even the land around it, hemmed in with a simple iron rod fence would have fit in here as well. The smells of sweat, Pledge, and cheap perfumes would fill the place up in the summers, nature's breeze the only thing to cool the space, unlike the titan pumps of the air conditioners in this edifice.

I felt God here no more than I did there, yet I found myself thinking I preferred my childhood place better. Poor and small it might have been, but those who worshiped there were family. This place was too big. Felt too impersonal. But maybe that was the point. I'd heard often enough from several of our elders, there was too much ceremony between the priests and His people and it only served to get in the way to God. Since I knew most of them had never even seen a part of a Catholic Mass, I wasn't entirely sure where their opinions actually came from.

About midway down the aisle, Jensen stopped and gestured that I should sit. I sat down, and he slid in beside me. For the first time, I realized he'd kept his gaze downcast this whole time. It was strange.

A door opened from the far right. A jolly looking man in a priest's cassock came out and spotted us immediately. A broad smile spread across his round spectacled face as he headed toward us.

"Father White, is that you?"

I turned in my seat and stared at Jensen. This man was a priest? He kept his gaze lowered but quickly stood up. "Please, Father, you know I don't go by that anymore..."

Jensen threw me a quick glance as if to see how I was taking this. His neck and cheeks had colored perceptively.

"Nonsense! Vows are vows. And I have it on good authority that though you may not have a church of your own anymore, you're still very much doing God's work." Before Jensen could think to protest, the older priest patted him on the shoulder soundly. "Now introduce me to your friend."

I sucked in my lips and tried to hide a smile, though I was having a hard time of it. I stuck out my hand hoping to circumvent a shoulder slap of my own. "Tamara Williams, pleased to meet you."

He took my hand in his but rather than shake it, he turned it and patted it with the other. "I'm Father William." His blue-eyed gaze sought mine. "I'm sorry for the things you've had to go through."

I suddenly didn't feel like smiling anymore. Did I now have a Scarlet Letter on me or something? A neon sign telling anyone with a clue I'd been possessed?

"Tamara..." Jensen stepped forward. "I told the Father you'd had some trouble and he offered to help."

I frowned for a second then realized what he was

saying. He'd not actually told the priest what the exact trouble had been. My face relaxed. "That's very kind of you, sir."

"It's what I'm here for." He gave me a soft smile then turned toward Jensen. "Maggie's here already. I set her up in one of the meeting rooms in the parish center. It's right this way."

He didn't let go of my hand and tugged me along as he led us to the closest exit. The school grounds were neat and very green. Either donations were respectable or school tuition was more than I wanted to know. Following a winding walkway, we made our way to the parish center. Father William chattered away the whole way talking about the parish and the school.

The parish center lobby was well maintained and painted in soft earth tones. It felt more accessible and friendly than the church had been. Two sets of double doors opened into an ample room that could be used for all manner of activities. A left hallway led off toward what looked like meeting rooms, while a set of doors directly to our right led elsewhere. It was there that Father Williams took us.

Past the doors was a large meeting room with a polished round table and tall-backed leather chairs. A blonde in her mid-twenties had a briefcase and laptop open on the far end. She stood up as we came in.

"Maggie, thank you for waiting!" Father William dragged me behind him further into the room. Jensen had said nothing else this whole time. If I hadn't glanced over my shoulder more than once to make sure he was still with us, I wouldn't have known he was there. He stopped just inside the door and to the side, leaving the priest to take charge of the proceedings. It felt rather odd.

"It's not a problem, Father." The woman gave him a

small smile then turned on a brighter one for me. "Hi, I'm Maggie."

The priest finally let go of my hand, so I was able to shake hers. She had a nice confident grip.

"Tamara."

"I hear you need some sketches made?" She sat back down indicating I should do the same.

"Yes. Of two young men."

Maggie nodded. "I've some special software for that type of thing I use at work. If you can describe them for me, we can get started."

All I had to do was close my eyes to see them. The memory of what they looked like got burned into my brain by the demon who'd been seeking them. As I rattled off their description, I looked at them myself. Two males, in their early twenties, possibly twins. One had black hair with ice blue eyes, the other an almost white blond with dark brown eyes and a small ruby pierced through his nose. They were handsome, actually more than that, they could almost be called pretty, even beautiful, yet I got no effeminate impression from them. I was sure they were male, because the demon had been sure, yet I supposed they might have been better labeled as androgynous.

Even their ancestry was hard to pin down. Aside from the fact they were Caucasian. Between the nose stud and their good looks, they weren't exactly inconspicuous.

For the next hour plus, Maggie changed the profiles as I agreed or disagreed with choices she made in the program. The final product didn't really do them justice.

It didn't keep me from going through a myriad of emotions though. These men were the reason I'd been possessed. Whether they knew it or not, they were responsible for the mess my life had become. I wasn't sure how I might react if we ever came across them. It might be better for them if we never met.

The briefcase had a handfed miniature printer, which she then used to print out a couple of copies of them in color.

Jensen finally came fully into the room and frowned as he looked at them.

"Do you know them?"

"No..." He didn't elucidate further as he just continued staring at the two drawings. After another couple of seconds, he looked up at the priest. "Is there a folder I could have to take these with us?"

"Of course! Let me get you one from one of the offices." He turned to Maggie. "If you want I'll walk you out."

"I'd appreciate that, Father. Thank you." Maggie replaced her laptop in the briefcase and got ready to go. "I hope you find them. If you want to file a missing person's report or talk to a detective, just give me a call. I'll put you in contact with the right people." She set a business card on the table and pushed it toward me.

"We'll think about it, thanks." I shook her hand and palmed the card away, suddenly glad I'd not given her my last name.

Maggie and Father William took their leave leaving me alone with Jensen. He'd set the two drawings on the table and was staring at them again.

"You said you didn't know them. But do they look like someone else you know?"

He put one on top of the other then turned them over. "No. There's just something familiar I can't quite figure out about them." He pinched the bridge of his nose for a moment then tried to smile. "I'm probably just trying too hard."

Figuring I had a couple of minutes, I decided to ask him about something else. "So you're a priest?"

He looked away from me, a pained look flashing across his face before he tucked it away out of sight. "Was. I *was* a priest. It was a long time ago."

My curiosity rose despite myself. "Was that before you were…?"

"Yes." He got up and turned his back on me, his shoulders tense. "I'd very much prefer not to discuss it right now. I'm sorry."

Guilt rose up and waved itself in my face. "I shouldn't have asked. I apologize." Of all people, I should have known it really wasn't a topic open for discussion. Mild as my own experience supposedly was, I wouldn't want to talk about it to anyone unless I absolutely had to. So why should he?

CHAPTER TWENTY

We sat in awkward silence until Father William came back. As promised, he brought a folder we could use to keep the sketches of the twins protected.

"Would the two of you join me for dinner this evening?" The priest glanced longingly at the folder in Jensen's hand.

"I'm sorry, Father, but we have to go. I need to show these to someone before closing time. And we may be leaving town straight after that."

My heart soared at hearing him say that. The hate inside me rolled with anticipation.

"So you won't be needing the room at the rectory either?" Father William looked crestfallen. He'd probably been hoping to get the scoop on what this was all about since Jensen called to arrange the meeting in the first place. I was more than happy he'd be kept in the dark.

"I'm sorry, but no. Though I really appreciated your hospitality and help. You made things a lot easier for me, and I'll always be grateful." Jensen offered him his hand.

Father William shook it hard. "I found our conversations most stimulating. So if there's any gratitude to be passed around, it is from me, I assure you. In this day and age, it is challenging to find those with an open enough mind to realize not everything around us is always as it seems."

Jensen bowed his head at the priest's words but said nothing else.

"May the Lord bless and keep both of you."

"Thank you, Father."

I thanked him as well, thinking he actually meant it and wasn't just giving some expected platitude. I followed Jensen toward the door.

"Oh! Wait, please. I almost forgot!" Father William shuffled forward, reaching beneath his cassock into a hidden pocket. He pulled out a thick envelope. "Your requisition came through. I can't believe I almost let you leave without it."

Jensen took the envelope without looking at it. "Thank you. This will be a great help."

The priest smiled. "If you find yourself in these parts again, please don't hesitate to drop by."

"Thank you again, Father." Jensen nodded to him, looking slightly uncomfortable, and hurried out.

The whole exchange was so peculiar I couldn't stop myself from asking about it when we got outside the range of other ears. "What was that about?" Jensen gave me no reply until we were outdoors.

"The work that I do… It's sanctioned indirectly by the Church. I'm allowed a stipend against expenses."

I nodded. "So you *are* a priest."

"No!" Anger, guilt, horror, shame, sadness, loss; they flashed across his face one after the other. "Not anymore…" He turned away. "We should get going if we plan to reach the storage place before they close." I followed him back to the car.

The ride to the Public Storage was quiet, the silence thick. I stared out the window not really seeing the darkening surroundings as they streamed past, thinking. It was easy to put two and two together. He'd been a priest when he'd been possessed and whatever the thing had done with him made Jensen not want to be one afterward. Yet despite the fact I guessed all that, I found a sick curiosity growing inside me wanting to know more. A demon possessing a Catholic priest. It was strangely mind-boggling, though it shouldn't have been. Priests were but men. Pious, good men if they were true to their beliefs, but men all the same. Why should they be any harder to defile than I had been?

With a pang of loss, I stared at the building I'd worked at for so many years as Jensen pulled into the storage place's parking lot. I could see my window clearly. The window which was the sole criteria on why my life had been devastated. And not just mine, but mine and everyone else's around me. Because it had been bored. Because, to it, we mean less than nothing.

The heat inside me rose to bursting, demanding I do something about this *now*. But there was nothing I could do at the moment, and it just made me that much angrier.

"Tamara, are you coming inside?"

Jensen was already out of the car and had ducked his head back in, a concerned look on his face. I'd never even noticed him getting out.

Gritting my teeth, I tried to give him a normal sounding answer even as my insides wanted me to scream. "Yes. Coming."

My nails were digging into my left hand, my right wrapped in a death grip on the door handle. I forced them both to relax before actually opening the door. My hands tingled as blood flow rushed back into both of them. I pushed the anger back until I could breathe again.

One monster had left me but inadvertently released the one I'd tucked away long ago. But I needed my rage, I needed it badly. Yet how I would keep it from destroying me in the end, I had no idea at all.

"Are you all right?"

Jensen's face was hidden in the deepening shadows,

but if anything his concern was more pronounced than before. Surely he knew what I was going through. Surely he'd felt this after his own encounter. "Weren't you angry? Didn't you think impure thoughts? A window, my soul was raped for a lousy window, that window."

My finger rose accusingly toward my old office. My whole arm shook. "It sat there, day after day, amusing itself at my expense, staring down here for a couple of men who might have never shown. It could have kept making more and more victims for years! Had been ordered to, if necessary. The fact it wasn't happy about it just made it that much more determined to take it out on everyone around it, especially *me!*"

The last word echoed around me, my throat hurting as I yelled it out with everything I had. I'd thought I could do this. I'd thought I could get past this. I had no idea what I'd been thinking about.

"Tamara..." He didn't come closer, but his voice was pitched low, so much emotion coating my name I didn't understand it, yet he seemed to be trying to soothe me. "It...will get easier. Not right away, but eventually, mostly... You just have to fight to hold on right now. Don't let it get the best of you. The work itself will help. We are doing something. Even if it doesn't feel like it."

He gestured toward the entrance of the storage place. "Let's go inside and get this done. Then we can move on."

Despite the forceful words, the tone was suggestive, consoling. I had no idea how the heck he could do that. Perhaps it had to do with his priest training, maybe it was just the fact he knew firsthand how explosive I was at the moment. In the end, however he did it, it seemed to do enough. I was able to grab hold of my inner self and pretend at some semblance of control. Everything we did would get me one step closer to what I wanted. I had to remember it, cling to it, master this thing, or it would consume me.

Reminding myself of this over and over, I took the lead.

Though I'd worked beside the place for years, this was the first time I'd ever been inside the Public Storage. The tan building with its orange accent had always seemed innocuous enough. The interior was no different. There was a desk/counter just inside the main entrance, a bank of private boxes lining the left wall. There were several other entrances from the outside to the larger storage areas for those who had keys.

"Welcome to Public Storage! How can I help you?" A thirty-something man with a badge of 'Roger' gave us a business 'welcome' smile. I didn't smile back. This seemed to give him pause. I even saw a twitch of possible alarm.

Then Jensen stepped past me flashing a bright smile of his own, pretty much eclipsing me and my foul humor. It was done so smoothly I was more startled than pissed by it.

"Evening. My name is Jensen White, and I really need your help." He set the closed folder on the counter. "Were you working here last Friday night?"

I moved deeper into the room, past them, then half turned back around so I could watch. The boxes around me beckoned to me. Each waving the fact they might have been the one the two men the demon had been waiting for came here to see. My eyes were itching again.

"Uh, yeah, I was. What about it?"

I could only stare as Jensen's whole face seemed to go through a transformation. The smile on his face grew warmer, brighter. He leaned against the counter totally relaxed, oozing trust and camaraderie. It was rather scary. Nowhere was the 'haunted priest chasing down demons' to be seen.

"I'm trying to help track down a couple of missing men. We got a tip they'd been seen here last Friday. Do these boys look familiar to you?" Jensen opened the folder and moved the two sketches to sit side by side on the counter.

Roger blushed when he looked at them. His Adam's apple bobbed up and down when he tried to answer. "Y-yeah, I seen 'em."

Not exactly the reaction I would have expected. He couldn't take his gaze off them as the blush rose up to his ears.

"I know it's probably against policy, but is there any way you could see yourself to checking what names they're going under? To be honest, they're in some trouble, and the sooner we find them, the faster we can get them out of harm's way."

Every last thing he said was true, yet could be taken to mean something else entirely as Jensen was pushing for it to be at the moment. Just how long had he been doing this type of thing? The more I saw of him, the more of an enigma he became.

"In trouble? *Them?*" Roger's eyes widened in panic. Again the reaction was way more than it should have been.

"Do you know them?"

Roger half turned toward me, his gaze still mostly on the pictures of the two men. "No. I don't."

This just got weirder and weirder.

"Do you remember their names?" Jensen touched him on the hand close to the sketches as if steering him back toward him.

"Yeah. I do. Are you sure they're in some kind of trouble?"

Jensen nodded slowly. "There's a bad man after them. And I don't think they know about it. If we can catch up to them, we can make sure they stay safe. I can tell you'd like that. So help us help them."

Roger stared at the pictures. "Jared and Ross Jenkins." He said the names with a wistful sigh.

They must have made a mighty big impression on him. I would never have remembered a customer's name from several days ago that clearly.

"Are they likely to come back here, do you think?"

Roger shook his head, his expression turning sad. "No. They took their package and closed out their box."

"Had you ever seen them before Friday night?"

"No…"

"Thank you. You've been very helpful." Jensen retrieved the sketches and closed the folder.

Roger looked even sadder than before. "Please help them." The guy was starting to creep me out.

"We will. Thank you again."

I followed Jensen out the door.

CHAPTER TWENTY-ONE

"Was that man acting weird, or was it just me?"

"He was rather odd." Jensen looked troubled.

"Drugs, do you think?" I had no personal experience with the stuff, but I'd seen a few of my childhood friends blasted a time or two.

"Hard to say. His aura was…" Jensen shook his head. "It made things easier at least."

"Did it? Because aside from a pair of names we don't really know much more than we did before." We got into the car.

"They picked up a package. It's possible whatever the contents are, they're somehow tied to why the demon was after them."

My brow rose. "If that's true, why didn't the bastard just go in there and get it? Why would it have to wait for them? I doubt he would have had any issues with tearing the whole place apart."

"The building was protected. It couldn't have gone inside to look for it."

"Protected? What does that mean?"

Jensen slipped me a sideways glance as he started the engine. "There are symbols, woods, metals, ceremonies that can protect or sanctify objects, places. Someone went through some trouble to make sure this would be one of them."

"A Public Storage?" It just didn't seem like the type of place someone would go to that kind of trouble for. But then again, what did I know? Until today I'd not even believed in demons. How much more was out there I had no idea about? It made me feel cold.

"Think about it. It's a public place, people would constantly go in and out. Unless you knew who you were looking for, it'd be highly unlikely you could figure out what had been protected let alone by whom."

I supposed it made a certain amount of sense. Except it hadn't worked. The two men had been expected. Yet the demon had been told not to follow them, which was odd. None of it made any sense.

"The drive to the casino is about five to six hours. We could get a motel close to Dallas and hit them first thing in the morning. Some dinner before then would probably be good as well." His tone was soft, casual, but from the way he didn't look at me directly, I got the feeling he wasn't sure I was going to take the suggestions.

Like everything else so far that day, not very well. Though I tried to rein the explosion in before it got anywhere. "Casino's normally run twenty-four seven."

"True, but we don't. If there's something to be found there, I'd rather we were rested to better deal with it." Then he added gently, "You've already had a very full day."

I glared at him then relented, knowing he was right. It was hard to believe I'd just found out by whom and why my life had been turned upside down only late this morning. It already felt like I'd been dealing with this for years.

"There's a GPS unit in the glove box, would you mind getting it for me?"

I didn't answer but moved to get it. His glove box was filled with a carton of different colored chalk, small plastic bottles with some sort of liquid, and a thin coil of rope. A strange combination. I grabbed the GPS and gave it to him.

Jensen activated and clamped the unit just below his rearview mirror after inputting a destination. A British male voice acknowledged his choice. I don't know what I thought the thing would sound like, but I liked it. You didn't hear that kind of accent much around these parts.

"If you'd like some music, feel free to find a station on the radio. I've currently got it set on 96.5."

The smooth jazz station…Interesting. I supposed three months was long enough to get acquainted with the local offerings. He just didn't look the type. But then again, I would have never pegged him for a Catholic priest either. I, more than anyone, should know better than to assume people's molds. "Jazz is fine."

He turned it on but kept it low.

We made our way to I-45 and headed north leaving Houston behind us. I tried hard not to feel anything, not sure I'd ever return.

To distract myself, I retrieved my laptop from the shoulder bag and worked in the dark to get my email and other new settings in place.

Jensen drove in silence, but there was nothing awkward about it. I wondered how long he'd been doing this job alone. Then I wondered why you'd want to. Had no one else ever volunteered to go with him? Or had none of them had a reason to want to? From the glimpses I'd caught of my unwanted visitor's mind, they wouldn't have had an agenda, but just done it and created chaos because they could. How had that not enraged them? Did they genuinely believe ignoring what had happened to them would make it go away?

Pain accented my thoughts, my nails biting into my hand again. It was harder to make it stop than it should have been. I needed something to distract me. Something to keep me from asking questions Jensen would most likely have no interest in answering.

On a whim, I opened a browser window, angling the computer on my lap to hide most of the screen. Then I typed his name into the search field and hit enter.

There were pages and pages of hits—44,700,754. Many were for pages with the words White and Jensen. Some were for a fireplace manufacturer, ear studs, and curtains. There was even a realty company by that name. I clicked on advanced search and forced the two words to be together. That narrowed the field a little.

I scrolled through the results, looking for I wasn't sure what, but doing it all the same. If he'd been possessed by a demon, there should be something on him out there somewhere. Researching him on my own wasn't the same as asking him to tell me, though whether he'd be any more pleased was another thing altogether.

Of course, there was no guarantee Jensen White was the name he'd been using back then.

About to give up, I ran across an entry leading to a news archive site. I went ahead and clicked on the link.

It was a story on Treepond, a small town I'd never heard of, located in Nebraska. The article was from a small newspaper in a neighboring city several miles away. It wasn't even really a story, but more of an editorial commentary. It insisted the tragedy in Treepond needed to be further investigated. Cover-ups were not a thing of the past and were happening right then on their own doorstep. Whole townships didn't just burn down on their own. There were also too many people missing. Jensen White was one of those listed.

The editorial posed a lot of questions but stated few facts. Surely if half of what this Perry Strauss insisted happened were true, I would have found more than this.

It was the type of news the big papers and TV media would have had a field day on. But aside from this, I'd found nothing. Yet the fact Jensen's name was mentioned, the fact I knew he'd been possessed at one time. Even the time frame agreed with what little he'd said.

But how had it not made the news?

I decided to change tactics and did a search on the town name instead.

Treepond was an unincorporated town servicing about four hundred people. Large enough to warrant a general store, church, post office, town hall, and small sheriff's office. No website, no real Wikipedia entry. Aside from some ancient stories about a forest fire, as far as the internet was concerned, the town didn't really exist. Even the fire was touted as being small and doing little, though yet undisclosed amount of damage to the city proper. There was no mention of casualties, missing people, nothing.

I decided to leave it alone for now.

CHAPTER TWENTY-TWO

The drive was uneventful. Dinner was a drive-thru off the highway somewhere for burgers and fries though I didn't really taste much of either. Jensen stopped for the night at a La Quinta Inn just south of Dallas. This particular location looked more like a standard modern chain hotel than the quaint older look of their Houston locations. The telltale Spanish tile was still in evidence, but the building itself had more of a cookie cutter look. The interior was a black and red chic but kept a retro style in the rooms, which surprised me. Guess they'd come a long way in the last few years.

I didn't pay much attention as Jensen booked the room, so was caught off guard when we ended up in the same one together. Double beds, sure, but so not the point. I doubted my virtue was in danger, but it seemed like odd behavior for a priest, even an ex one. Perhaps his stipend wasn't all that.

"I hope you don't mind." Jensen sent me a sheepish look as he set his bag on the bed. "It just seemed more expedient for our early leave-taking in the morning. I can get another if you feel it'll be a problem."

I looked away. Helping me or not, this man was a stranger. If he was left anything like me after his experience, probably not quite all right in his head. But now that we'd stopped and needed to sleep, I was suddenly grateful for not having a room of my own. I didn't want to be alone with just my thoughts if I could help it. So far, I'd pretty much been pretending that I was keeping things together. Left on my own, I knew I'd lose it completely. Masks were much easier to wear when there was someone to see them. "No, this will work fine."

He nodded, taking me at my word, then opened up his duffel. From inside it, he removed, of all things, a DustBuster and its charger. He plugged it into one of the free plugs on the far side of the room. As I continued to try to work that one out without asking, he removed a small spray bottle and a cylindrical canister. He opened the curtains at the back windows and sprayed the contents of the bottle liberally around it then thumbed the canister open and poured out a thin line of white crystals on the window sill. Murmured words left his lips just softly enough I couldn't make them out.

"What are you doing?"

Ignoring the question, he moved about the room continuing to mumble words and using the spray bottle. I jerked out of his way as he came near me and then proceeded to the room's door. There he lay down another line of white crystals. My eyes felt dry.

"Jensen?"

He sprayed the bathroom then came back out, head bowed and eyes closed. A moment later he opened them again and glanced in my direction. "Sorry, I needed to finish before I could answer you." The shy sheepish smile I was getting quite familiar with flashed for a moment. "I guess I should have explained before I got started."

He stashed the two items back into his bag. "Holy water and consecrated salt. To purify the room and set a general protection for the night. It's not powerful enough to be noticed outside of the room's area, but will serve well enough to keep us safe."

"Keep us safe from what?"

"Evil intent, restless spirits, demons." He shrugged.

"And the words?"

"A Latin prayer to reinforce their innate power with my faith."

I shook my head and sat down on the edge of the nearest bed. "This is crazy."

Jensen gave me an indulgent smile. "Salt has been used as a purifier and for protection for many thousands of years."

Sure, I'd seen it used in movies and TV shows, but those weren't reality. Although I did recall one of my cousins occasionally throwing a pinch over his shoulder for good luck. I supposed he had to have gotten it from somewhere. "And the rest of it?" I pinned him with my stare. "Catholicism and Christianity haven't been around as long as that, so why would anything from that religion slow anything supernatural down?"

The question came out a lot more antagonistic than I meant it to. It didn't seem to bother him.

"Since its inception, the Church has absorbed a lot of traditions and practices from other religions, usually as a way to make conversion easier for the new faithful. But it wasn't the only reason. Many of the old traditions were kept or at least retained the knowledge of, especially since things like this are useful when dealing with forces outside of what most consider normal."

I stared, stunned. He was actually serious about this! I gripped the cross he'd given me hoping it could somehow be true. A part of me wanted desperately to believe. It would mean I could actually be safe, that there were things we could do against the bastard who'd stolen my body and keep him from doing it again.

"I can teach you the prayer tomorrow if you like."

I shrugged, not sure whether I did or didn't want to learn it. He'd spoken about faith to power it. I hadn't had much of that for a long, long time.

He appeared to take that in stride as well. "We should turn in. No telling how things will fall when we get to Durant."

"Sure."

Digging through my hastily packed things, I found something modest to wear and changed in the bathroom.

By the time he'd taken his turn, including a long shower, I was already under the covers pretending to be asleep.

He shut off the lights and turned in.

I listened to the quieting sounds in the room wondering just what the heck I thought I was doing.

Next thing I knew, the alarm went off, jolting me upright. I'd never even noticed him set the thing. More shocking though was the fact I'd slept through the night, no nightmares in sight. Although it only felt like I'd laid down but moments before.

"Good morning."

I barely grunted a reply, still trying to catch up with everything. I felt slow, numb, lost. It didn't hurt my feelings when Jensen went for the bathroom first. He'd slept in black shorts and a black t-shirt. Was that standard priest nightwear or just his preference? What did priests wear to bed?

I was mentally blabbing to myself, yet I was weirdly curious, too. Getting out of bed was hard. But today was the day. Today we would get answers. Today we would sniff out that bastard's scent and start tracking him down. And when I found him...

A rattling sound startled me out of my thoughts. Glancing at the nightstand, I saw my watch shift and then just sit there. The noise was gone, and nothing was moving. Maybe I'd imagined it? I picked up my watch and turned it over in my hands. It seemed okay. Then what...?

The bathroom door opened and Jensen came out. "It's all yours."

I put my watch back down. "Thanks." Not looking directly at him, I got up, grabbed my toiletries bag and some clothes, and then escaped to the other room.

The hot water from the shower woke me totally up and by the time I'd cleaned my teeth and dressed I was feeling almost normal. When I came out, it was to find Jensen using his DustBuster on the lines of salt he'd laid the night before.

I must have had an incredulous look on my face because when he finished, he had an amused expression.

"I made the mess, so I figure it's up to me to clean it. The cleaning staff has enough to do as it is. Plus it leaves no curious memories."

Cautious, careful, I supposed one had no choice but to be those things to do what he did.

"We can have breakfast downstairs then head straight for the casino whenever you're ready."

His words fell on me like blinders on a horse. Though I'd woken up knowing this was what we meant to do, suddenly it was all there was. "I'm ready now."

My hands were moving as the words left my mouth, forcing them to be factual as I shoved all my possessions back into my suitcase.

I heard Jensen sigh, but his neutral face was back on when I glanced his way.

I didn't pay much attention to what I grabbed to eat downstairs at the buffet, just shoved it in and swallowed. Heartburn smacked me around because of it, but I ignored it. It was hard not to drum my fingers on the table, as unlike me, Jensen took his time to eat.

It irritated me to no end. "Tell me about Treepond."

CHAPTER TWENTY-THREE

I literally felt the temperature of the room fall a couple of degrees. The waves of unhappiness shooting from him as he stopped eating across from me almost made me drop it. Almost… "Come on, tell me about Treepond."

"You couldn't leave it alone, could you?"

"No. And if you don't tell me now, I'll just ask again later." I should have been ashamed of myself, I really should have, but I wanted to know. Desperately. This was as good a time to ask as any.

He put his fork down and wiped his mouth with his napkin then set it on the table. His gaze wouldn't meet mine. "Not here. On the way, in the car." I nodded, willing to concede at least that much.

He slapped some money on the table and left. I hurried to catch up to him.

Once we put our luggage away and got underway, he still said nothing. I stared at his profile as he drove, silently insistent. This man had revealed the truth of what happened to me, saved me from the torture of ignorance. Despite that, I wasn't being kind to him in the least. Yet even knowing this, I couldn't help myself. I had to know. Even if I didn't have any idea why that was.

Only after we were speeding along Central Expressway did he finally speak.

"Treepond was my first parish after seminary." His lips barely moved and I had to struggle to hear him. He kept his gaze locked out the front windshield. "I was placed under old Father Christoff. He'd served the small parish there for over thirty years, and that was after serving at other locations for twenty before that. He was looking forward to retirement."

Jensen grew silent after that. I didn't push. I could tell from his unchanged profile he would speak again.

"I'd been there for several years, taking on more and more of the Father's work, getting to know the diverse group of parishioners that populated the area. It was a beautiful place. Isolated from the outside world, from its ugly troubles, and everyone felt secure there. Our own little protected world...

"Father Christoff passed, died in his sleep. I missed him terribly. He'd been a kind, wise man and taught me much. But life went on, and I adjusted. Then one spring I got a call from the Richmonds—wealthy family, very old money, somewhat reclusive and pretty much the reason there was even a town. Their oldest son was visiting from college. Yet they said he wasn't himself. Asked if they could bring him to talk to me."

Jensen gave the smallest of shrugs. "I said yes, of course. Part of the job description. I tried not to make any assumptions since they didn't really give me any details, but many of the young people who left town for any amount of time always found it hard to assimilate back into the slow lifestyle when they came back... If they came back." A sad smile touched his face for a moment.

"I met them at the Town Hall per their request. It was after five, so the offices were closed for the day, so we'd have privacy. I'd seen David just that Sunday at mass. He'd appeared fine then. But the young man they brought with them to the Town Hall wasn't the boy I knew. He wore ripped clothes, dark eyeliner, his hair a gelled mess. I was sure he was just rebelling, probably going through a phase.

"He protested being brought there. The filth that poured from his mouth was incredible." Jensen's hands tightened on the wheel until they turned white. "Yet the moment his parents were out of the room, it was like a switch got flipped. He stared at me as if I was some fascinating toy and lounged in a chair as if all was right with the world. That was when he asked me… Asked me if I had the knowledge to figure out what he was. If I knew how to rid the boy of him."

My pulse sped up. Here was what I wanted to know.

"I was confused at first. I didn't know what he was talking about. Then he stood up and grabbed the desk and lifted it over his head like it weighed nothing and then set it back down while grinning at me. That was when I remembered some passages from seminary, beliefs held by the Church and its people ages ago. Things we were taught, but no one believed. We'd all just assumed it'd been a sign of the times. Things done to reassure the people, not actually things that happened, or were real."

Jensen finally glanced at me, his eyes dark and haunted. I felt more than a tinge of guilt for forcing him to talk about it. But at the same time, I couldn't work up my voice to tell him to stop.

"It wanted me to know what it was. Taunted me by speaking in several languages, some of which I don't believe have existed for millennia. Then it asked me what I planned to do about it. I almost ran…then I thought about David having this thing inside him, helpless, and knew I couldn't go.

"Though I had no real idea what to do, I also realized I was the best chance he had. So I pulled out my rosary and the pocket bible I always carried with me and began the chant of purification, praying, hoping it might have some effect."

Though the sun was just starting to peek over the horizon and traffic wove all around us, the longer he spoke, the more it seemed to me we were somewhere else, apart from the world, just the two of us and his memories.

"David looked shocked for a second then started laughing. He was laughing so hard I thought he would fall down. When I kept going, he just walked over to me and picked me up off my feet." Jensen shuddered. "It said to me, 'You're a sorry excuse for a priest. Not very well prepared at all. But let's have us some fun anyway, shall we?' That's when…that's when he switched from the boy to me. And all pretense was thrown to the winds." The emotion was gone from his voice. The words fell one after another in a monotone.

"It let me watch. It let me rage and plead and totally ignored me. It got canning jars, dish soap, a bottle of alcohol and pieces of cloth from the general store after picking up and throwing Jimmy Tompkins across the length of it just for saying 'welcome.' Then it went to the gas station down the block and filled the jars with gasoline."

"Oh…" I looked away, not wanting to see his pain as I guessed at what came next.

"It set the town on fire. Luckily most of the people had gone home for the evening, except at Lu Belle's, where the dinner rush was on. Those who came out got thrown back in. No matter what I tried, I couldn't stop the thing. And when it had had its fill, it left me—staring at my own burning church."

My hands shook as I risked a glance in his direction. He had no expression, his face was blank. That made everything he'd just said and lost so much worse. He hadn't lied when he said the demon had taken it easy on me. "And David…?"

I saw the blank mask crack. "He lived. Didn't remember anything clearly about what had happened but insisted that his parents get away from the Town Hall, and they listened to him. They must have seen something in my face when I walked past them. I never dared ask. But when it was over, they felt responsible and so helped keep matters quiet and out of the papers. Then the Church came and made sure."

I felt sick to my stomach. How many times had something like this happened before? How many times had people been silenced, the truth hidden, just to keep the masses in check? Although with an enemy that seemed able to strike through anyone, anywhere, perhaps they were doing most people a favor…

"And your scar?" I didn't realize the question had come from me until after I'd said it.

"A gift." He laughed. There was no mirth in it. "Toward the end it allowed me to partially take my body back to see what I would do. I grabbed a broken piece of glass and tried to take it with me, to rid the world of it, but it stopped me and left me this as a reminder of my powerlessness instead."

He turned his face toward me and like a coward I looked away again. Every time he looked in a mirror he would see it, he'd be reminded of what had happened, of his inability to stop it. And I'd made him dredge it all up again. "I'm sorry…"

I stared out the window at the green fields, the homes, the cars outside, trying to link myself back with the living. Though I didn't speak to Him often, I thanked God for the fact I'd had things as easy as I had.

CHAPTER TWENTY-FOUR

Mercifully it didn't take much longer to reach the casino. Though the day was warm, there was a chill inside me I couldn't quite get rid of. Guilt had grabbed hold and even my waiting anger couldn't burn it away. Fear nibbled inside me as well, the actual lengths these demons would go to now perfectly clear.

The recently built casino rose grandly toward the sky in a gentle curve, the right side extending outwards from the main as it rose almost like a hand reaching toward heaven. A quick count found twelve stories plus. The front drive was covered by a tall portico shaped into three pieces and put together under marble columns. On the front lawn, nine pillars rose in a circle increasing in height, framing metal rings that were stacked on each other and on fire.

Something this grand I would expect from Texas, but from Oklahoma? The guys at work would never believe it. With a painful twinge, I remembered I wouldn't be seeing them again to share.

Jensen parked the car but didn't get out. "I want to give you a couple of things in case something happens." He reached under his seat and pulled out a small Tupperware case. Inside were small plastic bottles, like for carrying lotion. He pulled two out and handed them to me. One was clear while the other had something milky white inside. "Holy water and consecrated salt. It burns them, but won't hurt the host. They'll buy you a few seconds." He took one each for himself and slipped them into his vest pocket. "Be aware though, some of the more powerful demons won't be affected by either."

"More powerful?" My stomach contracted into a knot.

"Running into higher level demons is incredibly unusual, generally. It takes a lot of power or a very greedy, foolish man to bring one over. But it's best not to assume whenever you can."

I noticed he wouldn't look directly at me. Was it because of what he was saying or because he was too angry to look at me for what I'd forced him to reveal earlier? I needed to find a way to fix this somehow.

Jensen got out of the car and opened the trunk. He pulled over the strange case I'd noticed before–the one that made my eyes itch. He unlocked the lid and lifted it. I scrunched my eyes half closed for a second, the itching going nuts before calming down again.

Inside were drawers and neat compartments full of I didn't rightly know what. There were labels on everything, but all in a language I couldn't read. He opened one small drawer and it contained weird looking letter openers in a bed of felt. He pulled one out then closed the luggage and the car trunk.

"This is just in case." He handed the letter opener over.

It had a broader blade than usual, giving it the look of a long leaf of some sort. But it wasn't steel, it was heavier, and it was a dark color, almost black. It had runes inscribed on both sides of the blade. "What is it?"

"An iron blade—unsharpened. But it's inscribed with several of the names of God. Both the names and the metal will protect you from demons. Use it only as a means of last resort, physical confrontations hardly ever go well. You should keep the blade on you in case, however, always."

I wrapped a hand around it and felt strangely comforted, blunt blade or not.

"Please stay close to me." Jensen started off toward the hotel.

Taking a deep, steadying breath and reassuring myself I was ready for this, I followed after him.

The lobby of the hotel was breathtaking. Brown marble flooring, black countertops for the front desk. There was a nook with a huge vase and exotic plants I'd never seen before. The back wall was done in strands of red and brown making it look like a woven basket. It was as if they'd taken nature or things people would relate to American Indians and made it chic. There was even a faux river/waterfall with a giant statue of a buffalo going across it. The light fragrance of incense wafting in the air was a nice extra touch.

Jensen avoided the front desk and followed the sounds of pings and whoops and clangs with bits of music that were a part of casinos everywhere. Machines were set three to four in a row, comfortable seats before each one for your gambling comfort. Though it was still early morning, several of the chairs were already occupied by people who looked to be planning not to go anywhere anytime soon.

Gently rising ramps led to a gigantic open bar area with screens for playing card games embedded into the bar itself. Jensen slowly scoped each area. A more sedate zone led to the Platinum High Limit Lounge. Soft grays and browns gave it a more laidback atmosphere than the larger lounges we'd come across earlier. The bar was smaller though still with embedded screens, there were also several large couches and conversation nooks off to the side.

Jensen's back stiffened as we walked in and he glanced

toward the bar. There was a woman about my age sitting there, nursing a tall drink with a spear of cherries. Jensen stepped toward her signaling for me to stay behind him. Was this someone like me? Was the same demon inside her? Fear welled up, but I pushed it back down as I let indignation takes its place.

"Excuse me." The ex-priest stood just behind and to the left of the woman's chair. As she turned around, he moved in close. I caught just a glimpse of the blunt knife. "It'd be in your best interest to leave this woman."

A plucked brow rose at this pronouncement. Green eyes took in his measure then flicked in my direction to take mine.

"I don't think so. I very much like this suit." She brushed long brown curls away from her partially exposed shoulder. Now that I could see her fully, I realized she was wearing a burgundy dress that while sophisticated also left very little to the imagination. Then the full truth of what she'd said hit home.

"Human beings aren't clothes…" I bit off the 'bitch' that was going to end the sentence, trying hard to keep my anger in check. This was White's show.

"To you maybe." She gave me a warm smile which totally clashed with her words.

"You might want to reconsider." Jensen leaned in close.

Her smile grew predatory. "I wonder if you've actually thought about what you're saying. We're in a casino after all. And casinos don't stint on security." Her gaze roamed to several places in the room.

Cameras stared down from the bar's lighting above us. I couldn't see anything in the gray tiled ceiling or the shelves of indirect lighting overhead, but that didn't mean the place didn't have eyes we couldn't see.

"Do anything at all and you'll find the police flashing your picture everywhere. Is that something you want?" She turned away to pluck the stick of cherries out of her drink and slowly sucked one of them into her mouth.

"You don't belong here, demon."

"That's only *your* opinion." She sucked another cherry into her mouth. "Mmmm."

"He's not the only one who thinks so." I fingered the small bottle of holy water, tempted to throw it on her. Jensen had said it would hurt the demon and not the host, so there'd be nothing the cops could make a fuss about.

Though it would probably get us thrown out. I was sure she'd call out to security and play the helpless white woman card.

"You really should learn your place, dear. There's no room in this conversation for someone like you." She stared down her nose at me.

I couldn't believe she actually went there.

"What should I call you anyway? Is it black or negro or African American? I forget." That warm smile was back on her face again. As if we were sharing pleasantries. "I remember fondly when your kind were just a commodity to be sold and traded like bales of cotton." She looked me up and down. "If not for the bad attitude, I'm sure you would have fetched a decent price."

My jaw hurt, the muscle along the jawline jumping, as the almost irrepressible urge to claw the bimbo's eyes out washed over me. I had to fight to hold myself back, telling myself over and over that a scene would only make things easier for her.

"Williams…" Jensen's soft voice caressed me with the lightest of admonishments. Shifting my gaze slightly in his direction brought the demon's drink into view. The glass and contents were shaking minutely on the bar. Was the creature doing that? What did it mean? What it did do was distract my focus, giving me the time I needed to grab full control of myself again.

"They know how to push our buttons. They always seem to know just what will set us off or hurt us most." Jensen spoke to me, but his full attention was still centered on the woman.

"That's right, *girl*. Listen to the white man. Listen to your betters." Her condescending smile couldn't have glowed brighter.

But it wasn't really her; it was the thing inside her, controlling her. She was a victim, just like me. The constant struggle to keep my boiling emotions in check made my knees weak. "You're a worse type of scum than any white man, demon. Let her go."

She laughed. "I'd like to see you make me."

My hands bunched into fists. Helplessness. I hated the feeling, hated it with a fiery passion. It was something I'd felt too many times in my teenage years. Feelings I'd pushed down and replaced with anger instead. Doing whatever I could, no matter how useless it may have seemed, to try to counter it. The clerk's job at the warehouse had paid almost nothing, and I'd had to confront other problems which made me just as mad, but unlike some of my relatives, rather than just sit around and begrudge my fate, I'd tried to do something about it. Just like my parents had slaved to do something for us.

The demon's glass distracted me again. It almost seemed to be jumping in place.

"We know about the twins." Though Jensen said the words softly, the demon jerked in place as if he'd shouted it to the room. Too late, she tried to make it look like it'd meant nothing.

Her eyes narrowed as she turned her full attention on him and studied his face. "You know nothing."

"I know your demon friend was sloppy. I know he came here to report on what he'd seen. I know who they are and what they look like."

Her eyes narrowed even further a snarl marring the stolen face. "You'd do well to keep your nose out of our business, *human*."

As the demon's anger rose, I found my own waning. The tables were currently turned and the very cameras she'd pointed out to stop us from causing a scene now appeared to be holding her back. Which meant this place was important somehow.

"This became my business the moment you entered this plane. And will remain my business until all of you have returned to where you belong." Gone was Jensen's neutral mask. Gone was any semblance of kindness or feeling. I felt a chill go through me at the open, jagged, righteous antagonism evolving on White's face. The scar seemed to pulsate on his cheek.

"I could snap your neck in an instant, insect."

Jensen leaned toward her. "But you won't. Because you *can't*. You're under orders."

My gaze jumped to his face, surprised. I should have figured this out sooner myself—and would have if I'd not been so distracted by my own emotions. If my demon had been told to report here, so might others. She was here to wait for them.

What could be so important about two men to have more than one demon on their trail? Or did they usually do things like this? The depth of my ignorance mocked me.

"You can pretend to know whatever you like, priest, but you'll get nothing from me." Her face smoothed out and she turned away from him and grabbed her drink.

I'd been too distracted to notice it'd stopped moving until she reached for it. Like the fact she'd called Jensen a priest. Had she pulled this from his mind or did she know him, or of him?

"Thank you for your time." White gave her a half nod, looking normal again, and backed away without turning his back on her. When he reached my side, he gently took hold of my elbow and steered me out of there. I was too stunned to resist.

CHAPTER TWENTY-FIVE

We rounded a corner putting us out of sight of the bar. I came to a dead halt. "We're, we're just going to leave?"

"Yes." His face was back to its usual neutral expression.

I jerked my arm away. "And leave that thing inside her? Let it do whatever it wants?"

"This is not the place to discuss this…" His knowing gaze met mine.

My hands clenched and unclenched as I tried to understand what was going on. This wasn't what I'd signed on for. I hadn't thought he would do such a thing—leaving an innocent behind with a demon inside. Could he only intervene once the demon was gone?

"Please, Tamara. It isn't safe here."

My face felt tight and the thumping at my temples drove small spikes into my head. "I don't…understand…"

"I will explain, I promise you, but *not here*." He didn't look at me as he spoke, instead searching everywhere around us. As if he expected trouble at any moment.

That decided me. "Fine." I put on my longest stride and headed for the exit. Jensen stuck close to me the whole way.

As we got in the car, he pulled out a cell phone and hit autodial. I strapped in, my mouth full of questions I couldn't yet voice.

"Jensen White. Durant, OK. Quatuor minores

Ordines dari possunt extra Missarum solemnia…"

I frowned at the odd words, thinking they might be Latin. My curiosity at whom he'd called bubbled up.

As he appeared to wait for a response, he started the car and drove from the casino's parking lot. He headed south, back toward Dallas. I glanced back toward the casino for any signs of pursuit. I saw none.

"Yes. Something is brewing. There is a definite increase and orders are involved."

My head snapped in his direction not wanting to miss anything.

"The Choctaw Casino off I-75. There's a woman there, in her twenties, brown hair, green eyes, a customer." His voice was low, and though it tried to sound impartial, I could hear a timber of emotion undercoating it all. "Yes, I'm sure. At least one other has made contact with her and I'm certain there will be others. The Order will need to get involved."

The car zoomed down Central Expressway, silent seconds ticking away as he listened to someone on the other end. "I can't." His gaze flickered toward me for a moment. "I have…someone with me. And we're already following a lead on what this might be about."

I frowned, not sure what possible lead he could be talking about. As far as I knew, we had no other trail to follow.

"Yes, yes. I understand. Thank you." Jensen closed the phone and tucked it away again.

"We have a lead?" It was the first of the multitude of questions to win free.

Jensen nodded. "We know who they're looking for and what they look like."

"But we don't even know what direction they were heading in! And they left several days ago."

He flashed me a smile—an impish one, which was terribly surprising. It made me wonder just what he'd been like before tragedy destroyed his life. "It won't be a problem. I have a plan. It'll only require some patience on our part, some prayer, and some luck."

Since he obviously didn't want to tell me the details, I went on to something else. "Who was on the phone?"

"Emergency contact for the Order I work with. They…they've trained for a long time to deal with the possessed. If they can trap it, they will free her. And any others who decide to show up at the casino."

I shook my head. "Catholic Demon Hunting Monks? Sounds like a bad SyFy Channel movie…"

Jensen laughed. "Not exactly. At least not like what they'd look like in a production from Hollywood. Mostly they're just prepared to act. Not since the 1400s have there been as many possessions as in the last couple of years. And as far as anyone knew, there was no reason for it. This is the first inkling we've had there might be something organized going on."

Demons organized. More possessions than had been seen in ages. Despite the little I knew about all this, it still made me uneasy, sure it couldn't be a good thing.

Then I realized that amidst everything that happened, I'd learned nothing about the demon who took me. It could have still been at the casino or moved on. I didn't have the faintest idea which.

The flash of disgust and hot anger caught me off guard. I glared around me before I could grab hold of it. There were priests or monks on the way, if it was still there, they'd find it. Although the idea it wouldn't be sent back to Hell by my hand rankled, I didn't have the proper knowledge to do it anyway. Helping Jensen would hurt it more. It'd been ordered to watch those men, meaning it wasn't entirely the source of what had happened to me. If I could mess up their plans, it would affect any of the bastards up the demon chain of command.

"Are you all right?"

Jensen's worried voice made me aware of the curled fists on my lap. I forced them to relax. "Yes… Just…yes. I'm fine."

A quick glance in his direction showed he didn't believe me, but he didn't press the point.

I needed a distraction. "How did it know you were once a priest?"

He threw me a veiled look. "Demons can sense things we can't. The rituals I went through, the purification, the vows, highly emotional things, they left traces. Like our bones, like tree rings, evidence is left of what's happened to us in our lives. It's similar to the things I can see in an aura, but much more complex. They can read them with total ease if they deign to take the time. It's how they gather ammunition to get under your skin."

My arms crowded with gooseflesh. It was bad enough being possessed revealed all my innermost secrets for one of the thing's inspection, but now it sounded like they all could pick up a large amount of information just by looking at you. No part of me was safe. "How, how do you keep them from doing that?"

"I'm sorry to say that you can't. You can school your mind to ignore their jibes, but that's about all."

He sounded as dissatisfied with the options as I felt.

"How many demons have you run across?" Though I was the one asking the question I found myself nervous as I waited for his answer.

"Only two."

"Then how…?"

A faint grin lit on his face for a moment. "Do I know

all this? The Order of the Niveus Miles Militis, the Order of the White Warriors. They've compiled information on demons for centuries. To be wary, to be prepared. To help mankind when it needs it. Like they helped me in my time of need, like I helped you in yours.

"The Church supports them, though they aren't spoken of. Very few are inducted, the knowledge they keep too tempting to use as it was not intended. In the ways of the Franciscans, most of its members are meant to be out amongst the people, ever vigilant—ready to fight in His name when called."

CHAPTER TWENTY-SIX

Everything that'd just come out of his mouth seemed ludicrous—demons, possessions, a secret order of monks supported by the Catholic Church—except it wasn't. I'd witnessed it, been a victim of it. Yet aside from a chosen few, no one knew. But something else he'd said sent a jiggle of alarm through me. In all the years since he'd been possessed, he'd met only two other demons. Yet in less than a week, I'd been exposed to just as many. The amount of possessions in recent years had increased. That could only mean that so had the number of demons.

And here I was traveling with a man who sought them out. Chances were I would encounter more of them. A part of me shook at the prospect, while another part, the raging part, couldn't wait.

I pulled out my laptop and tried to research this order, demons, anything I could use to distract myself, but mostly came up empty. There were a lot of pages on demons, even possession, but most of the information seemed to have been pulled out of movies or fiction books. I didn't know enough to sift the drek from the truth.

By the time I gave up, White was turning into a parking lot. To my surprise it looked to be another church—but a smaller, less ostentatious affair than St. Anne's, more austere. More surprising was the sign in Korean.

Jensen parked and threw me a glance. "I'll only be a few minutes, if you'd rather not come in."

"Why are we here?"

He picked up the folder with the sketches. "Father Nguyen has a copier and fax machine combo. I want to get these out to as many parishes as possible and use them to find these two for us." He gave that a couple of seconds to sink in.

"Oh." I felt stupid. This was how he'd planned to find them all along. "I'll wait here."

A fleeting smile surfaced for a moment then it was gone. "Suit yourself. Be right back."

I rolled down my window as he went, the day already heating up.

An old commercial I remembered seeing as a kid floated up in my mind's eye. He would do with the churchgoers what the shampoo did with those using it hoping they'd tell two friends, and they'd tell two friends and so on. It might get them somewhere, it might not. But it definitely had a higher possible chance of success than us randomly driving around looking for them. Now, all it had to do was work.

On a whim, I brought my laptop out again and did a search on the two names. I got some hits, but none were for the two we were looking for. Not unless Jared had been a production manager for Sesame Street or a funeral director up in Pittsburg. As for Ross, he could have been a men's wear and virtual artist from the UK, or a quarterback for the Louisiana Tech Bulldogs.

Like looking for needles in a haystack. There wasn't even any guarantee those were even their real names. The biggest question though was why demons would care anything about them in the first place. I was pretty sure my unwanted hitchhiker didn't have the faintest idea. His curiosity burned too brightly when he spotted them. I knew he even hesitated going to Oklahoma, trying to figure out if there was an angle he could exploit without getting caught by his superiors.

I closed the laptop and got out of the car and stretched, shaking loose from the bastard's thoughts and feelings. It would be wonderful if there were a way to scrub my mind clean of it once I'd gotten whatever I could from what it'd known while I was trapped inside my own body, but it wasn't likely. More bad memories I would have to just put up with and lock away as best I could. If they'd let me. The thing had cost me so much already.

My capped anger nibbled at me from the edges. But anger made it hard to think. Anger made you stupid. Although when used right, it could make you focused as hell. The time wasn't now though—alienating the only person who could help me monumentally moronic. If Jensen found me too much of a liability, he would cut me loose. I couldn't allow that.

Worse, there was no telling how long this hunt would take. I needed to become *indispensable*. I needed to be armed and prepared. My college self-defense course was a long way off. My ignorance on how to deal with the demons an even bigger liability.

These things needed to be remedied.

All I had to do was get Jensen to agree. But would he? I had no intention of joining an order, and it was highly likely they wouldn't indoctrinate a woman anyway. But Jensen never said he was part of the order, only that they worked together. Maybe the possessed were out, thought of as tainted, unworthy.

I rubbed the back of my neck, the muscles there too tight. There was no proof anything I was thinking about was even remotely true. I really was operating in a total vacuum.

Looking up, I stared at the baby blue Texas sky, large cotton ball like clouds drifting here and there, like sheep grazing in a field. Peaceful, quiet. How many afternoons had I laid under a tree as a kid and just lost myself in all that blueness? How long had it been since the last time I'd taken the time? Stare, let go, unfocus, think of nothing…

The sun warmed my skin and perspiration beaded on my lower back where I was leaning against the Taurus. The sound of light traffic and playful birds washed over me. Each of my muscles ever so slowly began to relax.

Then unbidden and out of nowhere a picture flashed in my mind. The demon in my body wearing next to nothing, staring at itself in a mirror and running its stolen hands all over me.

I yelped and tried to jump back as if I could somehow escape my own mind. My foot slipped on the asphalt and I went down, bumping my head against the side of the car. I barely even noticed, my heart lodged in my throat, fear and revulsion washing over me in an endless cascade.

"Tamara!" Jensen came around the car at a run, his face covered with concern. "What happened? Are you alright?"

I nodded, not having the faintest idea how to answer his question. What the heck was this? I rubbed my arms, strangely cold, as the feelings abated.

Jensen held out his hand to help me up, and after several moments, I reached out and let him. I had to lean against the car again, not feeling all that steady on my feet.

"Here, let's go inside. I'm sure Father Nguyen has some tea he wouldn't mind sharing with us." He reached for my elbow to help me, but I pulled back.

"I'm okay! It's over. I'm fine." I wouldn't look him in

the eye.

He leaned against the car beside me without intruding on my space. "What happened?"

I shook my head not wanting to talk about it. Then I remembered how just minutes ago I'd been telling myself not to be a liability. If I were a moody bitch all the time, he wouldn't want to keep me around. Why should he? I'd have to try harder. "I was just trying to relax. Something, an image from when I wasn't myself showed up. Surprised me, that's all. No big deal."

Jensen said nothing for almost a minute. His silence made me nervous.

"You're likely suffering from PTSD."

I gave him a shocked look. "Like the soldiers in Iraq?"

He wouldn't meet my gaze. "Like those of tortured prisoners."

I jerked away from the car, the idea repulsive and disturbing. "That's insane."

"Is it?" His soft voice coiled around me though he never moved from where he leaned against the car. "You were trapped in the most inescapable prison of all—your own body. You were shown things that wounded your very soul. Chaos and destruction done in your name and then you were left to deal with the consequences. No proof, and if I'd not found you, no memory available you didn't actually do any of these things."

What he was telling me was that I'd been helpless, that I'd been a victim. My old friend rattled inside me even as my fists clenched and unclenched at my sides. My jaw shut so tight it made my teeth hurt. "*Fine*. Call it whatever you want. But I'll deal with it. You don't have to worry about me."

"No, perhaps I don't. You're very strong. Stronger than I was." His voice lowered even more. "I doubt you've once considered taking your own life."

CHAPTER TWENTY-SEVEN

I snapped around at his words. The weight of what he'd left unsaid like a slap. He was, had been a Catholic priest. Suicide was considered a straight, one-way ticket to perdition by them. Yet he'd obviously contemplated it. Perhaps even attempted it. I kept forgetting how much worse his situation had been compared to mine. Yet here he was, still fighting, still moving forward. And he thought I was stronger? "You seem to be coping."

"I didn't always." His haunted gaze rose to meet mine.

I looked away, from cowardice or to let him save face, I didn't know.

"So how do I get rid of these PSTD's?"

"You probably won't like it."

That made me frown. "What's that supposed to mean?"

White ran his hand slowly over the hood of the car. "Talking, weirdly enough. Talking about the feelings, the experience itself. Feeling there's someone who understands and lays no blame."

He was right. I didn't like it. Speaking of these things to the psychiatrist had been bad enough, and that's before I remembered everything. There were things I didn't want to look at, things I didn't want to admit. "I'll have to think about it."

"It's your choice, of course. But when you need me, I'll be here." There was no disappointment, no expectation. Just someone who knew what this was about and how hard it was.

Gratitude filled me. It made no real sense as we'd not accomplished anything and I hadn't bared my soul, but I felt grateful and slightly better all the same. "Thanks."

He nodded then straightened. "We should probably get going."

"Going where?"

"Other churches, ones on the way to New Mexico anyway. There's a safe house there we can use while we wait for news." He went around the car. "It'll be a good spot to teach you some basics."

Now we were getting somewhere! "Just as long as it's not Roswell. I don't think I could handle finding out aliens are real, too."

Jensen gave a surprised laugh as if such a thing had never occurred to him. "Yes, it would be a little much, wouldn't it?" He gave me a small smile. "Actually, we're going to a place near there, the town of Hope. So if you do decide you want to check for aliens, it can be arranged."

"No thanks, I'll pass." I'd had more than enough surprises for one lifetime already. I wasn't about to go looking for more.

The somber cloud which had hung over both of us seemed to dissipate a little. Hopefully, we could keep it that way for a while.

As promised, we hit a couple of more churches on the way to I-20 and then headed west. It was amazing the number of churches he found along the way just off the freeway. More impressive was how many of the priests at these places he seemed to know by name. We crawled our way toward New Mexico.

We were stopped at a small gas station when my iPhone rang. Jensen was pumping gas. I scrambled to get the phone, not having the faintest idea who could be calling me. "Hello?"

"Miss Williams?"

"Yes?"

"It's Dr. Romero. I've spoken to Dr. Mitchell."

I jolted away from the phone as if he'd smacked me. Romero, the psychiatrist. I'd totally forgotten about him and the scans of my brain. With everything else that had happened, my visit with him felt as if it happened years ago instead of a couple of days. I forced the phone back to my ear. "Yes, thank you for calling me back."

"Is this a bad time?" His accent thickened. "You sound a little off."

"No, no, I'm fine. I just, I just hadn't expected to hear from you so soon."

A pleased laugh came from the other end of the line. "Mitchell hates being indebted to me, you see. Most of the wait was on the scans being processed and sent to his office."

I felt dizzy for a moment, a weird sense of the surreal sweeping over me. "I see... What did the scans show?"

"Mitchell says your brain is fine. No odd blockages, no growths. Totally healthy, as far as he could see. He mentioned something about higher activity than he expected, but said it was nothing to worry about. So at least we've been able to rule out the possibility of this being a physical mental issue. I think some blood tests would be the next step. Make sure your chemical levels are in balance. Then we go from there. How does that sound to you?"

I was in no way surprised the scans came out clean, but it did serve to reassure me all the rest of this wasn't some illusion of my making. "Dr. Romano, I appreciate all you've done for me, but I'm going to have to put the tests on hold. An emergency's come up and I'm out of state at the moment. But I'll call to make an appointment as soon as I get back."

There was only silence from the other end for a long, drawn-out moment. "Tamara, has something happened?"

"No. Nothing like that. A friend needs me is all." I was lying to a psychiatrist. I was sure that was illegal somewhere. "I'll call your office as soon as I can. Goodbye, Dr. Romero, and thank you."

I ended the call. There was no way I could tell him the truth. He'd lock me up for sure. Lovely.

When the phone rang again, I sent the call straight to voicemail.

Jensen stuck his head in the window. "Something wrong?"

I kept my expression neutral. "No. But I probably should change my phone number. Mind if we make one more pit stop along the way?"

CHAPTER TWENTY-EIGHT

The side trips for churches slowed down as the land flattened out and the heat went up. Trees got shorter then sparse, dried grass and weeds taking over the landscape. Rather than take 360, White stayed on Route 62 to hit Carlsbad and some of the churches there. Route 285 took us almost straight north past the Brantley Lake State Park. And I'd thought places in Texas were bare.

We reached a town called Artesia as the sun went down. My stomach made a sudden noise, not having had anything in it since lunch and not much at that. "How long till we get to Hope?"

"Not long." Jensen sent me a sideways glance. "But how about we stop for some of the best Mexican food in the area before we get there?"

My stomach must have growled louder than I thought. I stared out the window. "Sounds good to me."

White drove us to a place called Chapz Bar & Grill. A one-story flat building colored in a brownish red with red cloth awnings over the windows. There was even a sizeable awning over the entrance like those you'd see on hotels in New York on TV. Didn't scream 'good Mexican food' to me. More like a cheap strip joint. But I knew better than some not to judge by appearances.

The minute we stepped inside my mouth watered as we got hit with a wave of smells—hot fresh made chips, tangy salsa, and cooking meat. If these scents were anything to go by, the food would be fabulous. For the first time all week I was looking forward to eating.

The interior was dimly lit, medium round tables clothed in red set on the open floor, framing a small empty stage. Off to the side stood a large wooden bar with wine racks decorating the wall above it.

A young woman in a red t-shirt offered to seat us and once she'd done so left us to peruse the red menus. I was sensing a theme.

The place catered the usual fare you'd expect at a Mexican restaurant plus a few unusual items like cactus tacos. Not feeling all that adventurous at the moment, I ordered a mundane enchilada plate.

"Anything to drink with that, ma'am?" The waitress's hand stood poised over the order book.

"No, thanks. Water's fine."

She gave me a look like I was some kind of weirdo and after taking Jensen's order went on her way. He'd picked iced tea. He didn't get one of her funny looks. Did they do things differently here in New Mexico?

A guy came by and deposited a large basket of chips and a bowl of chunky salsa. They were hot, just out of the fryer. As I crunched down on one, my taste buds exploded, prodding my stomach to insist it wanted more of that. I didn't care if the enchiladas were decent or not at this point, these chips were mighty fine.

As I shoveled the fifth or sixth one into my maw, I noticed Jensen watching me, a little boy smile on his face as he took a chip for himself.

"You like?"

I forced myself to slow down, ignoring my stomach's protest at this, and gave him a shrug. "They'll do."

His smile grew wider. "I can see that. The food is just as good."

I looked down, grabbing another chip while I was at it, and made no comment. We'd see.

Less than five minutes later another waiter came by and deposited plates before each of us. I dug in the moment he left. White was right, this stuff was excellent. Before I knew it, I'd wolfed down over half of it. It wasn't like me. My stomach couldn't have cared less.

I pretended to ignore the muffled laugh across the table from me and kept eating.

"Holy shit!"

I glanced up startled as a quarterback sized guy in a muscle shirt and jeans made a beeline straight for me.

"It's you! What are the odds, man? This is fantastic!" He glanced over his shoulder at a guy only slightly smaller than him who sported a sweat rimmed cowboy hat. "Danny, get over here!"

I was pretty sure I'd never seen this guy before in my life. "Sorry, but I don't know you."

The man's face split with a shit eating grin. "Well, you may not know me, but I sure as heck know you. Visited your website often enough. Damn, but I love your work."

The blood just flowed out of my face. No, God, please don't do this to me. "You have me confused with someone else. Please, just leave me alone."

My stomach curled and soured up inside me, making me regret having eaten anything.

The guy never bothered to listen to me. As his friend came up, he put an arm about his shoulders to bring him close as he leaned over the table, as if doing him a big favor by sharing a great secret with him. "This here is the famous Chocolate Lover, man. You know, the one on the internet."

A meaty hand pushed up the cowboy hat as suddenly intent eyes really looked at me for the first time. Cold chills skyrocketed up and down my spine.

"I already told you, you have me confused with

someone else. Now *please* leave me alone." Fury flared deep in my insides. I'd never expected the demon's bored pastimes to haunt me like this.

Jensen stood up. "Gentlemen, we're trying to eat our meal. Please be on your way."

"Don't get your panties in a wad, old man. We're just trying to be friendly. This cute thing has warmed Danny and me many a night. She's our favorite."

I caught a glimpse of confusion on Jensen's face as his brows drew together then cleared. "Be that as it may, please leave us. She doesn't want you here."

"He must be wanting a taste of her, too, Bill." Danny's voice was low and slow. His gaze had yet to leave me. It seemed to be roaming all over me as if remembering things I didn't want to know.

I pushed my chair back and stood up. This type of thing was supposed to be long behind me. My nails bit into my palms. "I asked you to leave. I don't know you and you don't know me. I'm not this 'Chocolate Lover' of yours. *Go away.*"

Despite the music playing in the background something of what was going on must have radiated around because I could feel the eyes of the other patrons turning our way. It only made me angrier. Was it so much to ask to have a quiet meal without being pestered by a couple of horny assholes?

"Honey, I'd never mistake you for anyone else, never." Danny's lips curled into a lustful sneer. His meaty hand reached out and grabbed my arm before I could jerk it out of the way. I tried to pull my arm loose but he was gripping it too tight.

Who did this *bastard* think he was? My fist shot out and slammed into his chest. Futile as the gesture would surely be, I wasn't going to just take this.

Instead, when I hit him square in the middle of his torso, he launched backward as if hit by a bus. He crashed into the table behind him and brought the whole thing down sending chips, salsa, and guacamole flying up into the air which then landed in glops all around. Startled screams echoed across the room.

My ears roared as if under pressure and a pounding headache rose up behind my eyes, but I didn't really notice, too numbed by what I'd somehow done. The salt and paper shakers, plates, forks, and knives were jittering on the table beside me as if they were upset as well. This had to be some kind of nightmare.

"Tamara, we should go."

I half turned to look at Jensen, everything else passing weirdly by in slow motion. He reached inside his wallet then randomly threw some cash on the table. Bill's mouth was hanging open, Danny out cold on the broken table. Then he turned toward me, his face scrunching up with rage, one hand coiled into a fist while the other reached for me.

The roaring in my ears got louder.

Jensen cold-cocked him in the back, and Bill dropped like dead weight. Then White hurried around the table and grabbed my things. "We've got to go, *now.*"

I nodded and let him herd me toward the exit. He didn't touch me, just made the motions, but I moved just as if he had. I was sure I had to be losing it.

Once out of the restaurant and into the parking lot, the pressure and roaring in my ears disappeared. It was so sudden and such an unexpected relief I tripped and would have splattered all over the blacktop if Jensen hadn't been there to catch me. "Are you all right?"

My knees were shaking. Hell, my whole body was. What had just happened in there? "I-I don't..."

"Come on, let's get you in the car and then get out of here." His voice was very close to my ear. "I think we know now what talent you've been given as your 'gift.'"

CHAPTER TWENTY-NINE

"My *what?*" If he hadn't already had a hold of me, I would have definitely fallen this time. Jensen didn't answer me. Instead he kept me somewhat upright and got us to his car. I wasn't able to offer any resistance as he slipped me inside. All the strength had flowed out of me at once as if I'd been running all day.

White got in the car and started it, for the moment ignoring my question. He had us back on the road out of town before he slipped a glance my way.

"Remember the conversation we had on the day we met? The one about possession sometimes triggering other parts of the brain to start functioning?"

I went cold all over. "Yes, I remember."

"You've found out which one is yours."

It wasn't bad enough the thing had destroyed my life, stolen my time, used my body, now it'd also turned me into a freak? How many more minority categories did I have to be in? "I don't want it."

He threw another glance my way. "If you're going to really follow through and hunt after demons, there might come a time when you'll be thankful you have it."

Despite the fact it sent chills rippling over my skin, he had a point. But I didn't have to like it. "Why do I feel so awful then? If it's supposed to be useful…"

"It was your first time using it. Like trying horseback riding for the first time—it'll tire you and make you sore as you use muscles you've not had to before. Like any other skill or sport, the more you train to use it, the easier it should become and the less it will take out of you."

I slumped in the seat not even having the energy to argue. Still, if it could somehow end up being beneficial… It sure had gotten that creep off me at the restaurant. This could definitely come in handy. But it scared me as well. My anger had never had a weapon before. This could be trouble.

In less than a half hour, we reached the boundary of the village of Hope. Other than the sign, I didn't spot much that proved there was even a village here. Darkness lay on just about everything, making the place look even more desolate.

"This is it." Jensen turned down several two to one lane roads, the headlights finally illuminating a ranch style home with a porch in tan and brown at the end of a weed-filled, pebbled driveway.

I felt slightly less exhausted than before and sat up in my seat. When he turned the car off, everything was covered once more with darkness. It was as if the house didn't exist. Rubbing at my eyes to get used to the lack of light faster, I oozed out of the car.

The greater darkness that was the house stared at me. I then looked up and lost my breath. Stars, it was a sea of stars and brighter than I had ever seen them. More than I had ever seen. The dark spaces between the major constellations I was familiar with weren't dark here but were filled with tiny bits of light, millions of them. All my life I'd heard the illumination of the city ruined the night sky, but I had never had a chance to see if it was true. Now I had.

I could stare at it forever…

Even the air was different here—dry, crisp, clean. Houston this was not. Yet it also wasn't home. You could say what you wanted about the pollution and the months of chocking humidity and heat, but it's where I came from, what I had always known. And this wasn't it.

Underneath that endless sky, it was hard not to feel insignificant and alone.

I blinked as light suddenly flooded the yard blinding me momentarily.

Jensen was standing in the house's doorway motioning to me. "Come on in. Let's get you settled. Then if you want, we can sit out back and study the view. I have a couple of lawn chairs just for staring up. The dawns around here are incredible as well."

His smile was warm and inviting. A lifeline of sorts. I clamped onto it and shuffled on inside.

The entryway opened into a large living/family room. The rust and brown colored carpet was well worn but clean. A couple of sagging couches sat in an L with a large short legged worktable between them. The room was plain, almost austere, yet not unwelcoming. A big oil painting of a dense forest over the cold fireplace did much to soften the room overall.

There was one major peculiar thing about it, however. On the windows, glued to the bottom frame was a line of rock salt. Glancing back toward the door, which opened outwards, I saw there was one there as well. I was lucky not to have tripped over it. There also were symbols carved into the door and window frames, which made my eyes itch for a moment. They were very similar to those I'd seen on the case in Jensen's trunk.

"Kitchen's in the back. It leads to both the garage and the patio." He then pointed to the entryway on the same wall as the fireplace in the back of the room. "Bedrooms and bathrooms are to your right."

It was only then I noticed he had my bags. My cheeks grew hot as I realized I'd spaced out yet again. Had to be getting old for him. I nodded just for something to do.

"Come on." He stepped into the short hallway and then opened the first door on the right. "I don't have guests often, so sorry if it's a little bare."

Bare was an understatement, with only a twin sized bed and beat up chest of drawers, the room was otherwise empty. There was just enough dust on the dresser to proclaim it wasn't used often. Jensen set my bags down. "Let me get you some clean sheets and a blanket. Even in summer, it can get a little cold at night."

He left me there and I did nothing. Exhaustion suddenly dripped from me. All I wanted to do was sit down. Even with only a thin coverlet the bed looked incredibly inviting. I'd just sit down for a second before I fell down.

Without meaning to, I leaned too far and flopped over on the bed after I sat down. I'd never felt such relief in my life. I was just thinking I really had to be tired when I stopped thinking altogether.

CHAPTER THIRTY

I opened my eyes to sunshine. Bright and unhindered, it lit up the room and washed over me. I let it soak into my face, not thinking, not feeling, just being, as if born again.

The weird, peaceful mood didn't last long. My brain finally started kicking into gear, noticing the unfamiliar room and view out the window. Sitting up, I dislodged a comforter in rust, brown, and green from my shoulder. It was so cliché, so done, yet it touched me that Jensen had made the gesture anyway.

This didn't stop a flood of embarrassment from washing over me at having fallen asleep on him, though. The power, the uncalled for 'gift,' must have really taken a lot more out of me than I guessed.

Running my tongue over my teeth, the unpleasant taste of last night's altercation came back to me. I found my bags where Jensen left them, and after scrounging around inside, I pulled out my toiletries bag and some clean clothes. If I was going to have to deal with weirdness, I'd rather do it with fresh breath and a minimum of stench.

Sneaking out quietly into the hall, I found a bathroom a few feet down to my left. There were fresh towels on the racks and the lingering smell of scrubbing bubbles. My host must have done some work after I took my sleep dive. My embarrassment rose another notch. I'd have to find a way to make it up to him.

The tub was small and the shower head spit for several

seconds before a steady stream of warm water came through, but it felt great. Getting the weird mothball taste out of my mouth when I brushed my teeth felt even better. My hair miraculously didn't fight me too hard as I rolled it up into a kinked ball on the back of my head. Better still, no weird flashes of things I'd never done, yet been there to witness. The unfamiliar surroundings were weaving their own kind of magic.

Somewhat self-consciously, I made sure to put the cross Jensen had given me on again and tucked the iron knife into one of my pockets.

Ditching my dirty clothes, I walked barefoot back to the house's main room. The scent of coffee and syrup drew my attention to the kitchen. At the small table, I found a covered dish and a bottle of Mrs. Butterworth's syrup beside it. A frying pan and plate sat dripping dry on a kitchen towel beside the sink. Looked like not only had White woken up before me, but had cooked me breakfast as well.

A brown curtain ruffled as a bit of breeze snuck past it to roll around my feet. I remembered Jensen saying there were lawn chairs in the back. So taking off the cover from my breakfast, which revealed a rather neat stack of pancakes, and pouring some syrup over them, I then grabbed the plate and fork and pushed through the curtain to the open patio beyond.

There was an awning over a concrete patio with an old and beaten table and possibly matching chairs. Out in the full glare of the sun were a couple of reclining lawn chairs already seemingly prepped for night viewing.

Jensen was under the shade and sat with his back to me, facing out toward the open desert. I flopped down on the other chair and set my plate on the table then dug in.

"Good morning." He flashed a small smile in my direction then returned to staring out into the day.

"Morning." I shoved a forkful of pancakes into my mouth. "Sorry I wasn't up earlier."

"There wasn't any hurry. Plus I enjoy looking out at God's creations. Helps to remind me evil is not all there is. And that the strangest things can be quite beautiful."

I looked out into the desert only seeing scraggly bunches of grass, cacti growing in different mutant shapes, lizards darting between wind-beaten rocks. Desolation, struggle, death. Maybe I was too jaded to see what he saw.

It made me sad and angry at the same time. "After what happened to you, how can you still believe? Why would you even want to?"

He turned away from the view to look at me, not mad or hurt that I'd ask such a thing. "There are times I doubt, I won't deny it. Times when I want to throw it all away and pretend He doesn't exist. But in truth, I believe more now than I ever did. I've been fortunate to see behind the veil. To be witness to truths most men will never even suspect. And these things, these things only prove more and more how He is out there."

I shook my head. "How? That doesn't make sense." Though I'd only taken a couple of bites, I pushed my plate away, not hungry anymore. "If He even exists, He doesn't care. The world is a mess and always will be."

"But that is man's choice, not His."

I felt a sneer mar my face as I sat back in the chair and crossed my arms.

Jensen only watched me, not judging. "Life is about choices. About properly growing the seeds He's planted in our spirits. Whether we cultivate them or crush them has always been our choice."

I could name him a ton of situations lived by me or others that left little choice for those involved—accidents, wars, natural disasters, persecution, genocide.

"You may not have had a choice in what happened to you, but you do in how you deal with it. And you've chosen."

At the moment, I *chose* to ignore the remark despite the tension coiling inside me. "You still haven't explained how what's happened to us proves He's out there."

White nodded as if acknowledging fault. "Look at how we were made— made with the capacity of being ridden by an intangible being. How it's been set up so we're paid for delivering such service by the opening of skills we didn't possess before. The fact that by being made aware of what else exists, we're also given weapons to fight against it. It speaks of a grand plan. Of details thought of and followed through. It speaks of God."

CHAPTER THIRTY-ONE

The most horrifying part was that I had no doubt Jensen truly believed this. Not like a fanatic or smug man, just someone who was enlightened and saw things clearer than others.

It was tempting. Tempting to go ahead and just fool myself into thinking I'd chosen this, that I'd been compensated for my trouble, given a weapon to fight back with. Except I couldn't. It only served to show me once more how if He existed, He'd set up the machine then left us to rot on our own. What kind of attitude was that for a caring creator to take? Just make it and let it go, probably moving on to another project. Let the lab rats maintain themselves because they're too much trouble to care for. A book and some cryptic fables all we needed to get along.

My fork started rattling on the plate.

"I'm sorry. It wasn't my intention to upset you." Jensen glanced at the fork then at me.

Dammit it all! Wasn't it bad enough I had trouble controlling my emotions and keeping them from showing on my face I now had another telltale sign?

"I'm not upset." I looked away from him and out into the desert again, trying to find some of the elusive calm he somehow eked from there.

He stood up. "Finish your breakfast then come see me. There're things we should get started on."

I shoved my chair back. "I'm ready now."

"No." For the first time, his voice held a bit of an

edge. "Sit, eat, relax. You have to refuel your body, your spirit, and your mind or you'll burn out. We have to take these things and cherish them when we can. It'll be your first lesson."

I glared out at the landscape rather than at him. I sternly reminded myself how I needed to keep on his good side and bit my tongue. It was tough going. Plus I knew most of it was my own fault. "Fine."

"See you in a bit." Jensen left.

Dragging my plate closer to me, I took out my ire on the syrup soaked pancakes with sharp cutting strokes of my fork. I shoved a mouthful in and chewed without tasting it.

As the minutes passed though, I felt my annoyance trickle from me and slowed my pace. In the ensuing silence, things made themselves evident. Quick furtive movements with small echoing sounds marked the passage of lizards. As I stared at a far off cactus, I noticed bits of color on its extremities. Then a tiny colorful bird swooped in and hovered around them then drifted away. A furry rodent of some sort scurried across the open ground, too busy with its own business to pay attention to the human sitting across the way.

Thin wisps of shimmering air grew in size as the day warmed, covering the land like strips of sheer curtains.

There was more here than I ever imagined. It was relaxing and beautiful after all.

I wallowed in it until the rising heat drove me back inside. The rattle of a window unit air conditioner sounded from the living area, so I made sure to slide the glass door closed.

Jensen wasn't in the kitchen. I took my dishes to the sink and washed them, then set them to dry with his. A glass from a cupboard filled with water from the sink finished my breakfast. I put that on the towel to dry as well when I was done.

Having procrastinated as much as I could, I set off in search of my partner and teacher.

The living area was deserted. The door in the kitchen to the garage opened up on a converted room. Well used padded walls and mats on the floor covered up the concrete foundation and thin wood paneling. A boxing bag hung from one corner of the ceiling. A rack of wooden weapons hung from the back next to another portable air unit, though this one wasn't on. The smell of dried sweat and long hours hung in the air.

Stepping back into the house proper, I knew I was running out of options. My room was empty. But a door further down the hall was open on the right. I stopped in the doorway to take it all in. Unlike the other rooms, this one was filled to overflowing.

Maps covered every inch of the walls, the diffused sunlight coming from the covered windows swathing them in streaks. Every state had its own sheet, cut or folded so it could be joined with those surrounding it. California started it all on the right of the window and the maps wrapped around the room until New England ended it on the window's left. Looking up, I could see that the states there had been cut and parts of them were probably on the back of the door so that when it was closed, it would complete the US circuit.

The maps weren't bare, crosses of all religions marked different spots, phone and fax numbers written in a neat hand beside them. Most were small, but here and there I noticed a larger drawing. What that exactly said about the place, I didn't know.

A large desk took up the area by the window, several short file cabinets taking up the right and also shoved into the room's small closet. Jensen sat before the desk, a larger monitor than I would have expected from what I knew of him taking up a big chunk of it. A fax/scanner sat on one edge and seemed to be very busy.

"More churches?"

Jensen turned around, unsurprised to see me there. "Yeah. Yesterday was but a warm-up. The order has a small program to help distribute items like this. They like to be prepared."

"Just how bad, exactly, do they think things could get?" I couldn't see a holy secret order hanging around just for the fun of it.

He didn't look at me directly. "Bad. Very bad. I haven't seen all the texts myself, but there are warnings. There was a major infiltration back in the time the order was created, in the 1400s. They've been expecting a resurgence ever since. It's possible we're about to get one now. There's no telling how unpleasant this might get."

"A major infiltration..." The words left a sour taste in my mouth. Some flicker of a memory from my unwanted guest gave even more weight to them. A tendril of terror coursed through me. "Did they stop the demon at the casino? Get any information from it?"

Jensen shook his head. "They were able to exorcise it, and one more besides, but got no new information. They've left a small team there to catch any others that show up to report to the one we met."

My trepidation only got worse. "So we still don't know anything. Only that it's somehow tied to those two men."

"So it would seem." He looked no more thrilled by the prospect than I was.

CHAPTER THIRTY-TWO

"How do you fight them? If demons can pop in and out of anyone they like, do whatever they like, how do we stop them?" The mapped walls seemed to close in, screaming of the impossibility of just a few people covering such a large area. And this was but one of hundreds of countries at risk.

Jensen's gaze met mine. "The core of the order may be small, but they have many agents seeded throughout the world. Anyone whose life's been touched by the demons, changed by them, and who's willing to remember their ordeal is recruited as at least a pair of eyes and ears since they'd know what to look for. If you'd not been so eager to come with me, once I'd filed a report, someone would have come to see you."

I wasn't too sure how to feel about that. Though I supposed if they truly respected your wishes and left you alone if you didn't want to get involved, it was a decent way to go about it. Give the victims space, time to find their feet again. Then only those who knew the truth and could handle it would be involved.

"Hallowed ground will keep all but the most powerful out, so we have safe havens just about everywhere." He swept a hand toward the maps. "If someone needs help, it's easy enough to ask nearby churches for prayers to be sent their way. The unity affects them somehow. Humans have gifts they don't even realize. And of course, this giant network can be used as we're doing now. The faithful, though they don't know the truth, help us, glad in the knowledge they are assisting others."

The heavy pressure on my chest eased a little. What he said made sense. Even if they didn't know what was happening, if believers would extend a lending hand to those associated with the order, then there was help to be had all over. I stared at the maps again as I let that sink in.

A giant web of faith—a machine that covered the whole country, even the world. The demons might be able to roam as they pleased, but we outnumbered them. At least I hoped so, the word 'infestation' rising to haunt me again.

Then it occurred to me that I had no idea just what it took to consecrate church grounds and if all religions did something or not to make them so. I'd never needed to care about such things before. Despite the rising belief that more and more people were becoming atheists, the number of churches on the maps was impressive. Help would never be all that far away.

It was good to know we weren't really alone in this. Then something else occurred to me. I pointed at Houston and the different types of churches marked there. "Something doesn't make sense here though. Are you saying belief by any of these religions will help against them? Not all of them believe in God. So how?"

White scratched his hair dipping his head as if I'd caught him at something. "I'm not entirely sure whether they can or can't, but I list them anyway. Kindness, regardless of religion, is one of our strongest weapons. So I'll take it wherever I can find it."

People didn't always choose to be kind. But I supposed an organization could drive them in that direction when directed. Those who went solely on faith tended not to ask many questions.

"Any thoughts on how long it might take to find them

this way?"

"Impossible to say." He shrugged. "It could be in the next hour or the next year. Especially if after retrieving whatever they were storing they went to ground."

I started pacing, the thought of having to wait a year to act scraping me raw. "There's got to be something else we can be doing, more than just sit around waiting."

Waiting would drive me mad. I felt the sense of calm I'd gained from my first instruction evaporating. The endless droning of the fax machine wasn't helping.

"There is…"

I turned on him, part of me not entirely sure it wanted him to have something or not. "Like what?"

"Like learning how to fight them. How to use the knife I gave you. The words, the symbols, items that can help protect you and others. But better yet, learning how to use and control your gift." He looked right at me, his expression serious. I could see the scar on his face almost jumping in place. And his eyes basically said everything. If I was going to help, if I was to be allowed to stay, to get revenge, I wouldn't be permitted to get around this one thing.

Even if it sounded like total madness. "Just tell me what to do."

CHAPTER THIRTY-THREE

"You're trying too hard." Jensen leaned forward across the kitchen table. Everything had been cleared away from it except the salt and pepper shakers. "Relax. Don't force it."

As if it was that easy. I'd force him then see how he liked it! I closed my eyes and counted slowly to ten, wanting nothing more right then than to scream obscenities at him and tell him just what he could do with my supposed 'gift.' My rusty anger management techniques from high school had been getting a lot of use in the last couple of days.

Time waiting for news sped by quickly, but occasionally it seemed like it had stopped instead. Following Jensen's lead, I'd started watching the sunrise, the sunset, even the stars in the sky at night. During these times, with some effort, I could detach from myself, relax, and try not to think—something which I had a lot of trouble doing the rest of the time.

Thinking just made me angry or depressed. It reminded me of what had been done to me, of how I'd been used and tossed aside like nothing. Worse, there would be memories that would flash out of nowhere of things the demon had done with my body. Sometimes I was overwhelmed by an aching sorrow over all the things I'd lost and might never get back. But at night, at night my dreams would sometimes turn into nightmares, and I'd wake up shivering, filled with disgust and fear.

There wasn't much to do here except read, wait and

train. So I did. Going into town was not an option. The little scene at the restaurant wouldn't be repeated if I could help it. Jensen did all the supply runs alone.

Practicing my rusty self-defense moves eased things some. Gave me an outlet, a place to siphon all the ugly energy. The knife fighting even more so. I drove myself so hard I'd fall asleep exhausted and get a bit of rest for at least part of the night before the nightmares might come and get me up before the sun.

Trying to come to grips with my so called 'gift' though, just kept frustrating the heck out of me.

I opened my eyes and tied those feelings up in a spear and threw them at the salt shaker. Nothing happened. The darn thing didn't have the decency to even quiver. "It's not working. Maybe what happened at the restaurant was just a fluke."

"It wasn't." Jensen shook his head. "Maybe we're just going at this wrong." He stood up and massaged the back of his neck. Looked like I wasn't the only one frustrated over my lack of results.

He turned to look at me. "Tell me again what happened."

"You were there. You saw it."

"Tamara, humor me. Please? From the beginning."

I sighed and tried to think back to that night. "I was halfway relaxed for the first time since this whole thing started, actually enjoying my food for a change, then they came over, and reminded me of that thing. It pissed me off. Though the demon was gone, its stupid actions were getting me harassed. But when that yokel grabbed my arm, I got furious. All I wanted was the bastard away from me. I didn't figure it'd do any good, but I punched him in the chest. Then he went sailing across the room." I sighed again. "There was no intent, no focus, no nothing.

It just did what it did on its own."

Jensen sat back down staring at me closely. "You wanted him to go the whole time correct?"

I nodded, wondering where he was going with this.

"But only when you struck him did anything actually happen."

"Stuff was dancing on the table on its own, but I didn't ask for it to. Otherwise, yeah."

His eyes lit up. "Maybe what you're missing is a way to release it."

"What?"

"A way to release it. Like a trigger." His eyes weren't focused on me anymore but somewhere inside. "Something to direct the force inside you into doing what it is you want it to do."

I felt stupid, still not getting it. "Is that what you do to make yours work?"

"No. But I think it activates differently for each individual depending on who they are and the gift given to them." He gaze locked with mine. "The punch. Your punch is what gave your power focus and direction. It subconsciously told it what you wanted it to do."

Could it really be so simple?

"Try it again. This time make a movement while you concentrate."

Keeping my doubts to myself, I concentrated on the salt shaker and then flicked my hand as if batting it off the table. The salt shaker flew off, sailing past Jensen's ear, to smack into the far wall and then bounce on the floor.

The beginnings of what felt like a pressure headache buzzed around for a second in my head then went away. I barely noticed it, my mouth hanging open at what I'd just accomplished. "No way!"

"Apparently, yes way." Jensen looked pleased.

So was I. I aimed up on the pepper shaker next and sent it sailing after the first a moment later. The pressure headache didn't abate as quickly this time though. Something I'd have to keep in mind. This 'gift' had limits. It explained why I felt so horrid after using it at the restaurant. But for the moment I grinned from ear to ear. As Jensen had said, we now had a weapon. One I would make sure to learn to use very well.

CHAPTER THIRTY-FOUR

"I'd heard Latin was a dead language. I can see why..." I shoved the massive tome away from me. Though I'd not seen any books in other parts of the house, I'd come to learn there were a ton of them lining the walls of Jensen's room: Bibles in English, Hebrew, and Greek; Catholic manuals in Latin; the Koran; Torah; 14th Century reprints; Buddhism, Shintoism, Mapscos from all over the country; even some mystery novels.

The last I'd been surprised and totally pleased to see. First, it proved Jensen was human and did a mundane thing or two. Second, it gave me something different to read than old tomes and stuff to memorize. I found out he had even more books on his computer—about anything and everything. A satellite internet connection opened up even more possibilities.

"Wouldn't these things work just as well in English?" Rote memorization had never been one of my strong suits—especially when I didn't understand what I was memorizing.

Jensen turned away from the computer where he was going through email. "They work, but for some reason, the old language has a stronger effect." He held up a hand. "No, I don't know why that is. It just is. Though I personally feel it has to do with the fact Latin is used mostly for ceremony. That in a way, the language itself gained power over time."

I raised an eyebrow at that one. It was possible the ex-priest had spent way too much time alone.

He suddenly smiled. "Yes, I'm very well aware as to how that sounds. But it makes it no less true. You may see this for yourself someday."

My other eyebrow told him I very much doubted it. This time he laughed out loud. Personally, I wouldn't have been all that happy at someone thinking I might be bonkers. Soe people did think of me that way already and I definitely didn't like it. The letters I wrote before leaving Houston should have long reached all their recipients by now. They'd either written me off or were frantically looking for me, sure I needed long term medical care.

They wouldn't find me.

In some ways, I was strangely relieved by the thought. The last thing I wanted was inducting any of my family into the mess I'd been thrust into.

Plus it would require me to make fewer explanations—like why it was I could attack things with my mind.

"Think you're ready to say the exorcism ritual?"

I grimaced. "Maybe."

"Let's hear it then. And watch the pronunciation." He turned his full attention to me.

Taking a deep breath, I got started. "Quatuor minores…"

His cell phone rang. My feelings weren't hurt one bit at the interruption. Jensen threw me a glance as if he knew what I was thinking. My aura was probably giving me away. I needed to ask him about his ability at some point. Specifically, if there were ways to hide from it.

"This is White." He turned away from me, raptly listening to whoever was on the other end. He yanked open a drawer and pulled out a notepad and pen. Shoulders hunched, he quickly wrote down several lines of information.

My heart thumped hard in my chest as I tried to keep calm, the sudden idea of what the call might be about screaming through my brain. But it might not be. It could be something else. Raising my hopes would only get my spirit crushed.

"Thank you. You've been a great help." Jensen ended the call then slowly turned to look at me, his expression less legible than usual.

"Something wrong?"

"We might have a lead."

I blinked, not sure I'd heard correctly. A part of me insisted there was no way the two we were looking for had been found. "A lead?"

He nodded. "They've been spotted in a small town in New Hampshire." I couldn't breathe. I knew if I tried to stand, I'd fall flat on my face. Most of me was jubilant, but deep inside I was suddenly petrified. There was no telling where this might take me.

"I'm going to fly up there and check it out." I still couldn't read his expression. "You don't have to come with me."

Heat rushed through me. I was on my feet without thinking, hands curling at my side. "You're not leaving me out of this!"

His eyes grew wide. The window rattled behind him and the loose items on his desk jumped around.

After everything I'd been through. After all the restraint I'd had to force on myself, and he was just going to leave me behind?

"It could just be a fool's errand, Tamara, so I wanted to give you a choice."

Then just like that, my anger was gone. I slumped back into the chair and hid my face in my hands feeling ashamed. With total certainty, I knew I would have hurt him if he'd tried to deny me.

What was happening to me? It was as if the demon had never left. Or was I only now seeing what I was really like? Did gaining the gift just peel all the layers away and revealed my true self? I didn't want to be this way!

"Tamara, don't. *Please?* It's all right." I could hear him kneeling down beside me, his presence hovering. "I'm sure it's just part of the PTSDs. And you've no real reason to trust me anyway. We've not known each other all that long. You couldn't have known what I meant."

An ex-priest fighting the good fight to rid the world of demons and to help those who've been used by them? What was there not to trust? He should be the one thinking he couldn't trust me, not the other way around.

I was just too volatile.

But I could not, would not be left behind. It would destroy me.

So gathering every bit of self-control that I could, I pulled my face away from my hands and looked at him. "I'll do better. I promise you."

"You already are."

CHAPTER THIRTY-FIVE

"If we drove, we could make it there in thirty-five hours." I held my laptop in front of his face.

Jensen had been trolling the airline websites trying to get us a booking. Nothing flew the way we wanted to go until Monday morning, so that was twenty hours and then with two connections it would still take twelve hours on top of that to get there. Add in having to deplane, get our luggage (and we had a few items I'd no idea how we would even get through security), sign out a rental car, then drive up to the town. It would be at least as long. *Unacceptable!*

"We can drive in shifts." If I had to wait here doing nothing the rest of today to wait until morning to leave, I would totally lose it. "Since we can't get there any faster we might as well just go direct."

Jensen stared for several seconds at the laptop's screen, his own computer and then up at me. The pencil and pen holder started to dance on the desk, so I tried hard to clamp down on my growing impatience.

"Exhaustion will be a factor."

I shook my head. "No, it won't. Yeah, we won't sleep as good as we might otherwise, but you're not going to be the only one driving. We have to do it this way." Better to be moving, not waiting and being sealed up in a flying tin can. I could delude myself we were actually doing something if we were driving.

Jensen suddenly chuckled, color flushing up his neck. "Sorry. Lone wolf complex. Not used to thinking like two." He rubbed the back of his neck and clicked his browser closed. "Let's do that." His hazel eyes were bright.

I could have kissed him.

Packing took no time at all. We were ready to go within the hour. Jensen brought along a small cooler filled with drinks and sandwiches. More time we wouldn't have to spend off our chosen path.

I was putting my bag in the trunk when he came out with the weird wheeled case I'd seen before. My eyes started itching again. "Why does it do that?"

Jensen stared at me, the case on the edge of the trunk. "Why does what do what?"

"The case, the symbols in your house, something at the Public Storage, my knife—they make my eyes itch."

"They shouldn't…"

I could almost hear the wheels grinding in his head as he tried to make sense of what I was talking about. For the first time, it occurred to me that maybe this didn't happen to him, only to me. "They do."

I was suddenly sorry I brought it up. I already knew what my 'gift' from the possession was, so what the heck was this about?

"Huh…" He looked away and finished putting the case in the trunk.

Yeah, that didn't make me feel better about it. "You don't know, do you? Your eyes don't do that do they?"

He closed the trunk and glanced over at me, his expression neutral. "No is the answer to both questions, I'm afraid."

Something struck me then, making my blood rise to a boil. "If I'd been possessed more than once would I have gotten more than one 'gift'?" Had the bastard demon lent me out like a sweater or was there a gap of missing time somewhere else in my life I didn't remember?

"Tamara, please, calm down."

I barely heard him, the roaring in my ears smothering almost every other sound. That's when I noticed the trunk lid shaking in its moorings and the pebbles on the road and the dry land shaking as if in an earthquake. It wouldn't do.

I closed my eyes realizing my anger came from assumptions rather than anything I actually knew. Taking deep breaths, I counted with them, trying to bring myself once more under control. Twice in one day didn't say much for my abilities. Soon I might have to decide to become a hermit or run the chance of people seeing me doing this. Gift my aunt's ass!

One… Two… Three…

"Are you all right?"

His concern shamed me. "Yeah. Just give me a minute." I opened my eyes and kept counting. Five… Six… Seven…

By the time I got into the car, I was calmer. I mucked around on my phone, pretending I was doing something so I wouldn't be tempted to look his way.

"I know it's not easy… Needing answers and not getting any." His tone reflected his intimate knowledge with the subject. "I'll help if I can. The Order might have some ideas on how this could be."

Several movies with secret orders danced inside my head as well as government organizations that took unusual people away for experiments. While I knew the difference between fiction and reality, this was one aspect I didn't wish to test for congruence. "No. Please don't. I feel enough like a freak as it is. I don't need others thinking I am even more so."

He nodded, saying nothing. Jensen got us on 82 and

then to 285. We were on our way.

The rising dry heat of the desert fought against the rattling air conditioner of the car. 'Hot' in New Mexico was not the 'humid hot' of Houston. It could catch you off guard and smack you down if you weren't careful. With it being past noon, we'd be lucky to get it comfortable inside the car any time soon. I closed my eyes and felt a drop of sweat gather behind my ear and get sucked up almost immediately into the moisture deprived air. And this was monsoon season; the scorching part of the year had yet to arrive. If not for the cooling units in his house I knew I wouldn't be able to survive out here. Too spoiled as a city girl I guess.

"It's possible it has nothing to do with you directly." We'd been driving along for over an hour. The sentence came toward me tentatively, like a miner feeling along the floor of a dark cave, making sure he'd not fall over into a bottomless pit.

Guess that's what you got when you acted like an unstable nuclear reactor. Rather than let myself off the hook, I decided I wanted to hear what he had to say. It was better than leaving it to my imagination to figure out. Surely his idea would be less bleak. "Go on."

"Mind you, I've no real basis for this, so it's just a guess. But could it be that you've inherited this other skill? One that lay dormant inside you until more of your brain came into play?"

"Wouldn't that beat everything." I snorted. "What you're saying is some ancestor of mine was probably possessed at some point?" I shook my head. "What would be the odds of that actually being the case though? You said possessions were rare. It'd be like lightning hitting the same tree twice—astronomical odds."

He shrugged, keeping his gaze glued to the road. "It's

the best I've got. I'm a demon hunter, not a scientist."

I snorted again. White was full of surprises today. "You're a Trekkie?"

He shrugged again. "As a priest, it was helpful to have my finger on the pulse of pop culture. It didn't hurt that my dad was an SF nut back in the day so I'd been exposed to a lot of it as a kid. Easy enough to keep up with it from there."

"A Hip Trekker Priest. Who knew?"

"A Hip Trekker Ex-Priest, if you please." Though his tone was light, his expression had soured.

Way to go, me! Not.

Time to keep my mouth shut for a while. Besides, he'd given me something to think about. Us Williams's, or perhaps the Sane's on my mother's side, looked to possibly be cursed. I know I definitely felt that way recently.

But at least I was trying to do something about it.

CHAPTER THIRTY-SIX

About four hours into the drive, as we moved through Amarillo, TX, Jensen finally pulled over at a rest stop for a break and to switch drivers. After my foot-in-mouth comment, neither of us had said much, the radio filling in the ensuing silence.

I was quite shocked by the rest stop, to be honest. Never seen a place quite like it. But then Texas was usually anything but typical. A white building built like an adobe home, it stood proud and tall, the Texas flag and its large, lone star and the red white and blue flapping in the breeze. It had a massive playground on the side for the kids, and the interior was air-conditioned. The bathrooms were pristine and tiled in grays, blues, and greens. It even had vending machines. What bowled me over the most, however, were the interactive displays and the fact it had free wireless internet access.

I slinked in there to do my business, not making eye contact with anyone. This was the first time I'd been in a place with other people since the incident at the Mexican restaurant and found I was quite nervous at the possibility of a repeat performance. The internet was forever (despite my attempts to delete all the evidence) and viewable all over the world. There was a chance I could meet a 'fan' anywhere. Becoming a hermit was growing on me more and more all the time.

By the time I made it back to the car, my nerves were a wreck. Jensen had beaten me there. He was leaning against the car while staring off at nothing. He straightened as I approached. His brow went up. "Something happen?"

I'd had my poker face up, too. Damn that aura tattletale. "No. Just being paranoid." To prove it I threw a glance over my shoulder to make sure no one was following me. "That 'gift' of yours is a totally unfair advantage, you know." I had to fight not to pout about it.

He laughed. "I could read people long before my gift. You'd be amazed how many things are part of the calling."

I wasn't sure if he was bringing it up as some weird peace offering, but I wanted nothing to do with it. I felt guilty enough about souring the mood earlier as it was. "How about giving me the keys? My turn, I believe." I held out my hand for them.

He nodded, still looking at me, his eyes crinkled, probably laughing at my sudden avoidance, as he reached into his pocket. He dangled the keys over my hand for a moment before letting them drop. "Her best coasting speed is around sixty-five."

"I'll keep it in mind." The last time I'd driven in shifts was when Debbie and I took a trip to San Diego for a week. I made sure to keep my face turned away as I went around the car to the driver's seat, the memory of the fun we had going there and back a definite pang of pain. There were too many things that would probably never be mine again.

A rush of fury buried the pain but was so abrupt I stumbled.

The bastard would pay. And then, then I would find a way to fix things. I would get my life back!

"*Tamara!*"

With a gasp, I looked up at Jensen's hard-edged bark. That's when I realized several car alarms were screaming, the automobile bodies rocking on their wheels. Berating myself for being a total moron, I slipped inside the car and did the slow count while jamming the key into the ignition and started the engine. Backing out slowly, I then put the car in drive and left the parking lot at ten miles an hour. In the rear-view, I spotted people coming out of the building as the racket brought them outside. I speeded up to merge with the freeway traffic.

"What happened? Did you have a flashback?"

I was pretty sure Jensen was totally regretting bringing me along, and we'd been only at this for a handful of hours.

"No. I, I'm just stupid. I'm sorry." My blood turned chill when something occurred to me. "Oh lord, the station has 24/7 security. They probably got this on tape. Crap!"

White reached out and lightly touched me on the arm. "Calm yourself. No harm done. The video will only show us talking then you going around the car. Yes, the shaking cars will also be in it, but there won't actually be anything on there to tie the odd occurrence to us. As long as you can keep from doing something like this again, we should be fine. No one will be able to make a connection. All right?"

My mind zipped back and forth trying to see any holes in his supposition and couldn't readily find any. Forcing more counting and several deep breaths, I got a hold of myself again. "I won't be a liability to you. I won't! This just caught me by surprise."

"You weren't the only one."

I shot a sharp glance in his direction. Jensen had a smile on his face.

"Wasn't quite sure for a moment if I'd need to duck back inside again with a change of clothes."

He was serious! A moment later I was laughing like a loon, tears gathering at the edge of my eyes. My mother would have a fit if she ever knew I'd almost made a priest, an ex-priest, shit himself. Way more trouble than I was in already. Although the thought sobered me enough to stop laughing, the whole thing was too insane to let it sour my mood again. Guilt still nibbled at me though. "Sorry. I know it wasn't funny."

Jensen barked out a laugh. "Yes, yes it was."

I couldn't help the grin that tugged on my face after that.

CHAPTER THIRTY-SEVEN

We made good time and didn't stop anywhere for long. I had to admit that though old, White's Taurus drove quite smoothly and seemed to thrive on the highways.

The landscape over the day changed from flatlands to grassy hills, then to forests and granite cliffs where holes had been cut through to put in roadways. When night time fell on that first day, I reclined my chair during my off shift and actually slept. Though I didn't know Jensen well at all, some part of me seemed to trust him, some deep part, because as uncomfortable as the sleeping arrangements were, I'd not slept so profoundly in days.

A McDonald's offered fresh breakfast and also a chance for us to change clothes, freshen up a little, and Jensen to shave.

The more miles we put behind us, the more anticipation built inside me. I tried not to let it, knowing full well this might turn out to be nothing, but I couldn't stop myself.

"Booked us a place to sleep yet?"

"What?" I'd been half sitting forward knowing it would only be a couple of hours before we reached our destination.

He raised an eyebrow in my direction. "Surely you didn't think we would be going out to try and find them in the dark?"

I kept my mouth shut having expected precisely that. It was like the casino timing all over again. We were so close! How could he hold back like this? Maybe they beat patience into him during priest training.

"You'd had your laptop out earlier. I thought perhaps you'd booked us somewhere."

He wouldn't look directly at me, and the corner of his mouth kept trying to curl up. He'd thought no such thing. Probably waited to spring it on me till now in case I decided to get pissed. I was, a little. I clamped on it hard not wanting it to grow into anything more and possibly get us into trouble. "No, actually, I didn't. I'd really had my heart set on trying to find them tonight."

"Oh, did you, now?"

He was poking at me. I didn't really know what to make of that. Could this be a test or was he just some kind of sadist? "Is there something wrong with that?"

"Merrimack is a small town. They roll up the carpet early."

That never occurred to me. Houston was far from being a small town. There were places there open to all hours. "Huh."

I slumped in my seat, deflated, sure he was right. Unless I were willing to go door to door looking for them and waking up the neighborhood and possibly getting the cops called on me, I'd have no choice but to wait. Didn't make me like it any better.

But I wasn't about to let Jensen know that. Showing I could keep my temper, I pulled up my laptop and tried to find us some lodgings for the evening.

The closest thing I could find was the Fairfield Inn run by Marriot. It was but five to ten minutes away from the town proper. Assuming he'd want things like the last time, I booked a room with two queen beds. They had a pool, so shaking off some of my built up aggression might be possible. There were also several restaurants within a mile or less, and at least one of them delivered.

I was rather impressed with it when we got there. The construction made it look like a longhouse with windows in the attic rather than a glaring corporate-owned hotel. Inside, it was decorated in a genteel English style, which flowed over into the rooms. Almost as if we'd stepped back in time to a younger New England.

Unlike the last time we'd shared a hotel room, this time I helped Jensen place the protections about the place—it didn't take much skill to pour salt. It felt good being more than a bystander for once.

"Why Merrimack of all places?" I was pacing by the curtained window, dinner on its way. Jensen's suggestion of eating out had met with cold disapproval. I wasn't going to risk it, not when we might be close. The last thing I needed was another pervert making a move on me. I didn't trust that I'd be able to hold myself back.

Jensen was seated in a straight-backed chair, looking cool and collected. I wondered how he did it.

"No idea to be honest. Maybe it's just the fact it's a long way from Texas, and it's a nice quiet town." He shrugged. "We know too little for me to make a real guess."

"Do we even have a plan?" Up until this point, it hadn't occurred to me to ask. This wasn't like me. I wasn't sure I was fond of the person I now seemed to be.

"I spoke to Father Paul on our last rest stop. He'll be meeting with us at his office at nine tomorrow morning. Then we can go from there."

Perhaps a little research on the town wouldn't hurt. Better than pacing the room all night. I scooped up my laptop and setting up on the dark cherry wood table, did some electronic research.

Some quick reading told me the town of Merrimack

was founded in 1746 and lay near the Merrimack River. John Cromwell was said to have lived and traded in the area back in the 1660s. The Burnap Sisters, daughters of the first minister of the town, invented the Leghorn Hats, or bonnets. Merrimack was home to the Jackson Inn, where President Jackson was said to have stopped for dinner in 1830 on his way to Concord. Matthew Thornton, one of the signers of the Declaration of Independence retired there. Basically the types of things you'd expect from a town 300 plus years old. But nothing that rang of it having any significance to demons or people demons were hunting.

Since all of this started not much of anything had made any sense. The trend didn't seem to be about to change. With a sigh, I closed the laptop, hoping dinner would hurry on its way.

CHAPTER THIRTY-EIGHT

I was up early, so I quietly dragged myself outside to watch the dawn. Feeling off balance, I desperately needed the ritual. I wasn't stupid, however, not when we were this close. I kept out of sight, my protective cross and iron dagger with me.

Cool air brushed against me. Everything was so very green here. Moisture clung to leaves and grass, the trees towering above me. I'd always thought the trees in Texas tall, but not when compared to these. In some ways, it seemed like the total opposite of Hope, NM with Houston somewhere in between. But as the sky changed from deep indigo to brush strokes of pink, orange, and red, I was reminded again there was one constant that wouldn't change no matter where on the planet I might find myself. Not everything was different. Not everything would change.

And today, today there might be answers.

Calmer and with some growing optimism I went back inside. To my surprise, I found Jensen at the breakfast bar. "Did I wake you?"

He shook his head then sipped his coffee. "The cheese Danishes are good."

Somehow I didn't believe him but took the hint anyway. Maybe he'd been worried I'd go postal if not supervised. Not that I'd given him any reason to think differently.

The breakfast bar was well stocked. A Danish, cereal, yogurt, and some apple juice later and I was definitely ready for whatever would come. Or so I hoped. It'd helped a lot that the other boarders paid me little to no attention, and no one had come over claiming to know me. A tight band I'd not been aware of over my chest eased just a little.

"I thought we might drive around a bit, get acquainted with the town until it's time for our meeting." His hazel eyes glittered with repressed glee. "If you've no objections."

As if. Which was probably why he looked so amused. "None from me." I stood up. "Ready when you are."

So we left and drove over to Merrimack proper. The Daniel Webster highway proved quite scenic. Never in my life had I seen so many trees. Not that Texas didn't have its share of forests here and there, but up here they were thicker, taller, and I hated to admit, grander. The buildings we drove past all gave a sense of the Colonial, the old country. If we'd not been on such a serious errand, I would have enjoyed the view more.

But there was only one thing currently interesting me right then. I kept my gaze roaming about on the off chance we crossed their path before the meeting. It'd make things easier, anyway.

Merrimack had over twenty-five thousand residents, but you wouldn't think it from looking at it. With all the trees and winding two-lane roads, it was easy to lose sight of the other residences or businesses, making the homes seem a lot more isolated than they actually were.

Baboosic Lake road cut through the heart of the town. Our Lady of Mercy Catholic Church was on it, trapped between the Frederick Everett Turnpike and the Daniel Webster Highway.

The Last Rest cemetery spread out across the street.

The church had one large building with double doors

for holding services. A sidewalk from there led to a house and further on to another smaller church building, which I assumed had offices and perhaps a chapel for smaller services. An elementary school lay just a bit further off.

Jensen turned into the side street and followed it back to the parking lot for the church offices.

"Remember, this might turn out to be nothing." He gave me a long look.

I was already half out of the car and he'd yet to turn the engine off. I froze, fighting with myself to wait. "I know. I really do." And I did. Still didn't keep my heart from speeding up, my palms from growing sweaty, possible answers or direction so close at hand.

I closed my eyes and took several deep breaths, this time to calm myself from too much excitement rather than welling anger. By the time Jensen turned off the engine and got out, I wasn't quite as wired.

Sending a nod in my direction, he started forward with me close on his heels.

I could see the lights were on inside and considered it a good sign. With any luck, we'd only be here a few minutes and then off on our way after our quarry.

Jensen opened the glass office door and stepped inside then almost immediately stopped. I heard a low gasp from his lips, but I couldn't see what he was looking at, his higher shoulders and head blocking my view.

Expecting something unpleasant, I reached behind me for the iron dagger, even as I sidestepped from behind him.

Two men stood inside the reception area and were facing straight toward us. Their hands were in plain sight and held no weapons—although if they were possessed by demons that would have meant nothing. At least Jensen could easily see if they were with his aura viewing skills. Only he just stood there saying and doing nothing. Wondering what was going on, I finally took the time to look at their faces.

My heart squeezed hard for a moment. The two men before us were the very ones we'd been hoping to find.

CHAPTER THIRTY-NINE

"You need to stop."

Both men spoke in unison, standing in exactly the same pose. If not for the difference in hair and eye color, I would have sworn they weren't twins but mirror images of one person. It was eerie.

They looked like I'd described them from my suppressed memories, but here, up close, there seemed to be more to them than what I saw. They exuded a presence, a glow, something beyond the physical, and it was beautiful.

I was starting to understand the reaction of the clerk at the Public Storage just a little.

Jensen took several steps forward then dropped to one knee, jerking my attention from them. "Who, what are you?" Wonder coated his voice.

The almost twins traded glances, and I could swear words passed between them though neither said a word. They turned our way again. "Please do not search for us. It is imperative we do not attract attention."

Even in their well-scuffed boots, worn jeans, black t-shirts and worn jackets they'd be very hard *not* to notice.

Not waiting for a reply, they nodded at us as if we'd agreed and went around us towards the door.

Stunned, I realized they meant to just leave us here and take everything they knew with them. That wasn't going to happen. I wasn't going to be dismissed again as if I didn't matter. I turned around and reached toward them without actually touching them, then jerked my hands back as if I'd grabbed them by the collar. Though already halfway out the door, both men were picked up off their feet and yanked back inside crashing into the two of us.

Twisting on top of the closest one, I pulled out my knife and placed it on his throat, a small headache pounding in retaliation for my actions. Ice blue eyes stared into mine filled with puzzlement instead of fear or worry. I didn't care. "No one's going anywhere until I get answers!"

"Tamara, no!" The awe was still there but was now laced with fear. Jensen untangled himself from the other man and backed away. "They, they're not human."

Three pairs of eyes swiveled in his direction.

"What are you talking about?" I pressed the blade just a tad closer to the man's neck. "Are you saying they're demons?"

Horror flashed across his face. "No! By all that's Holy, no, they're not demons."

The blond of the pair sat up slowly, the small ruby in his pierced nose flashing. "You have the Sight…"

"You've been touched." This came from the one beneath me.

Jensen's weird reactions since he'd opened the door, the odd symmetry between the brothers and the lack of fear from the one which I held down with a knife at his throat—I was missing something. It didn't make me happy. "None of that matters for shit! What does is that demons are possessing people left and right to spy on you two."

Blue eyes stared at me obviously startled. Good.

I almost jumped as a soft touch landed on my shoulder. It was White. "Tamara, I beg you, please don't. Not like this."

His eyes and expression pleaded with me, not just his words. He obviously knew things I didn't. I tried to calm down, telling myself he knew way lots more about all this than I did and should follow his lead. My hand only trembled a little as I pulled the knife away from the prostrated man's throat and rose to my feet.

Jensen bent forward and offered the other a hand up. After a moment's hesitation, the dark-haired man took the offered hand and rose to his feet. He took a step back, which placed him flawlessly even with the other one without ever looking, almost as if he were intrinsically aware of where the other was at all times.

"Please, just listen to us for a few minutes." Jensen stared from one to the other, his expression earnest and also weirdly vulnerable. "We were looking for you to warn you." The two men did not react. "You are Jared and Ross Jenkins, aren't you?"

There seemed to be layers to the question. But if they weren't possessed by demons, what did Jensen mean?

"Yes. Those are the names we're going by at present."

"Which one is which?" I couldn't help myself. Besides, it kept them talking while I tried to figure out what was the matter with White.

"I go by the name Jared." This came from the blond one with the ruby stud in his nose.

The dark haired one said, "I go by the name of Ross."

If I hadn't been watching their lips move, I wouldn't have been able to tell which one was which. Even their voices were the same.

"What did you wish to say to us?"

Questions and accusations bubbled up my throat. Jensen's light touch on my arm, however, stilled my tongue, much to my own surprise.

He spoke instead. "A demon took over Tamara's form

for three months, keeping its nature in check as much as possible. We believe it was there purely to watch the Public Storage next to her office, waiting for the two of you to appear there. Once you did, it left her, picking another host to head to Oklahoma where it reported what it'd seen to another of its kind. This second demon seemed to have been placed there purely for gathering reports from its fellows and despite our threats wouldn't leave. We're assuming it couldn't leave and once it received intelligence, it was then reporting it to other demons sent there for that purpose. All of its activity and actions were highly unusual for their ilk. And both of you seem to be at the center of it." The brothers traded glances, their expressions suddenly grim.

"You're right," Jared said. "We needed this information. And we thank you. Things have progressed more than we guessed."

I took a step forward. "But what does it mean? Why would they go to this kind of trouble? What makes you so special?"

"Tamara!" Jensen's shock filled face turned toward me.

It was only because I looked his way that I saw it—a car crossing across the grass of the side road gunning straight for us. "Shit!"

CHAPTER FORTY

I grabbed Jensen's arm and pulled him back as with my other I made a sweeping gesture which shoved the other two men back in the opposite direction. My light headache skyrocketed, but it didn't matter, I had no time for it. The sound of a revving engine trickled in from the outside as the blue Ford Aspire's small grill grew large in front of us then burst through the glass office-front sending screaming shards everywhere.

Jensen and I hit the floor hard, my ears ringing. The smell of burnt car oil and rubber filled the air. Dazed, I saw the car was half in and half out of the office, splitting the front area in two, ours a little on the not much room side. The driver's door opened with a screech of metal. The man got out, blood dripping from a cut in his forehead. He straightened with a broad grin, and it was then I noticed his collar—the man was a priest.

With a sinking feeling, I was pretty sure he was the one we'd come to see today in the first place.

"So sorry I'm late to the party." He turned his head from side to side as if to relieve a kink in his neck. "Don't think the donuts I brought quite made it through my entrance though."

"Demon." Jensen staggered to his feet. An angry scowl disfigured his face. "Release Father Paul, or it will go badly for you."

Using the wall to hold me, I was able to get up. My head was thumping and not just from using my 'gift.' Warmth trickled over several places of my body where I'd been caught by the flying pieces of glass. Now that I was upright I was able to spot Jared and Ross, who'd luckily not been turned into roadkill. The two brothers stood side by side to the right of the back of the room, where a small hallway led into the actual church offices. They appeared unharmed.

The possessed priest laughed then ignored Jensen entirely, turning his attention to the brothers. "I know you have it. Give it to me."

The brothers raised identical eyebrows. "It is not for the likes of you. And we very much doubt you're the one who was to come to retrieve it."

Though I could only see part of his face, the demon didn't look like he appreciated the comment. I had a feeling 'someone' decided not to follow orders, trying to get whatever the brothers' possessed for themselves.

Jensen moved beside me. Water arched past the car to splash the demon on the cheek. Vapor rose where it touched him as if the water turned boiling hot on contact. "Get thee gone from here!"

The possessed man hissed and took a step back, his arm going up to protect his face from further assault.

I remembered my own flask of holy water and pried it out of my pocket. The container was small. For the first time, it occurred to me it really couldn't hold all that much inside it. So the protection it might bring was limited. My knife, which would have given me much more comfort, was hiding somewhere beneath the wrecked Ford in front of us. At least I still had the cross. Though none of the three would have saved me if I'd been hit by the car. Safe seemed to be a very relative term around here.

Weren't church grounds supposed to be consecrated? Maybe the blessing hadn't extended to the offices. Even if they were, it wouldn't have kept the car out, but it might have driven the demon from its host. Unless this one was one of the more powerful ones Jensen had mentioned before. Great.

The demon maneuvered himself closer to the two brothers, but this time kept a modicum of his attention focused our way. "Give it to me, or I shall take it from you."

Ross took a step toward him. "You're welcome to try. But remember, there's a reason *we* were given this task."

Jensen still had his knife and inched along the side of the car to leap over the hood if necessary. The demon's face twisted with indecision as if slowly realizing he may have bitten off more than he could chew.

Noise filtered in from outside. Cars were filling up the parking lot, their drivers getting out and staring at the wreckage. A siren wailed far off yet grew louder by the moment.

"Is everyone all right?" A husky forty-some year old in a blazer crunched on the glass that had ricocheted back outside after the Ford's abrupt entrance. The car was fully wedged where the glass and frame used to be so anyone wanting in or out would have to climb over the automobile.

"If you're going to do something, now would be the time," Jared said. "There'll be too many witnesses for you to make a clean getaway if you don't. And even then, I doubt your master isn't already aware of what you've tried to do and will be hunting for you soon."

Ross gave him a cold grin. "If you make it out of here first, that is." He took a step forward.

That seemed to decide the demon. His stolen body went perfectly still and then seemed to quiver in place for a moment. My eyes felt prickly for a second then stopped.

Father Paul dropped to the floor, blinking in confusion. "Oh, oh."

From the sudden relaxation in Jensen's pose, I realized the demon had gone. The stupid things were invisible when not in a body? I felt something graze by me, like a gentle gust of wind—its icy fingers dragging past my face. My necklace felt suddenly heavy. I had the weirdest feeling it'd just saved me from being ridden again. Revulsion caused bile to rise up my throat. The demon had thought it could use me to hide.

Jensen slid over the front of the car to get to the other side. He immediately went to check on the priest.

I made my way across a little less quickly.

"We should leave this place. Too many eyes and ears." Ross and Jared were staring out at what could be seen of the parking lot. To my surprise, they seemed to be including us in that statement.

"Father, I'm sorry about all this. Help is just outside so you'll be seen to presently. But we have to go." Jensen put a handkerchief to the priest's bleeding cut on his head then placed the man's hand over it to hold it in place before standing up.

"I don't understand." The priest just stared at him like a lost child.

I saw a flash of sadness and regret cloud Jensen's face then clear as he turned toward the two brothers while gesturing me to join him. "We can probably find a way out through one of the offices. There should be windows facing the other way."

Without a word, we all headed down the hall.

"Hey! Where are you people going? Hey!"

Jensen opened the door leading to the chapel rather than head toward the small offices. The two brothers looked to have no trouble walking on consecrated ground. I felt my respect for White growing, sure this wasn't only an escape route but probably also a test for our companions—just in case. An exit sign beckoned to us from the chapel's far end. We were in luck. I turned around and locked the doors we'd just come through in case one of the good Samaritans decided to chase after us and try to help.

Without prompting, Ross headed straight to the outside door. He tapped it and locked or not, it swung open. The harried wailing of sirens poured inside much closer than before.

"I'll go around and get the car. Be right back." Jensen took off on foot.

Despite all the trees I'd seen all over the place, this piece of Baboosic lane was pretty bare. The closest real cover lay across the street on the far end of the cemetery, and we'd be fully exposed getting there. The chances of people remembering a black woman and two youthful, handsome men all leaving the area of the accident would probably be high. So instead we loitered behind a small pine tree against the off side of the chapel.

The brothers appeared at ease as if there were nothing to worry about despite the fact cops were coming, and a demon was on the loose. I couldn't quite exude the same level of tranquility and tried to keep my attention everywhere at once. I needed to sit down desperately, but the brick wall holding me up would have to do. I'd never used my 'gift' to this extent, and it was making me pay for it. Add in almost getting run down and peppered by shards of glass, and I was at my limit. I needed sugar, caffeine, and food—*now*. Energy bars would have to become part of the things I carried around with me if I was going to actually try to pull off this demon hunting business.

"He's almost here."

Jared's comment didn't seem to be aimed at anyone in specific, yet it still felt like it was for my benefit. If my head hadn't been pounding and my knees not felt like melting rubber, I would have pursued it, even asked questions. But it took everything I had at the moment just to keep myself standing.

Jensen's Taurus came down School Street at a slow pace, just another morning person going about their regular routine.

He slowed to a stop by us, and I pushed away from the wall to start making my way over there. That's when the world tried to tilt over backward. Before I hit the grass, both brothers were somehow to either side of me holding me up. I didn't resist as they helped me over and into the car.

The moment I felt the upholstery beneath me, I gave a big sigh and remembered nothing else after that.

CHAPTER FORTY-ONE

I gasped and opened my eyes as something cool settled on my forehead. I wasn't in Jensen's car anymore. He sat beside me on the edge of a blue flower print couch. Had I fainted?

I tried to sit up, staring around me. Jensen let me, standing up to get out of my way. A wet washcloth landed on my leg, but I paid it no attention.

It looked like we were inside someone's home.

A large wood fireplace jutted across from me, a framed painting of a forest glade with a fawn drinking from a bubbling brook above it. A clock sat on the mantelpiece surrounded by miniature deer figurines. The scent of lilacs hung in the air. I spotted a matching loveseat and chair as well as a large coffee table. Then my attention homed in on the plateful of sandwiches and the glass of orange juice sitting there.

"Go ahead. They're for you."

I didn't need any more prompting. I reached for a sandwich and chomped it down, not caring what type it was. The orange juice followed not long after. "Where are we?

"A residence in Merrimack. Where they've been staying."

No need for him to state who 'they' were. "Are they here?"

Jensen half turned to glance at the arched hallway leading deeper into the house. "Yes…" The note of wonder I'd heard from him at the church offices was back.

Feeling better by the moment, I reached for another sandwich but kept my gaze locked on him. "At the church, why did you keep staring at them like that? What did their auras tell you?"

He turned his full attention back to me a serene expression settling over his face. Even his scar appeared a little muted. "I think they're angels."

"What?" I'd been prepared for just about anything except this. It felt like someone had punched me in the gut.

"Servants of God..." The need, the joy, the confidence which shone from him at this was uncanny.

It gave me chills. Good or bad I wasn't sure yet. But it made sense in a way. If there could be demons, why not angels as well? "So they took over the bodies of a couple of guys?"

"No. These corporeal shells are our own."

We both jumped where we sat, twisting to look in the direction of the hallway. Ross and Jared both stood there, expressions blank.

My throat felt unusually tight. "Is it true? You're angels?"

The two brothers exchanged a sad, amused look. "Not exactly."

My stomach clenched. I wasn't sure if it was the 'angels' or the 'not exactly' part that affected me more. "What does that mean?"

Jensen placed a hand on my arm as if asking me to restrain myself though he never took his attention from the two across the room. He might not admit it, but I was sure he was as horribly curious about them and what they meant as I was.

"Many things, actually." Ross's eyes gleamed with amusement.

"What my brother means to say is that we're not going to tell you." Jared sent him a reproachful look. "You did us a good turn. And we appreciate it. But you won't be getting further involved.

"As soon as you feel well enough, we'd like you to leave."

Jensen rocked where he sat, obviously not having expected the dismissal any more than I had.

Ross took a step forward as if trying to soften the already launched blow. "Before then, however, we'd greatly appreciate it if you'd inform your fellows to stop looking for us."

A rough laugh escaped my lips as I shoved away from the couch to my feet. "Really? We just saved you from getting run over by a car driven by a demon, gave you information you needed, and you're just going to throw us out? I don't think so."

"Tamara, don't..." Jensen finally half turned to look at me.

"Why not? My life was destroyed because of them!" My arm rose up to point at the brothers, filled with my righteous indignation. "I've lost my family, my friends, my work. The least they can do is tell me *why*!" I glared at them, daring them to say different.

"Whatever's happened to you is not of our doing." I found some of my own defiance reflected back at me in Jared's brown eyes.

"Is that right? Because it seems to me, they have a reason for wanting to find you—something very specific. Which is why they felt the need to disrupt my life in the first place. So forgive me if I think you're *full of crap*!"

The figurines on the mantle started vibrating. I knew I should try to reign myself in, but I just didn't care. They wouldn't be tossing me aside like I was nothing.

"Telling you what you want to know won't change what happened to you." Ross' expression was full of loss and regret. "It could also place you in even more danger."

"I. Don't. Care." Other things started rattling around the room. My head started pounding again. I let it.

"Tamara, please," Jensen said. "This isn't the way."

I ignored him.

Jared leaned against the wall, his arms crossed over his chest. "I'll give you the name of the one who wore you. Would that be enough for us to be rid of you?"

My mouth instantly opened to say 'yes.' Knowledge of the one who hurt me was what I needed if I was going to bring about my vengeance, but I caught myself in time. The one who'd destroyed my life was but a flunky— someone following orders. Something else was truly responsible. Whatever it was they were after, I wanted to make sure they never got it. I wanted all of them to regret ever having taken my life away from me, not just their errand boy. "No. It will not."

Jared pushed away from the wall, his long blonde bangs falling over his forehead and half concealing his eyes. "Then I guess you're out of luck." He glanced at his brother. "We need to go. We've been here too long already."

They weren't going anywhere. Not if I could help it.

CHAPTER FORTY-TWO

I brought up my hands and made grabbing motions at both of them. The brothers astounded gazes twisted my way.

"Tamara, what are you doing?"

"What I have to." I didn't look at Jensen, not wanting to see his disapproval, but mostly because I had to concentrate. I didn't want to hurt the brothers, just hold them. Yet this was something I'd never tried before. "They're going to answer my questions." I squeezed them just a little. "Aren't you?"

I didn't get quite the reaction I was expecting. Instead of looking upset or pained or even panicked, Ross just seemed unhappy, and Jared annoyed. The latter's gaze locked with mine and suddenly I was shoved down into the couch behind me hard enough for me to lose my breath.

No one had moved when this happened.

With my concentration broken, the brothers were free again. My head pounded like a drum, my 'gift' not all that excited about being called on so soon, and less at being cut off abruptly. So I just sat there and tried to concentrate on breathing.

Jensen scooped up one of the sandwiches still on the plate. "They're not like us. You're way outclassed. Please don't try that again?" He held the food in front of me as if it were a treat for good behavior.

"You should listen to him."

My eye twitched. I didn't much care for the simultaneous suggestion from the two strangers. But I also didn't have a choice. I was done. It didn't make me very happy.

Jensen handed me the sandwich when I did nothing. I wolfed it down, keeping my gaze locked on my knee.

It was over. The bastards would leave, and I'd be left with more questions than I had before we got to this stupid town.

"Brother, would it really be all that bad to tell them?"

I looked up in surprise at Ross' statement.

"Don't." Jared shook his head looking even more irritated than before. The ruby stud flashed as if in agreement.

White spoke up then, making me even more surprised. "It would be polite if nothing else. Plus, it would give me more of an incentive to get the search for the two of you to stop."

The ex-priest moved in front of me as if to shield me from them if they decided to get angry. He astonished me more and more with every word that left his mouth.

"If our planet is about to have an infestation like it did in the 1400s, we need to know. Some of us are prepared to fight against them."

Even Jared looked to have been caught off guard by this. "You know of the cycles?"

I saw White shrug. "We know that in the last year or two there've been more possessions recorded than have plagued us in 600 years. We know that a trial is coming. And I know that somehow the two of you are in the middle of all that is to happen."

He took a step toward them. "The more information we have, the better the chance we can minimize casualties. To use what resources we have to best effect. So please, I beg of you, for the billions of souls that may soon be placed at risk, tell us what you know."

I held my breath, sure this was our last chance. If Jensen's words didn't move them, nothing would. I gingerly leaned out so I could see the other two.

"Brother…" Ross stared at Jared, his gaze asking permission once again.

"We were punished for consorting with their kind before. You think He will like this better?" Jared wouldn't look at his brother directly, his expression closed.

"That was different, and you know it." Ross touched him on the arm, and the other jumped though he didn't move away. "Besides, if they know what's coming and can fight against it, our enemies will have to divide their forces, which would only help us do as we must."

I held my tongue knowing there was nothing I could do to help this decision. If I tried, I might very well wreck it. My batting average wasn't so good so far. If not for Jensen, the game would already be over.

Jared sighed and made a vague hand gesture.

Ross broke into a smile. "Thank you." He looked over at us. "The veil between the realms is thinning."

That didn't mean anything to me, but by the stiffening of White's shoulders, I could tell it meant something to him.

"The cycle is not constant. It can occur within a few years or a couple of millennia. And the grade of the weakening itself varies. But this appears to be a Grand Cycle, where the fabric between what you refer to as dimensions will grow thinnest. During such cycles it is easier for the Others to come across, their tether to their own plane of existence easier to tap and maintain. Some will be able to generate physical form because of this, though most will prefer to find hosts. During a Grand Cycle, even the weakest of their kind can cross for a time if they wish."

A shiver crawled up my flesh. The thought of demons of all types roaming unheeded across the land was horrifying. And some would make bodies of their own? With horns, rows of teeth, multiple arms, and legs? But then why bother? When there'll be billions of bodies readymade that they can take. The more I thought about it, the harder it got to breathe. Thousands, hundreds of thousands, for all I knew, millions of demons would cross to Earth and take the flesh of others to take a vacation in, leaving murder, horror, and chaos wherever they went.

Jensen sat back down next to me. His pale face showed he was as excited about this news as I was.

"Can we…is there some way to stop it?" Jensen's voice shook.

Jared threw a glare in our direction. "No. There's not. Which is why you'd have been better off not knowing."

That got my ire going again. It was better that way. "That's your opinion, not mine!"

"If you have others like you, you can at least prepare somewhat," Ross added, obviously trying to derail me and his brother from a fight. "Possibly stem some of the damage they'll try to cause."

"You shouldn't give them false hope," Jared said this quietly. "You know how it's been before…"

That sounded ominous. It also made me wonder if his reticence before was to give us the blessing that came from ignorance, the type of blessing best given when there was nothing you could do to change your fate. Not that I agreed with that.

"How long will it last?" Jensen was not looking at them but at his clasped hands. He grasped them so hard, the knuckles were pale.

Warm sunlight came in through the window, draping over us. I could hear the sound of birds frolicking outside. Not the type of thing you expected when talking about the possible end of the world.

"There's no way to tell. Though it hasn't reached its peak yet." Ross sent a quick glance toward his brother. "The Others have a hierarchy. Much will depend on whether there is an agenda or not. And how many decide to cross into this plane regardless. Many will find it too much of a temptation. It will override their better sense."

"Yes, an agenda. Like the two of you." But why? Yes, these two were more than they seemed, but what would make demons toe the line to gun after them?

"Azza, enough of this!" Jared cut in front of Ross to keep him from saying anything further.

At his comment, however, Jensen jerked where he sat. Had that name meant something to him as well?

He rose shakily to his feet. "Are you, are you Azza and Azzael?"

The room grew suddenly quiet and very still. Both brothers weren't moving, weren't breathing. They just stood and stared at Jensen as if he'd frozen them in place with his words. Or perhaps more like two cobras waiting to see what he would do before deciding to strike.

CHAPTER FORTY-THREE

"Jensen…" It felt weird for me to be the one pleading caution.

As if realizing his sudden danger, White sat back down, saying nothing.

After several stretched, taut moments, something gave. While not exactly safe, the mood didn't feel quite as dangerous.

"I take it you've heard of us?" The lightness in Ross' tone didn't quite make it to his face, which was as set as chiseled stone.

Instead of answering, Jensen reached slowly into one of the many pockets of his vest. He brought out a small book with letter tabs on the side. He flipped it open at the 'A,' found an entry then turned the handwritten pages in their direction. "I've come across you in some of my readings."

The awed tone was definitely back in his voice. I was dying to ask what he knew about these two but held back, the situation still feeling way too volatile.

Jared stepped forward stiffly and took the book from him, then scanned the page quickly. "Some of this is accurate, some of it is not." He gave the book back without shedding any more light on what he'd seen.

It was eerie, but I felt I was seeing the brothers more as who they were than before. There was an edge to them, a waiting wariness, and if possible, they were even more striking than before, an unexpected maturity showing in their young looking faces.

"So you are them?" Jensen's question was barely more

than a whisper.

"Perhaps." Jared stepped back. He and Ross traded glances again. "Tell us about those you mentioned. The ones ready to fight. What have you told them about us?"

The question sent alarm bells ringing in my brain. In all the movies it was just the type of question captors asked before disposing of you permanently. Jensen hesitated, probably thinking something similar. Yet if we weren't willing to trust them, why should they trust us? They probably had more to lose than we did.

I figured White reached the same conclusion because he told them the truth. "At present, nothing. The Order knows I'm out following a lead but not what. And the faxes with your likeness only say you're in trouble and need to be found. No names, no other reasons."

"And why exactly did you not mention us to your order?" Two pairs of eyes, one light, one dark, totally focused on him.

Jensen rubbed the back of his hand against his jaw. "Honestly? Because I wasn't sure if it was anything. I don't involve them unless it's something big I can't handle on my own. They gave me a purpose again, a way to serve. I won't waste that by crying wolf when I don't have all the facts..."

He left the last open as if giving them an invitation to resolve the matter. Fat chance they'd take him up on it.

Jensen went on. "As long as it doesn't impose a threat on others, I can keep all I know and anything you care to share between us. You have my word." He glanced in my direction. "I am sure Tamara will do the same."

I nodded, considering it an easy concession. Who would I tell about any of this anyway?

While they seemingly thought about it, Jensen handed the book to me open on the same page Jared had read.

There were names in neat handwriting with information attached below them. I scrolled down to the entry for Azza and right below it Azzael.

Sometimes considered one angel, though according to others, two distinct ones as well. Fallen for having had carnal knowledge of women. Possible parents of the *sedim*. Trapped between heaven and earth for their transgressions, though other sources claimed they were fettered in iron and left in a spot no one could visit. Ranked as *maskim*. Forced by Solomon to reveal mysteries to him.

There was a bit more, but like a lot of the previous information, it meant little to nothing to me. Though the name Solomon sounded familiar. I wondered if it was supposed to be King Solomon—the wise king from the Old Testament in the Bible.

Still, if this was right, they were indeed angels. Or at least not human. They'd been alive for thousands of years. Looking at their young faces, it was almost impossible to believe or even wrap my mind around it. As to having carnal knowledge with women, well, I was sure there were ladies out there who'd force themselves on the two brothers on the slightest pretext if they could. If your tastes only ran skin deep… I closed the book and stared at them.

As if they'd been waiting for me, they spoke as one. "Long ago a responsibility was placed upon us—an object. This object has power. Once made it could not be unmade. And there are those who would seek it. From this world and from the other. But they shall not have it."

Their eyes shone from within with light for a moment, then it was gone. I blinked several times but couldn't be sure I'd actually seen what I thought I saw. "Is it a weapon?"

Their heads cocked to the side as one. "Not directly. Yet it could be the key to insurmountable amounts of power. Chaos and order are within its purview, but the object itself chooses neither."

I wondered if speaking vaguely and not actually telling one anything was how these two got their kicks. If they genuinely were as old as it seemed, I suppose they were entitled to an eccentricity or two. Still, it was getting on my nerves. "Either tell us what it is or don't, okay? Quit playing games."

Their expressions returned to individual ones, Ross looking amused and Jared's irritated again. "We were only answering your question."

"It's the Ring of Solomon…"

Again White seemed to have shocked the two men, angels, or whatever they were. I possessed no idea of what he was talking about.

Jensen wasn't looking at them but at his hands clasped on his lap— which were shaking. His face was pale; the scar on his cheek almost seemed to glow. "It fits. The fact it's the two of you who're guarding it leaves room for nothing else."

"What are you—" My words cut off as a weird increase in pressure filled the room. Though their appearance hadn't changed, my eyes ached, and I got the odd impression there wasn't as much room in here for all of us as there'd been a moment before.

"You will share this knowledge with no one."

Both men drifted forward toward us. The pressure increased. Their totally blank expressions did more to scare me than anything they'd done so far.

CHAPTER FORTY-FOUR

"Whatever it is you're doing, stop!" I moved to stand in front of Jensen, goosebumps covering me from head to toe. "We promised you we wouldn't tell anyone! There's no reason for this!"

For the first time, my anger did little to stem back the cold tendrils of fear. It was finally seeping through my dull brain that these two really weren't human—they only looked it.

The two stopped, and the pressure seemed to draw back almost immediately. When I saw them share one of their looks, I exhaled in relief, sure it meant we might live a little while longer.

There was too much I had no knowledge of. I needed time to regroup and pump Jensen for answers. "Demons are looking for you and probably us, too, right this minute. I think you had the right idea about the need to leave here. So come with us. I'm sure Jensen knows a safe place we can hole up at for a while."

I was making some assumptions but figured if I was wrong, we could wing it.

"We don't have to travel as you do." Ross quirked an eyebrow then disappeared, reappearing on the opposite side of the room.

I jumped in shock. Yet it answered one question for me. I now knew why the orders for the demon who took me didn't include him following them. He probably wouldn't have been able to. But if they'd picked up something a creature wanted, this Ring of Solomon, why didn't they just ambush the brothers at the storage place?

Too many things still didn't make sense. "So you could have left the church offices any time you wanted?"

Jared took this one. "Of course. But using power would have also let all the demons in the region know where we'd been. At the time, there was only one to worry about, so why advertise our presence if we didn't have to?"

Ross walked back to his side. "We *have* been doing this a long time."

"And your little display just now? Didn't that send up a flare?" I asked.

The dark haired man grinned. "I just moved fast. I didn't actually Travel. My bad."

Had an angel, or some proximity thereof, just pulled a joke on me? This just got weirder and weirder.

"There are numerous ways out of town." Jensen's face had regained some of its color. "Let us drive you. If there's only one of them here at the moment, it can't cover all the roads. It'll also keep them guessing as to whether or not you've actually left once he lets the others know."

White stood up, swaying slightly. Though he'd made the shocking revelations, I was starting to wonder if perhaps he wasn't the one most shaken of all. It just didn't make sense to me…yet.

The brothers looked to consider what he said a moment then traded another of their looks. At Jared's almost imperceptible nod, Ross gave us both a big smile. "Since you've offered, we'll go ahead and take you up on that. It's probably best if we keep an eye on the two of you for a while anyway."

His smile grew. "It's been some time since we met a human who was able to figure out who we might be. Isn't that right Azzael?"

His brother frowned. "It'd be best if they used our current names if any need be used at all, *Ross*."

"I'm not the one who made the slip."

Jared's frown grew more pronounced. "Ross…"

Something was going on. Were Azza and Azzael not their real names either? Just how many names did these two have? I turned away before I was tempted to ask them. I was pretty sure it'd be a futile gesture.

Instead, I followed Jensen.

He moved through the house to the immaculate kitchen and the phone there. He half glanced in the direction of the brothers who straggled behind. "I'm calling a friend of the Order. He'll get the word out that you've been found and all is well. I'd rather not use our cell phones for the time being."

The brothers made no comment, so Jensen went ahead and dialed after looking up the number in a small contacts book in one of his many pockets.

I spotted a fruit bowl, so I grabbed an apple as we stood around waiting. It was then that I noticed all my cuts from the flying glass back at the church offices were gone. I bit into the apple to hide my surprise. Had the brothers done this or did I have yet another weird 'gift' to contend with? I really, really hoped it'd been them. I wasn't sure I could deal with having another one.

I'd have asked them while we waited, but I was pretty sure they'd give me the run-around. Besides, they were way too focused on Jensen and his quick phone conversation. I wasn't sure what they thought he might actually say other than what he'd told them.

Less than a minute later, he hung up the phone and headed for the door leading to the garage.

Jensen's car was the only one in there. I was pretty certain the house didn't belong to the brothers. Were they house sitting or, the more likely choice, squatting? Lawbreaking angels. Who knew? But hadn't it said in Jensen's notebook the two were also Fallen Angels? Wouldn't that make them demons? Another item to add to my list of things I needed to find out about.

"Tamara, would you bring up a map on your laptop and look for a roundabout way for us out of town?" All signs of awe, surprise, shock were gone. Nothing about him said we'd be riding along with creatures, possibly thousands of years old, in his back seat, who could probably kill us without blinking. We were just going on a friendly little drive.

I tried to emulate him and did as he asked.

Ross and Jared climbed on board moments later.

When the garage opened, I saw we were in a neighborhood with large lots. Trees were everywhere. A two-lane winding blacktop sent us past quaint two storied homes.

I navigated us through a myriad of back roads which eventually led us to New Boston road. From there we took the 114 through Goffstown and just randomly wove our way across the state.

The brothers were so quiet it was easy to forget they were back there. Not that I could.

The sun started its descent in the horizon, making a rainbow of shades in the mostly cloudless sky.

"Can you find us someplace to stop for the night?" Jensen's voice sounded rough like he'd not used it in years. Made me wonder what he'd been thinking about. I'd been trying to do as little of that as possible though I was burning to ask all sorts of things. I just didn't want to be near the brothers when I did it.

A quick Google search got me to the Sunapee Harbor Cottages site. The small buildings had upstairs and downstairs sleeping arrangements. The location looked private, somewhat off the main tourist paths, but still full of amenities. The back of the cottages faced a forest, which might prove useful if things got out of hand. Number four would be perfect and didn't look to be currently booked. It had the added bonus it couldn't be located correctly on map searches per their web info.

I just hoped Jensen had enough cash. The fact Father Paul had been possessed when he came to see us might indicate the demons had used us to find the brothers. This meant our enemies knew who we were. And if they possessed someone in the police or FBI, they'd have the resources to track us down. I was sure it was one of the reasons Jensen had wanted only rural roads despite the addition of time. They didn't usually have cameras or tolls.

"Got one. Hopefully, they'll let us rent the spot when we get there." Though slightly surprised they had an opening at this time of year, I'd take any breaks we could get.

With any luck, I'd get a chance to pry some answers out of Jensen while I was at it.

CHAPTER FORTY-FIVE

"The web was right, they'd had a last minute cancellation, so one of the cabins was free. We can spend the night and get moving again in the morning."

We'd all been waiting for Jensen in the car, parked at the parking lot to the side of the office and out of view from the street. As we got out, he tossed a key to the brothers and pointed at unit number four. "If you'll go on ahead, we'll get our bags."

I kept quiet, not fooled by Jensen's friendly tone and manner. What mattered was that he'd contrived a way to give us a few moments alone.

Jared and Ross nodded and went on, seemingly unconcerned. I shifted from foot to foot as I watched them go, not wanting to let my stacking questions out until the other two were out of range. The moment I figured I was safe, I moved to the trunk to talk to him, yet kept my voice to a whisper still feeling paranoid.

"White, what's going on? What's this ring you mentioned at the house?"

He didn't look at me, going through the motions of getting our stuff, albeit slowly. "The Ring of Solomon…also known as the Key of Solomon…" He shook his head as if not entirely believing his own words. "It's a lot of things. Some believe it to be a pentagram, drawn circles and stars with runes, used for rituals to gain power and exact control over demons and spirits. Pentalpha, the five-pointed star of five alphas joined at the base—a pentacle."

I'd seen enough horror films in my life I thought I

knew what he was talking about here. Mystic circles and weird runes making a spell that could summon a demon and hold it. Upside down five pointed stars linked to Satanism. But those types of things wouldn't be something you could hide.

"Other sources insist it was a physical ring or vessel given to Solomon by God. King Solomon supposedly used the ring to force Azza and Azzael to reveal the mysteries of the universe to him and make demons help him build the great temple."

Jensen shook his head again. "A book with these secrets was supposedly buried with him in an ivory box, illegible to anyone not deemed worthy. It was seemingly recovered later by Iohe Grevis, who'd been given permission to read it." He swung a couple of duffels over his shoulder and handed me my suitcase, then closed the trunk after pulling out the roller suitcase that made my eyes itch.

"You can find a copy of it out there called the Key of King Solomon. It's bunk. All of it. A trick of misdirection with kernels of truth to make it seem authentic. A trap for the greedy and stupid." He started toward the cottage with me close at his heels. "A means for the Order to throw people off the scent. Keep them from trying to find the real texts so the knowledge wouldn't be abused."

"Okay, I think I get all that." Then it hit me. "Wait, did you say with this ring demons could be controlled?" Jensen nodded.

"Then that's good, isn't it? We could use the thing to stop the demons coming through this veil thinning problem, right? Until it got strong again?" I knew the idea had to have occurred to him.

We were coming up on the cottage. His pace slowed. The lights were on, and we could see the brothers' silhouettes in the upstairs window through some lacy curtains.

"I don't think they'll let us. From their reaction, I have the deep suspicion no one is supposed to use it, ever."

That froze me in my tracks. "No way! There's a means of grabbing hold of these intruders and keep them from hosing up the world and other people's lives and they're not going to use it? That's insane!"

Jensen glanced back at me, his eyes filled with sadness. "You forget, they're not human. They don't follow our ways. They might not care." He sighed. "If the notes in my book are correct, they lost their status and were cast out because they consorted too closely with our kind." He shook his head. "We don't know enough about them, but their actions so far speak of non-involvement in humanity's plight."

That couldn't be right. It just couldn't! Demons crossing to Earth in droves to do who knew what for who knew how long and these two possessed a means of stopping it and they wouldn't use it? No. Oh no. They'd help humanity or else!

I shoved forward to get past him. He grabbed my arm. I half turned glaring daggers at him. "Let me go, or I'll make you."

"Do you think I don't want to go in there and make them help us any more than you do? To make sure the horror we've suffered doesn't happen to anyone else?" His hot gaze trapped mine. "But we cannot *make* them. They're too powerful. Besides, violence and anger won't sway them to our cause."

"But they could disappear whenever they feel like it!"

"And the wrong word or move will only hasten that. As long as they remain with us, we have a chance to change their minds."

What he said made sense, but I didn't like it. What could two measly humans say to beings who'd been roaming the planet for centuries that they hadn't seen or heard already? A fatalistic sense of helplessness nipped at me. It was the one emotion I could not stand. But anger couldn't save me from it this time. "And how do you suggest we do that exactly?"

Jensen suddenly looked as helpless and lost as I felt. "Pray. Pray with all your heart and hope He hears it."

CHAPTER FORTY-SIX

I stepped through the threshold into the cabin, more depressed than I'd been since all of this started. Jensen wanted me to pray. He might still cling to the self-deluded assurance something like that could bring, but I'd disassociated myself from it years before. I just didn't believe in it. In Him. Even with everything that had happened. For surely the fact there were demons and possibly angels, meant there was a chance God was real as well.

But if He did exist, things would be crueler still. He'd not come to help or save us. He'd allowed this Grand Cycle thing to happen. Made humans so we could be vehicles for demons. He allowed these creatures to leave their realm to come and terrorize mine.

I left my luggage by the door and sat down on the futon couch. The place was tiny, yet arranged in such a way it took as much advantage of the space as possible. There was a queen bed behind me and just enough room to get to it. To my left was a small counter with a sink, a toaster over, a microwave and a mini-fridge. A small table, two wooden chairs, a tiny TV and a mini wood stove, rounded out the rest. Off white walls and wooden floors with quaint rugs were supposed to give it a homey feel. A set of stairs led upstairs. I assumed the brothers were up there as there was nowhere they could hide down here.

It was probably best for all concerned if they stayed up there.

The moment Jensen closed the door, however, they

clomped on down.

"Now that's interesting!" Ross reached the landing first and was staring with fascination at Jensen's special suitcase.

Without saying anything, Jensen lifted it onto the counter then stepped back behind me, his hand falling on my shoulder. I wasn't sure if it was to reassure me or to restrain me.

"Brother, come look at this!" Ross ran his hands slowly over the top of the case then opened it. Jared joined him, none of his brother's interest or excitement showing on his face at all. I half turned to look away, their mere presence making my anger bubble. I felt a momentary squeeze of my shoulder–a definite reminder to behave myself. I would have slapped his hand away except I suspected he was feeling pretty much the same things I was. I doubted I'd ever have his control. I forced myself to count inside my head anyway.

"You made this?" Ross sounded like a little kid at Christmas.

Jensen did not. "Yes."

"I've not seen some of these symbols in ages. Hittite, Sumerian, Babylonian; some Enochian, too!" He gave an unexpected giggle.

I was curious despite myself. I'd heard of one or two of those languages but not all.

"Your order does seem to know a lot of things." Ross ruffled through the contents. "Yes, a lot of things."

The more pleased Ross sounded, the less content Jared looked.

"I should set up the protections." Jensen stepped forward and took possession of the trunk. "Tamara, if you wouldn't mind helping me?" He pulled out a container of consecrated salt and handed it to me.

"Sure, I'll take the upstairs." Without glancing at either of the brothers, I went up to the second floor.

Three twin beds, a rocking chair, a couple of throw rugs and a dresser were all that was up there. It wouldn't take me long to salt the two windows, but I planned to make it last. Until Jared showed up.

He'd come up noiselessly from downstairs and almost made me drop the salt when I turned around to find him there, his stare boring into me.

"What do you want? I'm busy." I hadn't really meant to sound harsh, but he startled me pretty badly.

"You're not the same as before." He stepped up close, intruding into my personal space. The coat was gone, leaving his well-contoured arms bare for view.

I forced myself to hold my ground, not about to let him intimidate me. "I don't know what you're talking about." My hand moved on its own to the iron dagger still tucked in my back pocket.

"You're feelings have changed. You're upset about something."

I didn't normally go for white meat, no matter how pretty the packaging, but there was something about him that was hard to resist up close. The blonde hair and moody brown eyes added to that almost androgynous beautiful face called to all sorts of things inside me. I had a feeling he wasn't even aware of it, or if he was, he didn't care. It was tempting to just wallow in the fact he was so close. But I was getting really tired of everyone around me being able to read my aura. Not everything was meant to be shared. Plus I knew he didn't think much of me anyway.

I put my hand on his chest and forced him back a little. "As if you care. Especially since the reason I'm 'upset' is because you twins are unfeeling, uncaring pricks."

Jared actually dared look astounded at this. He took another step back. "What do you mean?"

He had to be kidding me. "Hello? You have Ring of Solomon, the one object that could be used to hold back the demon hordes coming through the thinning veil yet you refuse to use it? What part of that sounds feeling and caring to you?"

I crossed my arms and glared at him. So much for my nurturing some good feelings and keeping us in their good graces. Part of me panicked at the realization, but the rest of me wasn't going to back down. They were in the wrong, not me, and I wasn't about to sugar coat it.

Jared's expression closed up. "You don't know anything."

"Really? Then why don't you *enlighten* me?" I was giving him attitude, but I just couldn't help myself. How many times in my life had I run up against the same close-minded attitude? Just because I was black, or female, and now add to that *human*, there were those who assumed I could never understand anything. "Why not give the lowly, stupid monkey a chance? Or is that too much for you?"

His eyes narrowed, the ruby stud flashing with the movement. "It is not. But things just aren't as simple as you believe they are."

I shifted my weight to one side, tapping my finger impatiently against my arm. "Still not hearing much of anything coming from you."

The edges of his mouth turned down. Weirdly enough it made him look bad boy adorable. I shook my head. Did they exude something when they got real close? This wasn't like me.

"The ring has power over them and others, yes, but it

isn't a blanket power. You can't use it to stop all demons everywhere at once. If you have their proper name, you can call them to you and subvert them to the ring's will, or if they are physically before you. But you can't use it on any whose name hasn't been procured or is not in your presence."

His voice softened. "Even if my bother or I could use the ring, we couldn't stop what's coming."

CHAPTER FORTY-SEVEN

I reeled back, the denial clamoring to jump out at his words. There must be something that could be done. Otherwise, this ring was veritably useless, so then why… "Why do the demons want it then if it's so useless? All they'd have to do is steer clear of you, make sure no human got a hold of it, and even then you're saying it wouldn't be much of a threat anyway so…"

Was that what they'd been doing when they took me and destroyed my life? Only making sure they knew who had the ring so they could steer clear of it?

No. It didn't add up. It just didn't. The one who took me was under orders. Orders that had given it no reasons and brooked no questions. There must be more.

Jared was lying to me. He had to be. I clung to that hope like nothing else before.

"The reason they want it has nothing to do with what humans might do with it. This isn't the first time we've been pursued by them." The last came out sounding tired and stripped of emotion.

A cold chill leaped up my spine. "Are you saying demons can *use* the ring?"

"I said this wasn't simple. So no, they cannot. At least not directly. But a human could do it for them."

That was insane. Why would anyone in their right mind get a hold of an object of that much power then use it on a demon's behalf? I sat down on the edge of the nearest twin bed, knowing I had to find out and already sure I wasn't going to like the answer. "Why would they do such a stupid thing?"

Jared looked away. "Why do humans do anything? Power, money, but mostly the promise of a longer life."

My nails dug into the fabric of my jeans. "They can give them that?" While I tried to believe people were inherently good, I knew there were some out there who definitely weren't and would love to grab an opportunity like this.

"Some can. Though it never works in the human's favor in the end. It's not in a demon's nature to allow it. They must always have the last laugh and at their victim's expense."

"Still, what would a demon have them do with the ring?"

Jared glanced my way. I could see him trying to decide whether to tell her or not.

"Please. Just tell me."

The sigh that followed was heartfelt and long. "The demons have a hierarchy. One built on power and blood. The strongest rule, the rest are beneath them to do with as they see fit. There is a balance of sorts. But the ring could change that. If a demon were to obtain it and find a human to use it, he could get the human to subdue any demon above it if it had its name, and command it to follow or submit. Depending on how the command was stated, it could be made to last indefinitely. The balance could be tipped. And one willing to do this might have no qualms about using it to destroy other things, like the restrictions on the veil, for instance, thus opening the door between dimensions and expanding their sphere of influence."

I closed my eyes for a second trying to absorb all this. It was just plain crazy. "Why would anyone make a ring that could do that if it's so dangerous? Why not just destroy the stupid thing!"

The smile that flashed across his handsome face was bitter. "It's not allowed. The ring is an object of Choice."

"What the *hell* does that mean?" Was he just feeding me a bunch of bullshit?

He shook his head. "I've said too much already. Just understand that we cannot stop what is coming." He turned away.

Before I could think better of it, I reached out for his arm to try and stop him. When skin met skin, I got a small jolt like from static electricity. My eyes itched liked they'd done at other times, but I didn't understand it. I didn't get any time to think about it as Jared turned on me, snatching his arm away, eyes blazing.

"You *dare* touch me?"

I took a step back, the animosity blaring from him almost a physical force. It made no sense. "I'm sorry! But you were just going to leave me hanging, so I had to do something!" I wasn't sure exactly why but I felt bad about this. "Did I hurt you?"

I saw a glimmer of something I didn't understand cross his face then the heat coming from him dampened and died like a flipped switch. "Just don't do it again."

Then he was gone.

The door slammed downstairs so hard it shook the wall.

I was still trying to figure out what'd just happened when Jensen peeked over at me from the stairs. "Are you all right?"

I nodded, though I wasn't entirely sure. "Is Jared downstairs?"

"No." Jensen didn't come any closer. "Did something happen?"

Guilt poked at me, but I ignored it. "He said the ring can't be used to stop all the demons. Though it's possible he might have been lying."

Ross's dark head popped up right behind Jensen's. "We don't lie. It's a thing. Obfuscate, sure. Lead you astray, maybe. Outright lying, no."

Seeing him made me feel a little better. It meant that for the moment, I hadn't driven them away. There were still too many questions. "Sorry. I didn't mean…"

But hadn't I? Would all this not be easier if I did think he was lying? Give me some kind of twisted sense of hope? "It's a lot to take in. And I don't like feeling helpless."

Both men looked flabbergasted at the admission. I guess I was too. It wasn't like me to share. I really must be tired. I rubbed at my face. "Guys upstairs, girl downstairs? I call dibs on the shower."

CHAPTER FORTY-EIGHT

I surprised myself and slept like the dead. After the other two got over their shock at my words, they'd finished setting up the protections and turned in. I'd tried staying awake until Jared returned, but after the hot shower and the food Jensen got from somewhere, I crashed hard. If he'd come in while I was sleeping, I never heard him.

I was up before the sun, so I quietly got dressed, while deep snores echoed from upstairs. Either Jensen also slept deeper than usual or 'maybe angels' had breathing problems. It was also possible Ross had done something to us, but since I felt more rested than usual, I wasn't about to be ungrateful about it.

Grabbing a jacket just in case, I slipped outside. It would be nice seeing how this dawn differed from the ones I'd been watching these past weeks at Jensen's place. I needed all the tranquility I could get.

Dew covered everything, the scent of trees and greenery descending over me with just a tang of something fishy thrown in. Walking past the tiered flower garden, I took the back of the parking lot to Lake Avenue. I could just make out the lake, a yawning dark maw, as the sky began to lighten.

There was a gazebo in the public commons, so I aimed for that instead of the docks. Though it was early, the sound of eager fishermen getting ready for a day of leisure at the lake came down my way.

As I neared the open-walled structure, I realized someone had already beaten me there. I was even more astonished when I realized it was Jared.

I slowed, staring at his back. He was so still it was almost like he was a statue instead of a living thing. He stood unmoving, hands in his jacket pockets, seemingly staring out toward the lake. He was covered with the leftovers of an early morning fog. Had he spent all of last night out here?

I found myself loathe to disturb his solitude. If he'd wanted company, he would have come back to the cabin. I'd just have to find somewhere else to go.

Quietly turning away, I'd not taken a step when his soft voice reached out to me. "If you don't hurry, you'll miss it."

I turned back around, but he was still staring off toward the water. "Miss what?"

"Sunrise. Isn't that what you're out here for?"

He had me there. "I didn't want to disturb you. You've not been seeing me at my best plus I figured you wouldn't welcome my company after yesterday."

One shoulder rose then dropped. He'd yet to turn around. "If the thought of company offended me, I would be invisible."

I found my curiosity peaked even as I moved to join him. "You can do that?"

Instead of answering he seemed to shimmer for a moment and then was gone. My heart skipped a beat. A moment later he was back. He'd not moved an inch.

Hiding the fact he'd unnerved me, I stepped up to stand beside him and stared with him out onto the water and beyond.

Fog still covered parts of the lake like a blanket slowly being pulled back. Small fishing boats followed in its wake. The sky lightened making bands of color across itself like an inverted rainbow. Taking slow, deep breaths,

I tried to make the tranquility flow through me, fill me, steady me while letting everything else go.

I heard Jared let out a heavy breath of his own as if he too were seeking something from the sunrise. Perhaps he was. Maybe even for my benefit. "You and your brother have been guarding that ring for a long time, haven't you?"

"It became our task not long after it was made, yes." His voice was barely more than a whisper.

I tried to imagine it. Guarding the Ring of Solomon, letting no man or demon take it. Hiding, running, wondering who'd be foolish enough to make a move on it, on them. And when the veil thinned... Who could live like that? "Life must be hard for the two of you."

Though I was still staring out at the lake, I felt him shift beside me. After several seconds he said, "It is what it is."

He was nobler than I was. "Haven't you ever thought of quitting? Of giving the responsibility to someone else?"

The pause was longer this time. "I can't."

I waited, but he said no more. From just the two words I couldn't tell if it was because he had an obligation, it was payment for some indiscretion, or who knows what. I desperately wanted to look at him, hoping for a clue, but I was sure that whatever precarious calm we'd reached together would be over if I did.

"They'll find us again. Possibly sooner rather than later. We'll need to go our own way."

I bristled at the words, yet the unexpected sadness, almost longing in his voice stopped me cold. "I thought you wanted to keep an eye on us? Make sure we didn't betray you or something. Even maybe use our safe house for a while."

Despite the fact the ring might be no help at all against the thinning of the veil, the demons wanted it. And anything they desired I wanted to make sure they absolutely did not get. Even if I didn't understand everything it meant.

"I don't think it will be necessary. I believe you'll keep our secret."

This time I couldn't help myself, I gawked at him. Surely this wasn't the same person who'd seemed so vehement to have nothing to do with us. It's not like we'd really done anything to prove ourselves to him. "Who are you and what have you done with Jared?"

Now it was his turn to gawk. "What do you mean?"

I felt my mouth tug in a grin. "Well, the Jared I met is not quite this trusting, you see. A real hard-ass that one."

To my utter amazement, he blushed. I'd made an angel, energy being, alien, whatever, blush. I think I rather liked it.

"Getting close to people is not…"

A popping sound echoed all around us. I stared as Jared's head rocked back, a dark hole appearing in the middle of his forehead.

CHAPTER FORTY-NINE

I screamed. I'd never thought of myself as a screamer, but I was one today. As Jared's body fell, I dropped with it. I grabbed him by his coat and tried to pull him with me under one of the benches in the gazebo, trying to get us out of sight if more bullets would be coming. A head shot, he'd taken a head shot. He was dead. I knew it but refused to believe it. My head kept turning as I tried to look everywhere at once, except at him, not having any real idea where the shot had come from.

I jumped when a hand landed on my arm and almost screamed again when I saw it was Jared. His eyes fought to focus even as the gaping wound in his forehead seemed to flow backward spitting what remained of the bullet to clatter onto the ground. It was smoking.

"Are you all right?" My voice shook. My whole body shook. I'd just seen him shot. I saw him die. Now he was alive again. My brain was having a little trouble with the concept.

His eyes focused on me, his hand on my arm closing around it. The pain as he gripped me too hard felt very far away. Jared's lips barely moved as he said, "Iron...how?"

His head suddenly twisted in the direction of the cottage. "Ross?" Voices and running feet were advancing on the gazebo.

Before I could think of what to do, Jared rose up, bringing me with him. Then he swept me into his arms and ran.

Everything around me turned into a blur. I was

pressed into his body, pressure pushing me into him. I had to work at getting a breath. Then it was over. Though it took me a second or two more to catch up with myself.

Somehow we'd ended up back inside the cottage.

Jared set me down, my legs not so sure they wanted to hold me up. The sound of fighting clumped down from upstairs. Jared didn't spare me a glance before rushing up there.

Knowing I was in no state to try to help, I ditched out of the view of the windows, and coming up beside them, made sure to pull the curtains closed. No sense making it easier for the sniper than we had to.

Then I pulled out my iron knife and flattened myself against the wall between the window and the door, which also let me keep an eye on the stairs. I smacked the wimpy door lock closed, comforted despite the fact it would probably cave with a single kick from outside.

It got quiet upstairs. Too quiet. I got ready to throw myself to the side just in case. "Guys?"

Ross's blonde head peeked over the wall into the stairwell. "Tamara, come upstairs. Quickly!"

I was halfway up before I realized what I was doing. As I came past the half-wall, I could see the room had been trashed. The smell of gunpowder and something metallic tinged the air. A crumpled form filled the middle of the floor, a gun with a silencer next to it.

Jared stood over the body, his face a closed mask. I stared at the lump, knowing it had once been a man, knowing now he was dead. We'd breached a threshold. And there was no way to go back. A fist closed over my heart and squeezed. Yet I'd known there was no way back some time ago. This just shut the door even more firmly behind me.

"Tamara!" Ross waved me closer. I noticed his torn

clothes and a burn on his cheek. It took me a moment, but I looked back at it wondering why it was there. Jared had been shot in the head and come back from that, the injury healed and gone as if it had never been. So why was Ross's wound still there?

Yet even as I came forward, I saw it was indeed healing. Just nowhere near as rapidly as his brother's. It wasn't right. But there were other things to worry about more than this at the moment.

Jensen was sitting against one of the tipped beds cradling his arm. I could see something red spreading out over his fingers.

"White, are you all right?" I skipped past the brothers and the body to get to him.

His face was pale, his lips thin with pain. "Just, just get one of the pillowcases, would you? I need to stop the bleeding."

I stripped one of the nearby pillows and brought it over. "What do you need me to do?"

"Tie it tight just above my hand. Then get another and wrap it like a bandage." He grimaced. "Then we need to get out of here."

"Was this your doing?"

I tried to do what Jensen told me even as I glanced back over my shoulder at Jared. The blank mask was still in place, but his eyes were smoldering, something inhuman shinning inside them. It pissed me off. So much for our calm neutrality. "Are you *mental?* Do you not see he's bleeding here?"

Ross got between us, facing his brother. "He tried to help me." Ross sounded sure and surprised at the same time as he threw a quick glance back in Jensen's direction. "He's been hurt on my behalf. I don't believe this was their doing."

"You should go." My head snapped back around to stare at Jensen at his words. "Our plan didn't work. Someone knows you're here. Go ahead and travel the way you spoke of before. Get out of here."

"No!"

Jensen winced as I inadvertently tightened the pillowcase too tightly on his arm.

"Tamara, it's not safe for them here."

I avoided his gaze as I continued to bind his arm.

"Our attacker wasn't possessed." Jensen's tone grew gentle but with steel hidden beneath. "He even used iron."

I hung my head, already knowing he was right. These people knew more than they should. They'd shot Jared in the head. Whoever this was played for keeps and I doubted they were doing it for altruistic reasons. My need for answers would just have to wait. "Jensen's right. You should go. There could be more of them."

Concentrating on what I was doing, the rest of my senses were primed to see if I could tell when they left, my heart hammering for reasons I understood and for some which I did not.

"We agree. We should go. And you should probably come with us."

That surprised me. From the shocked look on Jensen's face, I could tell it surprised him, too. I turned around where I sat on the floor, half sure it was just a joke. That they'd disappear the moment I dared believe it.

Though I still couldn't read Jared's expression, he stood beside his brother, a lighter mirror image.

"Won't we slow you down?" The question stunned me, especially since it came from me. Didn't I want to stay with them?

"Not how we'll be traveling." Ross's attention shifted

to Jensen. "This safe house you mentioned before. Have you been there?" White nodded.

"Good. Close your eyes and think of it. As detailed as you can. As if you were there but also seeing it on a map." Ross knelt down beside us as he talked and took our hands in his.

There was no shock at the touch. No itching of the eyes as with Jared. Were they perhaps a different species from one another despite the fact they looked the same? More questions to add to my list.

"I'll leave their goods to you then?" He threw a glance at Jared.

The latter only nodded and disappeared. There was a twirling breeze around the room for a moment then it was gone. "Let's take a trip together, shall we?" Then we were gone too.

CHAPTER FIFTY

It was…disturbing…

One moment we were surrounded by the damaged trappings of the cottage, the next we're outside a stone and wood cabin surrounded by woods. The change in smells alone, from lakeside water to cloying tree sap and dense vegetation, was like a slap in the face.

Ross let our hands go and stood up slowly. "Oh, very nice. This must have taken years to prepare."

I wondered what he could see that I couldn't. My eyes itched, but that was the only thing about the place which seemed unusual. "What do you mean? What's special about it?"

I glanced at Ross then Jensen as I asked this, then reached down to help the latter to his feet. His face grew paler for a moment, but he was able to hold his own.

"Oak trees and oak wood for protection. Granite stone with sigils carved on them then hidden by vines. A circle of iron and rock salt buried in the ground around the house and an iron fence farther out. And that's only what I can sense from here." He turned around his eyes full of amusement.

"I can't wait to see what else you've done."

A crooked grin flared on White's face. "I'm glad you approve."

Then Jared appeared out of thin air. I cringed as a brief flare of pain, like seeing a flash of light, struck my eyes. Except there'd been no light. Nestled in his arms were our bags, the rolling case beside him, the handle in his full hands.

His eyes widened a tiny bit as he glanced at our surroundings before his focus locked on his brother. "I didn't find anything. No homing glyphs. No power signatures."

"You mean someone was tracking us?" I tried to herd Jensen up the cabin steps to the porch. He was doing okay, but that wound needed looking after. I'd just ask questions at the same time.

"Must have somehow. We were found too quickly."

Jared's accompanying scowl to Ross's response clearly stated he didn't like it.

The front door into the cabin wasn't locked, but visible glyphs were drawn all around the door frame. The mat just inside the door surely hid an ingrained line of rock salt. I expected much the same of all the window frames and any other doorways.

"You don't think they had time to put a tracker on Jensen's car do you?" Then another idea hit me. "Do you and Jared carry cell phones? If anyone figured out your names, they could have turned on your GPS." I steered White toward the nearest chair.

Ross was right behind me. Jared brought up the rear with our gear as if it weighed nothing. Only the space it all took seemed to be awkward for him.

"We don't need such things." Ross circled past me. "May I?" He gestured at Jensen's arm.

My reluctant mentor gave a small nod. "There should be medical supplies in the storage closet in the bathroom."

"I'll get them." I zoomed off in the direction Jensen indicated with his head, glad to be of some actual use.

The cabin was just one large room with walls dividing some of the space, making a miniature maze of sorts. My eyes itched almost constantly the whole way through, then seemed fine. A couple of false turns later I found the bathroom and the storage closet. I grabbed the large medkit there and hustled back.

Ross had removed the bandage off Jensen's arm and ripped the sleeve but left the tourniquet on. Jared still stood by the now closed front door, our stuff on the floor off to the side.

"What about yours?"

"What?" I placed the medkit on the small table next to the rocking chair and glanced over at Jared.

"Your cell phones. Your GPS."

That brought me up short. I saw his point. It didn't necessarily have to be something of theirs. Not if the demons knew we were with them. Though the fact their attackers, one of them anyway, hadn't been possessed inferred all kinds of other things. "I suppose that's possible? But who'd be following us? We only caught up to you yesterday." Then a horrible thought hit me, one that made goosebumps burst all over my skin. "Unless the demon inside the priest was the one who possessed me before?"

The bastard was the only one who knew my name and other personal information about me. Enough that he could fake being me—*again*.

"No. The mark upon you is Rosier's. He wasn't with us at Merrimack." Jared's words screamed over and over inside my head. I finally had a name. Rosier. And he'd left it behind for anyone to see. My hatred flared and scorched me from the inside. "The bastard left a *brand* on me?"

Jared appeared taken aback. "It is usually their habit. A way to keep a tally and also to claim you if your soul ends up in their domain."

I felt both relieved and horrified that it wasn't an

automatic thing. It'd never even occurred to me they might actually want people's souls.

"Would you read mine?" Jensen's voice sounded as strained as my own.

Before Jared could answer, he held up his good hand. "No, don't tell me. I don't need to know." His scar throbbed as he fought against the raging torrent I knew so well and won. I would never be as lucky. Not on anything dealing with demons. Yet Jensen had. And he lost so much more than me. I felt awe and jealousy clawing at me at the same time.

"Hold still please." Ross placed his palm over Jensen's wound, his other beneath the opposite side of his arm. Jensen's face went sheet white, his jaw clenching in pain. My eyes started to itch. Ross yanked the hand over the wound away. A piece of something dark popped out after it as if being pulled by a magnet. It clattered to the floor near my feet.

I stooped to pick it up as Ross clamped his hand back against the wound again, forcing Jensen to grit his teeth.

There was no blood on the small caliber bullet as if Ross had separated it from anything Jensen. It was heavier than I expected.

A loud gasp made me look up. Jensen was breathing heavily as if he'd just stopped running. Ross was taking bandages out from the emergency kit. The tourniquet was off, but the wound didn't seem to be bleeding anymore. I could swear it looked better than a minute ago.

"I've accelerated the healing process, but it will still take some time for the wound to completely heal," Ross spoke as he placed the bandage on Jensen's arm and taped it down. "Like the TV says, keep it clean and dry until it gets better."

Jensen stared at his arm as if he'd seen a miracle. I

suppose in a way he had. Ross's own wound had totally disappeared by this point. "You'll need to eat. A lot. Is this place stocked?" Jensen only nodded, his eyelids suddenly drooping.

"I'll go make something." Ross headed off toward the back of the cabin as if he'd lived here all his life.

I wasn't sure what was more astonishing, that angels watched TV or that they seemingly could cook.

Shaking my head, I tried to get back to business. "This bullet. It hurt you and Ross. But the two of you aren't human. How could it do that?" I offered Jared the lump in my hand for inspection.

He wouldn't touch it. "The core is cold iron. From the resonance, I'd also guess there were glyphs on the casing." His tone was flat. "Whoever did this was very well informed."

"Isn't cold iron for faeries?" I was sure this had been in a movie somewhere.

"It affects many things. And normally would be of little concern to us. Unless certain steps were taken." His face took on a faraway look as if he remembered some past event. From the expression which followed, it couldn't have been pleasant.

"So it could have killed you?" The incongruity of what I'd seen at the gazebo rose up to haunt me. I'd been sure he was dead. But he hadn't been. And yet I was starting to get the feeling he should have been. So why wasn't he?

He shrugged. "What's important is we now know they can do that." He pointed at the bullet in my hand. "They can get at us like no generation has been able to before. Even from a distance."

He rubbed at his forehead for a moment then turned away.

CHAPTER FIFTY-ONE

I stayed with Jensen as Jared moved off to explore the rest of the cabin and then the outside. The scent of brewing coffee and baking bread trickled its way from the hidden kitchen and made my stomach rumble in response.

My hand went to the knife in my pocket when the heavy front door opened. The moment I spotted it was Jared I relaxed. He threw me a look as he came in almost as if sensing what'd just happened. "All's well?"

"Yes. Everything's fine."

He nodded. "Breakfast is ready, by the way." He headed off toward the back. The smell of pine trees trailed after him.

"Thanks." I half turned to wake Jensen only to find his eyes were already open. "Food's ready."

"Good." He got up slowly, but his color was better, and he didn't seem to be in pain, although he did cradle his arm on the way to the kitchen. Still, it was a great sign as far as I was concerned.

A thick table close to the wall had a plate of dried meats, one with slices of cheese, another with still steaming bread slices. Several jars of preserves and jams sat in a line as well. Coffee had already been poured into four large mugs. The large window slats I'd noticed in the front room windows were here as well but had been pulled up and hooked to the ceiling. If trouble came, cords hanging were from them that would allow one to pull and slam the slats closed in seconds.

Sitting down, I glanced at the kitchen proper. There was a wood stove as well as an electric one. An oven, refrigerator, and microwave as well. Old and new put together to cover any eventuality. It must have its own power generator or solar panels. As many trees as I'd seen outside, I got the impression this place was way off the beaten path. Someone had spent a lot of money here.

The hot bread called to me and my stomach, so I grabbed a piece and lathered it with orange marmalade. The moment I bit into it I went from hungry to ravenous. Jensen was way ahead of me, having already made a thick sandwich for himself and chomping it down in only a few bites. He was already halfway through a second before I reached for more.

Jared and Ross sipped their coffee, each having taken a piece of bread for themselves as well. Ross ate his plain, but Jared had covered his with orange marmalade as well. The latter was currently staring out the nearest window, seemingly deep in thought, while Ross was intently watching us eat.

Wolfing down my second slice, I figured we should probably get back to business. "About the GPS's in our phones. To be on the safe side, Jensen and I can get rid of ours. We can always pick up disposable phones later. They should have a much harder time trying to track us with those."

Jared turned from the window. "No. Keep them. If they're giving away our location, that means they probably already know we're here. We will stay, and they will come." His voice sounded sure as if he'd somehow seen the future. Maybe he had.

Ross picked up where he left off. "Knowing they'll be coming will make us better prepared. Better to be attacked here than somewhere on the road where we wouldn't be expecting it. Especially since they seem to know more than they should." He reached for another slice of bread.

"Do you eat because you have to or because you want to?"

Ross grinned at me, bread peeking past his teeth. He chewed for a moment. "Want to. Don't have to. Food is fun."

Jared hadn't stopped him from answering, didn't even seem to be listening. There could be an opportunity here. "Are those bodies yours?"

"Yes. They're our corporeal shells. We can have them or not in this realm as we choose." He closed his eyes for a moment obviously savoring his culinary handiwork.

"Angels of the 6th Chorus…"

I glanced at Jensen. "What's that?"

He looked startled as if not having realized he said it aloud. "Oh, nothing. It was nothing."

I could swear he looked embarrassed.

"That system of classification is a human invention." Jared stared at us. "I've never understood why your kind feels the need to fill in every single gap of information, even if it is with falsehoods."

"I'm sorry. I meant no offense." Jensen definitely looked embarrassed now, color rising up his neck to his ears.

The man had done nothing but try to help them. This made me mad. Not that it took much anymore. "Jared, could you cut it out with the bad attitude? If we have everything so wrong, why don't you *enlighten* us then?"

"What exactly would be the point of that?"

I tried to hold myself back, but it was hard, so very hard. "Are you listening to yourself? Do you hear what you sound like, you pompous blowhard?"

Jared shoved his chair back and stood, eyes blazing.

"Tamara, Jared, please!"

Loud laughter erupted and echoed from the non-involved side of the table. "She's got your number, hasn't she?"

Jared glared at his brother which only made Ross laugh even louder.

Then much to my surprise, Jared sighed and sat back down. "I apologize. It's been some time since we've tried to be social. I'm rusty at it."

I was sure that had nothing to do with it but let it go. If he could be gracious, so could I. "Sure. No problem." I made myself take another bite of breakfast just to prove it.

Ross leaned forward, putting his elbows on the table and resting his chin on his folded hands. "We're angels, we're djinn, we're elementals, we're something in just about any lore you have ever heard of and some which have disappeared with the ages. There are seeds of truth everywhere.

"We have been here since the beginning, and we will be here at the end." His blue eyes seemed to grow darker.

Jared snorted. "We exist. We're not human. Leave it at that."

"You do take the fun out of things sometimes." Ross rolled his eyes. "Anyway, what else would you like to know?" He looked pointedly at Jensen as if expecting a particular question.

The ex-priest didn't disappoint him. "King Solomon is spoken of in both the Jewish Midrash and the Bible. You guard his ring. So does...God exists as well?"

An odd little smile graced Ross's face for a flickering moment. "Which one? There are many to choose from according to all your human religions."

"Don't toy with them." The glare Jared sent his brother this time was cold and definitely unamused.

Words passed unheard between them then Ross sighed and sat back. "A total stick-in-the-mud."

Jared ignored him, turning toward us instead. "There is but one Creator. He too has many names, played many roles. Giving humanity 'choices'."

The words were shocking enough, but the layered, clashing emotions behind them even more so.

It was my turn. "If He exists then why the hell is He not doing something about, about everything?"

Jared's expression went blank. "Then what would happen to his gift to you of 'choice'? Not all are so fortunate."

Could it be that black and white? Could He be that deluded? Nothing worked in absolutes in life. Nothing. And what did Jared mean not all were so fortunate? Was this strange veiling of 'choice' not given to all?

"No. They are not. Are they…"

I snapped a look at Jensen. He was staring at Jared and Ross with a strange intensity. I was really tired of feeling out of the loop all the time.

Then it hit me. Jensen meant the brothers themselves.

CHAPTER FIFTY-TWO

"I don't understand what's going on." I grabbed another dish and dunked it into the soapy water with more force than necessary.

Jensen and I were on clean up duty. Breakfast had broken up after the ex-priest's last pronouncement. The two brothers citing different reasons for leaving as if they'd grown suddenly shy of where the conversation was leading.

"I may know a little more, but there's no guarantee what I know is right." Jensen favored his arm as he dried one of the coffee mugs.

"More than what was in those pages you showed me?" I wracked my brain to recall all that I read from them. There'd been a lot of distractions at the time.

"Not much more. But in several religions, angels have no free will. They exist merely to serve. The gift of 'choice' has been denied them."

I scrubbed the plate as I thought over what he said. The strong scent of Palmolive floated around getting stronger as I worked.

If what he said was true, then it would mean Jared and Ross were really no more than slaves. My shoulders twinged so I took a slow, deep breath to relax them. Whites over blacks, humans over angels. Universal discrimination. It didn't make me like Him any better than before.

"Your book said they'd been punished though. For carnal sins? So they must have some will of their own.

They even chose to take us with them." I handed over the plate.

"There are higher choices they cannot make. Whether to believe in Him or not. Have faith or not. Do evil or not."

I shook my head, not sure it wouldn't be a better way for humanity to exist. If we knew for a fact He was out there, even if He didn't take an interest in us directly, wouldn't we all be better off? Yet as I thought this I knew I was wrong. As Jared stated before, mankind was full of greed and selfishness. There would always be someone trying to place himself above others. Corruption could breed anywhere. How many scandals had been on the news about this or that religious group? If the fact He existed didn't stop angels from breaking his rules, why would we fare any better?

We were made in His image. And we were flawed. What did that say for everything else He touched? Or Himself for that matter?

I rubbed a soapy hand over my forehead feeling a headache coming on. "Doesn't matter. We have more than enough filling our plates at the moment, don't we?"

His silence was agreement enough.

"What else can we do to prepare for whoever's coming?" I pulled the plug in the sink, letting the water escape down the drain. As I watched it go, it really pounded in how much money actually went into making this place. If it was as isolated as I thought it was, it would have cost a fortune to get running water up here. I wouldn't be surprised to find out it was some kind of self-contained system.

Jensen put the last plate away and draped the drying cloth over the sink edge. "Come with me."

He led me back to the main room. "Would you mind

moving that?" He pointed at the large coffee table made from two chunks of sliced raw wood.

I stared at it for a moment, wondering how in the world I'd be able to even shift it but moved to give it a go anyway.

"Oh!" It was light. Though the exterior looked like a solid slice of some giant tree, somehow they'd hollowed it out, so it wasn't really that heavy. Most would have never tried to move it assuming it weighed a ton.

As I dragged it out of the way, Jensen leaned down and pulled back the round red and brown carpet off to the side as well. Beneath it was a trap door. The moment he touched the hidden latch and it popped slightly open, the brothers appeared in the room with us.

"What's this?" Ross bent forward to look down the opening as Jensen pulled the door all the way up.

Jensen flipped a switch on the wall in the stairwell revealed before them. A whoosh of stale air buffeted us as light flooded the room below. The echo of fans and machinery coming to life wafted from beneath. "Come see."

I descended eagerly wondering what we'd find. I wasn't sure quite what I expected, but this was so much more. The room below was large, possibly even more extensive than the whole cabin. Bunk beds filled one wall. Shelves of dry goods and MREs filled another. Yet a third had hooks holding a strange assortment of weaponry from guns to iron spears. The last wall was a panel of screens with a desk and computer equipment.

"Last line of defense. Also where the camera monitors and movement sensor feeds are kept."

Ross glanced around, his head slightly tipped to the side. "More salt infused iron. Very nice. I'm assuming if the trap door is closed, it can be locked from the inside?"

"Yes. It also has an air filtration system and other perks." Jensen sighed softly, looking suddenly tired. "I honestly never thought there'd be a need to use this place. Always figured it was just a waste of money for the Order. I was wrong."

"Have you not needed it before?" Jared stared at the revolving pictures of the surrounding woods on the screen. One semi overgrown dirt road flickered by occasionally.

"The upstairs area, yes. It's useful as a refuge when things haven't gone well with the Work. But it's the first time I've had to contemplate locking myself down here."

"We probably won't have long. You two should rest while you can." Jared still hadn't taken his attention from the screens.

The implied dismissal was obvious. At least to me, anyway. Jensen nodded and started up the stairs. Ross sent a glance my way, a hint of a grin flashing for a moment, then he went up after Jensen.

Whether this was good or bad, I had no idea. Ross was playing at something, but it was hard to say what.

"You should rest."

I ignored Jared's added hint and strolled around the open room. The Bunker—that's what this place called itself to me. I might have to spend some time locked up in here, hiding from demons, from greedy men. Meanwhile, utter chaos would be mounting in the outside world as the veil grew thinner and thinner. There would be little to nothing I could do to help in either case.

But there was one thing I could take into my own hands—trying to get answers.

"Were you really punished for a carnal sin? Chained for a thousand years?" I ran my hand over the wooden side of one of the bunk beds–more protective oak even down here. I glanced at the ceiling and saw a massive pentagram with symbols of all types. They really didn't want to take any chances here.

"Why do you want to know?"

I risked glancing his way, surprised he'd responded. He didn't even sound mad. Yet... "Because I want answers. I want to make sense of all this mess. I want to know just who you and your brother are, inside. Anything. Everything." I threw up my hands in the air not knowing precisely what I wanted or why I wanted it myself.

"Just like we were, humanity was His creation. His ultimate creation. What He'd striven for millennia to make just so. You are His children while we are but servants." He still stood before the screen of feeds almost as if talking to himself. "Despite that, I loved them, loved them because He'd made them. But because Choice was His ultimate goal, He interfered with them little. And how they struggled. In the beginning, life was very hard."

I sat down on a bottom bunk, fixated to his every word.

"We watched them for Him. Sometimes saved them from the Others. Delivered messages. But never were we to interfere unless He bid it.

"Yet because I loved them, it hurt to watch them suffer. I wished to make things easier for them. So once we'd finished a task set for us, I convinced my brother to take a detour. He has many servants, I was sure we wouldn't be missed for a time. And I wanted to help them, get to know them. Since He made them, surely being closer to them would also make me closer to Him."

Silence ruled for several long seconds. I sat still, not wanting to disturb it, hoping he'd continue.

Jared sighed. "Our shells were pleasing to them. Our

skin light compared to their own. They tried to make us into gods, but I wouldn't have it. We toiled with them. Worked with them. Taught them. Nurtured them. But they taught us things too. Too many things…"

He shook his head. "I fell in love… And that led to other, less tolerated… Forbidden things…"

Though I'd meant to keep silent, a question left me before I could stop it. "What was her name?"

He gave a short laugh, unconsciously running his hand through his hair. "Ross would be cross at you for the assumption. But you're right, it was a she. Her name was Leja."

Thousands of years of sorrow coated the name as he said it. I found myself feeling jealous all the same.

CHAPTER FIFTY-THREE

I stared at the floor, weighed down by his pain. Pain I didn't truly understand. I'd had boyfriends, relationships. But none had been serious. None ever even approximated one percent of what I heard in his voice. To be so close to anyone, so dependent on one another—it scared me. Caring for family and friends was bad enough. But to love another so profoundly, so completely? I wasn't sure I was capable of it. Yet it called to me all the same. "Would you tell me about her?"

Gaze still glued to the monitors he said nothing for a while. Then, almost as if dredging each word out bit by bit, he told me.

"Her body was born twisted, malformed. Yet her soul was the most beautiful I'd ever come across. She soaked knowledge up like a sponge—a revered wise woman even in her youth. Unlike the rest, she saw us for who we were rather than our outer visage. She warned the village not to take us too seriously. Not to make us false gods. They were going to kill her for that, thinking it sacrilege, but Ross and I intervened. We tried once more to get them to understand the truth of what we were, not what they wanted us to be. Fearing they might try to hurt her again, I kept her close. Too close. After falling in love with her, I wanted to share in the ways humans expressed their affection and succumbed.

"And we were happy. So happy I forgot about Him. I forgot about my duty. Unknowingly, I'd made a choice."

For a moment a look of such bliss flickered across

what I could see of his face, I was forced to turn away.

"Then they found us. And those who'd never bothered with a corporeal shell judged us. They found my brother and I wanting. Thought us tarnished. So we were punished. I was given this so I would not forget and everyone would know." He tapped the ruby stub at his nose. "We were chained and locked away where no one would find us. To think on the things we'd done and how we'd failed Him and His commands."

I stared at my hands and then rubbed them slowly up and down my legs. "And you never saw her again?"

"No. Her body turned to dust millennia ago. Her spirit rose to where my kind are not allowed to go."

It was awful. I should have stopped there, left him to his thoughts, but I couldn't. "How did you escape?"

"We didn't." He threw a glance in my direction, his expression unreadable. "King Solomon found us. Used the ring to bring himself to us. Used the ring to command us."

I frowned. "I thought the ring was only for demons, not angels."

"I told you, we're not angels. We're what some call Fallen. We're no longer enfolded by His Grace, so we're susceptible to certain things we would not have been under His protection." He took a step closer toward the monitors as if having had enough of this conversation.

I couldn't let it go. Not yet. To be honest, I wasn't sure he could either. "What did the king have you do?"

A loud sigh reverberated through the room, but he answered me anyway. "Impart him with wisdom, with knowledge, what some might call magics. And despite the fact Solomon commanded us to do it, he still tried to intercede on our behalf. To have us set free and give us hope…in a manner of speaking…"

Something about that didn't sound good. "How so?"

"The ring… Over time Solomon came to realize the danger it could pose to humanity. The baser feelings it could bring to the surface. The damage it could cause. He didn't want his descendants to be either tempted by its power or for those ruthless enough to try to take it to come upon them. So he spoke to Him. Offered a possible, though not perfect, solution. One that left open 'choice.' We could be released from our bonds and placed as keepers of the ring. Bind us to it not only through His Word but by the ring's own power. And if we managed it, whenever the game went on long enough, we might be allowed to rejoin His ranks again."

My mouth went dry. And I thought my people had been held in bondage. It was nothing compared to the sentence of millennia given to the twins. My hands clenched in my lap. Why would anyone ever dare say God was just?

"Do not think badly of Him. We are His creations after all. It was a mercy. Better by far than the chains and the mountain pit."

I found Jared staring right at me, his expression serene. It made me livid. "So that just makes it okay with you, does it?"

The veneer of calm disappeared, and he took a step toward me. "Oh, so you'd rather I shake my fist in the air and curse Him to eternity, do you? As if you could even partially conceive what this feels like."

This was better. Much better. The real Jared, the one I'd caught glimpses of before. The one that seemed more human. "I'm not the one lying to myself. I'm not the one bending over."

"I see. You're so much better versed than I. Please, tell me how I should deal with this. Tell me how to spit in the eye of our Creator and how my following obliteration would be so worth it. Tell me how giving in to my rage and pain will make my existence so much better! Perhaps even as good as *yours*." His face twisted with his mockery of me.

My whole body shook as an irrational need to lunge myself at him and punch him vibrated through me. But he was right. Who was I to tell him how to live his life? Or what he had of one. He'd been dealing with this for thousands of years. I'd only struggled with these topics for the blink of an eye in comparison.

Despite the fact it was probably not a good idea, I closed my eyes, cutting him from view, and tried to calm down. With my eyes closed, I became even more aware of his presence. As if seeing him helped encapsulate him, but out of sight, the closed boundaries compressing all he was were no longer there. A being of vast power and abilities who could destroy me with a blink and whom I kept recklessly pushing at anyway. Maybe there was nothing wrong with him. Maybe it was all me.

I opened my eyes and found he'd stepped away and turned his back on me, his attention back on the monitors. As I struggled to figure out how to apologize or what to do next, I spotted movement on the far upper screen. We had visitors.

CHAPTER FIFTY-FOUR

"They got here awfully fast." Ross rushed down the stairs in a blur and stared at the monitors from Jared's side.

Jensen took a bit longer to join us.

A large minivan had stopped before the chain locked iron gates. A woman in a black jumpsuit got out and approached it. Her brown hair was pulled back in a tight bun. Her expression was hard, her eyes cold. At the gate, she half turned so we got her full face in the camera, as if she knew exactly where it was.

She started talking, but the camera had no audio. Thanks to Ross, that didn't matter.

"Jensen White, by order of the Niveus Miles Militis, you are to stand down. Those under your protection are higher demons in disguise and are not affected the same as most others. You have been duped. It is in your best interest to stand aside and allow us to do what we must."

The voice that came from Ross's lips was not his own. Goosebumps rose up my arms; pretty sure the woman sounded just like he reproduced her voice for the rest of us.

"If you do not comply, we will assume you are a willing participant in this travesty and treat you likewise."

That said, she pulled out a key from her jumpsuit and unlocked the lock on the chain.

I glanced at Jensen. "Do you know her?"

He shook his head. "No. I've only had contact with a handful of members. She isn't one of them." He turned to face the brothers. "If you run at speed, you could make it out the gates before they were the wiser. I'm sure we can come up with some excuse as to how we ended up here. If they believe you both to be high-end demons, they know how easily you could escape from here."

The woman watched the minivan go through then came inside and locked the gates behind them, keeping the protective circle of iron intact. Whether they thought it or not, they didn't look to be taking any chances.

"While it's true it would just be easier to leave, it wouldn't get us anywhere." Ross gave us an impish smile. "We did say we wanted the enemy coming at us at a place of our choosing, and this is it, and here they come." His hand made a sweeping gesture toward the monitors.

The van continued up the semi overgrown road then stopped. Six figures hopped out, weapons in hand, and spread out in different directions. Looked like they wanted to surround the house and make sure we didn't run out the back way. I had the sneaking suspicion they were here to keep us bottled in until more reinforcements or their superiors came.

A drop of cold sweat trailed down my back. Going after demons was one thing, but these were people. People who, though not possessed, were being used just as thoroughly as I'd been. And I would have to fight them. I wasn't sure I was ready for that. The realization startled me.

"Be right back." Jared zoomed up the stairs in a rush. Fast thumping sounds came from upstairs then he was back with us. "At least one of them has a rifle. I'd prefer not to be shot that way again."

I for one didn't blame him. I wasn't the one who'd been shot and I never wanted to see the effects ever again. Jared must have dropped the heavy shutters down.

"I'm assuming we don't think there's any way we might reason with them?" I had no hope they'd actually listen to us but felt it should at least be brought up as a possibility. My track record for getting people to believe me had been on an all time low of late and I didn't expect my ratio to get better anytime soon. But perhaps one of them would have better luck.

Jensen shook his head, a saddened expression on his face. "They won't believe anything we tell them. Skepticism toward others is a part of our survival matrix as well as total obedience to the Order. They would never believe a superior has betrayed our cause. Any proof we brought forth they would assume was somehow created by the demons we're harboring or being used by. As far as they're concerned, the two of us have been compromised and can't be trusted."

Something worse occurred to me then. "They'll have powers, too, won't they?"

"It's possible." Jensen didn't look any happier at the thought than I was.

"So what do we do?"

Jared answered that one. "We watch and wait. Let them make the first move."

It didn't sound in the least bit productive, but aside from going out there and incapacitating and possibly killing them, something I wasn't sure I could do, no other options were forthcoming. I just wasn't very good at waiting. That ability had degenerated since this whole mess began.

Thankfully, it didn't mean we weren't busy. While Jared continued keeping an eye on our visitors, Jensen and I went through the cabin to ensure it was locked down tight. Then we moved even more provisions downstairs in case we were forced to lock ourselves in the bunker.

The window covers hugged the frames so tight we were forced to turn on lights. It got easy to lose track of time.

Knives were sharpened, paper runes written, guns cleaned and oiled.

I knew almost nothing about the last two, so I kept my mind occupied trying to learn as best I could. Aside from the runes, I did most of the work, Jensen's wound bothering him. I wasn't sure how he could keep on going. He'd not had any real time to heal or rest since he'd been shot.

Ross sat on the floor next to the stairs with legs crossed, eyes closed and hands resting on his knees. I couldn't tell if he was resting or using some sort of power to keep tabs on those outside.

Just about the time Jensen and I ran out of things to do, Ross spoke up.

"Go downstairs and sleep. My brother and I have things well in hand for now. We'll wake you if anything happens." He never once opened his eyes though his face turned toward us.

I wasn't sure I could sleep, though it would while away a few hours. Jensen looked the worse for wear. His face drooped as if his exhaustion were physically pulling him down. Yet I was sure if I decided not to go he wouldn't either. So I had even more reasons to at least try. "I'm beat. I think I'll take you up on that."

I saw Jensen's shoulders slump as if relieved when he thought I wasn't looking. It should have occurred to me to turn in before now. We made our way slowly downstairs. Jared stood in the exact same spot he'd been at before. He didn't even glance our way as I insisted Jensen take the bottom bunk and I hauled myself up to the other.

CHAPTER FIFTY-FIVE

I was wrapped in total darkness. I could see nothing, feel nothing. Yet the overwhelming sensation I wasn't alone screamed through my senses sending spiking fear through my veins. I'd felt this before. I knew what it meant even as a part of me shrieked with denial.

A stranger inside my own form. Pushed to the back to become a passenger rather than the driver. A passive figure unable to move, to speak, to choose or have free will. A prisoner inside my own skin. Actions done in my name as I rotted in helplessness.

Light flared before me, expanding into a floating screen showing me what my eyes could see. I couldn't help a soul-wrenching groan. I knew what this meant as well. It was a glimpse of the outside world only doled to me to make me suffer. My pain something to wallow in as they caused me plunge into the deepest pits of despair.

I tried not to look, but I had no eyes to close, no hands to use to hide from what was before me.

Jared stood before the TV screens watching our surroundings. My body slipped from the bunk bed and stealthily moved forward. My hand raised itself before me, the iron dagger Jensen had given me held tight. One step, then another, until I was right behind him.

The dagger and its runes seemed to glimmer as it was raised high then plunged toward the back of Jared's neck.

I bolted up with a resounding gasp. My chest felt tight as if I couldn't get enough air. Dread tickled all my nerve endings. I leaned forward, head between my knees, trying not to hyperventilate, trying not to see my hand coming down, again and again, the point of the dagger connecting with flesh, the warmth of splashing blood splattering on my face and arms.

"Are you all right?"

I jerked back at the touch of flesh on mine, jolted with a spark of electricity. My face rose before I could stop it and it was Jared beside me, a look of unexpected worry on his face, alive, breathing, not crashed to the floor with a dagger jutting from his back.

My breath hitched inside my throat. For a moment, I was unwilling to believe the reality around me because if it were false, it would be too painful to swallow. Seconds passed yet he remained–breathing, alive, real.

I blinked several times, something in my eyes, and it was only then I felt the wet heat trickling down my face. I was crying. Me. In front of a veritable stranger, an infuriating non-human, and I didn't know exactly why.

"Tamara?"

I hiccupped, feeling suddenly confused as concern glimmered in his eyes and beautiful face, even in his voice. This from the person I'd pissed off repeatedly since we first met.

"I'm okay." The way my voice shook told a different story, but hopefully, he wouldn't notice. "Just a nightmare. No biggie."

I hooked a leg out of the bed knowing there'd be no more sleep for me this night. Jared offered his hand, so I took it and jumped down. No electrical bolt this time, just warm, smooth skin. The touch calmed down my still hammering heart. He was alive. I was not possessed. I was my own person. I was *free*.

"Someone's here."

To my surprise, this came from the bunk below mine.

Jensen was awake as well. Looking at his haggard face as he got up, I wasn't sure he'd slept at all. He moved to the control console. After flipping several switches, the screens turned greenish, but everything was suddenly a lot sharper and more visible than before.

Another van and a suburban were at the gate. A man jumped out to open it and left it open after the two cars went through. I wasn't sure why, but that bothered me.

Ross joined us, shutting the door leading upstairs. "I think things are about to get interesting."

The two vans parked next to the suburban, left their headlights on to flood the area with light. An older man in a long robe that looked like something between a wizard's get up and a pope's stepped out as well as another nine men and women wearing the same type of jumpsuit as the first group. All were armed. A couple pulled out a huge trunk from the inside the second van. My eyes itched. I was pretty sure that wasn't a good thing.

Between their guns, no-nonsense stance, and the walkie-talkies they pulled out to talk to their already positioned comrades, they looked more military than religious. Since they called themselves the White Warriors, I shouldn't have been surprised, but I was. Jensen had been the only member of the Order I'd met so far, and he definitely didn't fit the mold I saw out there.

The man in the robe pulled out a phone from a hidden pocket. I half jerked around as Jensen's phone rang with a loud rendition of Tubular Bells, the theme from The Exorcist. The ex-priest had an ironic sense of humor I'd not suspected. With a look of disbelief on his face, Jensen moved to pull the phone from the pocket of his vest.

It looked more and more as if the Order had indeed used Jensen to locate the brothers as we'd suspected.

"Yes?" Jensen put the phone on speaker and set it on the console.

"White, why have you not complied with the wishes of the Order? Why are your doors closed to your fellow brethren?"

Rather than answer his question, Jensen posed one of his own. "Did the Order sanction the attack in New Hampshire? Have you been using my phone to track us? These men need our help. They need to be protected."

"It is not for you to determine what is and what is not to be done, brother." His tone pounded the words as if telling an errant child something he should have already known. "That is the Council's duty. And as a member of that body and sworn to obey, I order you to open your doors to us."

"He's not the only one here, asshole." Jensen gasped beside me. Whether he knew it or not, I was saying this *for* him. He was the one at the front line, the one actually helping others and taking risks. I wouldn't have his efforts, or ours dismissed as so much trash. "And the rest of us don't have to listen to you."

The silence lasted for several seconds, growing heavier by the moment.

"Ah, Miss Williams, I presume? I was sorry to hear about your troubles." His body on the screen stood in a relaxed pose. I could even see the condescending smile which matched his tone over the phone.

"How kind of you to say so. Now go away."

"I'm afraid I can't do that. You and Brother White are in danger. It would be unethical of me to leave."

I could swear he was enjoying himself. Who exactly was this bastard? It was almost as if he weren't really talking to us, but putting on an act for those around him. I decided to see if I could test that. "We know what you're after. Why you're really here. And it's definitely not to save us from some high-level demons. You want the ring."

The man went on as if he'd not heard me. Or at least not everything I said. "Of course the highest of demons can overcome normal precautions. They have power you've never dreamed of. Whatever these men have told you is a lie."

The brothers stood immobile, just spectators in the current exchange.

Jensen though, looked diminished, as if even up till then not truly believing he could have been betrayed by the very people who'd given him a purpose again.

"Why do you want it? What do you plan to do with it? It won't help against the demons crossing over. Not fast enough."

A sad expression crossed the other man's face. "You must reconsider. Please, for your soul's sake."

I'd had enough of his game. I disconnected the call.

The older man hung his head as if defeated, but I caught a glimpse of a smile. Looks like I'd played into his hands after all. It only made me madder.

"I think we've found the pawn." Jared looked far from happy about it.

Ross nodded. "The veil is thinning rapidly. They'll have to act soon or possibly lose the opportunity."

As if hearing his words, the robed man pointed at the few people left with him, and they ran up toward the cabin. Once they were gone, he turned to the last man left with him and pointed at the trunk.

After opening it, he shooed the man away from it and sent him after the others. Reaching inside, he removed a jar with something dark moving inside it. Opening it, he then released the contents. It had wings and hovered before his face.

There was something wrong about it, but I couldn't figure out what. "What is that?"

"An imp." Jensen's reply was rough as if struggling just to say it. "A lower form of demon." As if against his will, he leaned over the console and zoomed on the image.

The thing was dark but had no feathers—looked more like a miniature pterodactyl than a bird—leathery and full of wrinkles. Its eyes seemed to burn, its face was all teeth. It also had two sets of wings instead of one and neither seemed to beat in any particular pattern.

The old man spoke to it, and it seemed to answer back. Then it spun in place until it became nothing but a blur and disappeared. My eyes itched. "Where did it go?"

"Probably to report to its true master." Jared's lips barely moved his entire focus on the screens. "And test the weakness of the veil."

Dread trickled through me. "And if it's weak enough?"

"Then we'd better be prepared to fight like never before."

CHAPTER FIFTY-SIX

"You could still run." I wasn't sure why I spoke. I didn't know if it stemmed from fear over their welfare or my own or something else altogether.

"If the veil thins as much as we believe it is going to, running will only make things worse." Jared shook his head. "We've tried it before. Last time, Europe paid the price for it. Despite what you may believe, we don't wish ill for humanity.

"Perhaps drawing the attention of a powerful one here will keep the others restrained as they wait for matters to unfold."

It sounded like wishful thinking to me. But what did I know? If the chief demon hunting for them was high enough, he could force others to toe the line in case it decided they were needed. Yet the very thought only made my dread deeper. If a demon called upon his legions, how would two ex-angels handle that? What about Jensen and me?

But what choice did we really have?

"The two of you can still leave if you want to." Ross stared at us intently. "We can carry you to the gate. You can be gone before they were any the wiser."

"And do what? Go where?" If a demon apocalypse was coming, no one and nowhere would be safe.

Jensen straightened. "My place is here. It's my fault you're in this situation in the first place."

"This is not your doing. They would have found us eventually, in any case." Jared sounded unusually kind.

"Even so. As a true member of the Order, I will do whatever I can to keep you and what you carry safe."

The brothers nodded in acknowledgment, neither bothering to point out there was likely little Jensen or I could actually do.

I glanced at the monitors, trying not to let it show on my face how the fact chafed.

The traitor was at work again. "What is he doing?"

The old man had pulled a small rake from his trunk and was using it on a patch of flat road. The imp was back and sat on his shoulder as if whispering in his ear. It gave me goosebumps.

Pulling out a tripod when he finished with the rake, he extended it to its full height. He attached an arm to the top of it, making what looked like an oddly shaped protractor.

As I watched, he drew a large circle on the cleaned space.

Jensen's face drained of color. "No… He wouldn't…"

"With the veil as thin as it is, that could very well do it." Jared's face was a blank mask. I was sure this didn't bode well for us.

Positive I wouldn't like the answer, I pressed on anyway. "Do what? What is he doing?"

Ross rolled his head as if to loosen tight neck muscles. "Drawing a magic circle. He's probably about to summon the demon he's working for. Give him the final pull so he can get through the veil."

"Won't it need a host?"

"No. He'll be able to pull the power to be corporeal." Jared sounded very far away.

My dread shot up a couple of more levels. It was one thing to be possessed by a demon, but to have one running around in its own body? How much more could it do that way? "You don't think we should try to stop it?"

"No, because he'll come here or he'll come elsewhere. But he *will* come." Ross almost sounded eager.

I tried to process all this as the man on the other side of the screen continued his efforts. His movements were slow and sure. You'd never guess he was attempting to bring a demon up from Hell.

One that when it was done with us, if it won, would then be free to terrorize the rest of the planet. That's when I realized maybe it didn't have to be that way at all.

"One of the two of you should go close the gate. *Now.*" I half turned to stare at the brothers. "Even if it comes across and others follow it, they'll be trapped because of the iron and other defenses. Correct?"

It must be true, it just had to be. In a way, it would mean we'd be fighting back.

Ross laughed out loud, a look of pleased surprise on his face. Even Jared seemed more at ease than a moment ago.

"Yes, I believe it would at least annoy their master for a minute or two if not more." Ross grinned. "Allow me."

He didn't run from the room but popped away, making my eye twitch. I spotted him on the monitor at the gate, closing it up. He threw away the lock and did something to the chain. I had a feeling no human would be opening it anytime soon.

He disappeared from the gate area but didn't reappear with us. I didn't realize what he was up to until he started showing up on some of the other screens. He materialized next to each of the members of the Order keeping an eye on the cabin and touched them on their arm or shoulder or face. They dropped where they stood or crouched. Only the woman who'd first talked to us was able to make half a move for a weapon before she too collapsed like all the rest.

My throat grew horribly dry. "Are they dead?"

Jared didn't even bother glancing my way. "Unconscious. It will keep them out of the fight and hopefully safe."

The relief at his words staggered me. But then again everyone here except the old man was fighting for humanity, trying to keep it safe. We were on the same side. They didn't deserve to be duped and killed by those they wrongfully believed in.

Ross reappeared in the room toting several guns. "I brought *presents!*" He held them out to Jensen and me. "You might as well have something that might actually affect whatever's coming with a little more kick than a knife. Just in case."

I stared at it a moment then took mine. The .45 felt heavy in my hand. I'd seen plenty of guns, especially in my youth, but never handled one before. I'd steered clear of the things, having seen first-hand how tempting they were to use in anger. For once the damage was done, there was no way to take it back. My friend Jerome had eventually taken his own life after his mistake. He'd only been fifteen.

I made sure the safety was still on.

CHAPTER FIFTY-SEVEN

The camera angles weren't decent enough to see what the old man was drawing in his circles, but even if they'd been, I wouldn't have known what they meant, so it made little difference. It took him a while though. Long enough I started to get bored and more than a little antsy.

Whatever way this was all going to go, I was ready to get on with it.

"He's almost finished." Jared threw me a half amused glance.

I didn't say anything. I wasn't going to give him the satisfaction. But my pulse rate did go up.

As promised, the old man looked to complete what he was drawing after just a few more minutes. He stepped back, surveyed his work, and seemingly satisfied, repacked his trunk—except for the jar which had contained the imp. That he put the lid back on and placed in the middle of his circles. Then he lit the candles at five points along the inside of the outer ring.

Unfurling a small carpet, he knelt down on top of it. Then he brought out a small knife and bowl from within his robe. Setting the dark metal bowl before him, he emptied into it a packet of what looked like herbs. Brandishing the knife, his lips moving in some low voiced litany, he pricked the middle finger on his left hand. Eyes closed and lips still moving, he squeezed a drop of blood into the bowl.

Shooting pain stabbed my eyes for a flaring second, almost dropping me to my knees. "Crap!"

"Tamara?"

Hands grabbed for me, but I shook them off, straightening up on my own. "I'm okay!"

Blinking rapidly, I stared back at the screen. The old man rose to his feet, staring at the jar in the middle of the circles. It was full again, the imp flashing teeth as it rattled around in its prison.

Looked like this had been a test to make sure his circles worked. They did.

He spoke to the thing in the jar. The imp must have been able to make itself heard because the old man nodded then put it in the trunk. He also removed a flask of what looked like water and rinsed out the bowl and then dried it. He put everything but the bowl and knife away. I wondered if he was naturally this meticulous about everything or only around such dangerous things. It made the minutes pass slowly, that was the only thing I knew for sure.

The old man returned to his kneeling spot.

He repeated the first few steps he'd done before, refilling the bowl with more herbs. This time, however, he didn't cut himself right away. He spoke into the night, the air taking on a shimmering quality around him. My eyes itched but in a subdued way, and I could definitely feel it building.

"Maybe you shouldn't watch this." Jensen's concerned face turned my way for a moment.

"It just caught me off guard before. And he's doing it differently this time."

"Yes," Jared said. "He's building power on this side to help with the crossing, unlike before."

Not long after, the old man cut his hand, placing a lot more blood in the bowl than he did the first time. There was no abrupt pain, but the itching did increase. A spot above the middle of the circles looked wrong. As if reality around it were being siphoned off to somewhere else.

The spot elongated as I watched. It looked like something out of a high budget fantasy movie. Except it wasn't. This was real.

Thick gas like a fog appeared to fight against an invisible current and poured from the rift. The old man sat still, his lips continuing to move faster and faster. He squeezed his hand and sent more blood into the bowl.

I couldn't help but gasp as everything seemed to ramp up two-fold.

The fog continued to pour out, twisting around the opening with a life of its own. It turned and turned, folding, feeding on itself, growing. It took form, solidified, became whole.

My eyes felt like someone was raking razors across them for several seconds, then it calmed down. The pain left me wheezing for air.

I heard Jensen gag beside me then run for the facilities, the sounds of his insides coming out echoing in the main room. His aura skills must have shown him more than what was there. Because the package the demon chose to create for itself didn't look threatening—it was the body of a young Asian boy.

The old man rose to his feet, not entirely steady. He and the boy traded nods before the boy's full attention fell on the cabin.

He opened his mouth and a voice unlike any I'd ever heard reverberated around us like a weapon. As if no walls separating us at all. "GIVE ME WHAT I WANT…"

I put my hands over my ears to tone it down yet it made no difference.

Jensen stumbled back into the room looking pale.

"OR I SHALL TAKE IT."

The boy smiled a twisted, cruel looking smile. It was apparent which way he wanted this to go. The brothers would oblige him I was sure.

They stood there watching him through the monitors, their answer in their silence.

The boy's smile widened. "SO BE IT." He spread his arms wide.

CHAPTER FIFTY-EIGHT

The air around the outside of the circles shimmered and popped as it got displaced. Twenty, fifty, one hundred mutated and deformed beings stood, hovered, or rolled then bowed as one to the boy.

They had hooves, claws, arms, legs, some a combination of all of the above. Every monstrosity people had envisioned in art or nightmares stood there right then, in amplified night vision green. All possessed only one purpose.

Never looking at them, the boy gestured them forward.

His grotesque horde lunged toward the cabin.

"Will the protections hold?" I glanced sideways at Jensen.

He still looked a little pale. "They should. I hope. I don't think the Order ever imagined this many coming at it at one time when they built it."

"They will hold." Jared's confidence was absolute.

The demons slammed against the porch and walls and bounced back and away from it. Several were smoking, their appendages twitching as if in pain. The boy raised his hand and pointed at the cabin. After a slight moment of hesitation, the demons tried again, and again and again. To no avail.

The old man spoke to the boy, who seemed anything but pleased. He looked even less so after whatever the old man told him. Then he reached up as if to grab something from the sky. My eyes hurt.

Though the camera view did not reach upwards, we could see some of what was happening. The wind picked up. Fallen leaves and tree limbs swayed and moved. The demons slinked back away from the cabin, watching, waiting, expectant. Whatever the boy was up to I had a feeling it wouldn't be something good.

I wasn't wrong.

The boy closed the fist on his raised hand. An almost palpable crackle filled the air and then a boom crashed above which shook us all the way down in the bunker. The screens and lights flickered but stayed active. The air smelled heavy with ozone, and I had to work my jaw to make my ears pop. A strange buzzing filled my ears.

"We have to go." Ross and Jared spared us both a glance, then were gone.

"There!" I pointed to the screens. One of them showed a flickering picture as if the camera were struggling to work but couldn't quite make it. The brothers showed for a moment, then were gone again but with speed rather than teleportation.

The horde outside rushed to the giant, smoking hole the boy had made for them. That's where Jared and Ross fought them—two blurs against the mass of teeth and claws. Though I'd never seen them with any weapons, they had some now—shafts of colored light, like a Jedi's lightsaber, except these were an extension of their arms and not something they held onto.

They pushed the fight onto the porch, dark ichor splashing everywhere as they slashed the enemy back and forth, up and down. Heads, arms, legs, split torsos littered the yard, the pieces propelled backward they'd been butchered with such force.

Jensen dropped to his knees beside me, scaring me for a moment until I realized he'd put his hands together and was praying—praying for the brothers, for us.

He must have realized what would happen before I did. The boy opened his arms again, and more demons appeared to enter into the fray. These looked bigger, tougher, meaner than those who'd come before. Some of these blurred as if they too could move faster than expected. The brothers no longer gained any ground. They looked to be struggling just to hold onto where they were.

An imp appeared beside the boy, this one looking like a floating snake with tiny arms. Whatever it said didn't seem to be to the demon's liking as he, in a barely perceived move, plucked it from the air and crushed it. It never even had a chance to scream.

The boy closed his eyes and smeared the ugly mess over his chest. Wounded demons close to the circle suddenly found new life and hobbled, stumbled, some even crawled, back toward the fray. The old man hurried to the van and came back with a small box.

Meanwhile, the boy raised his arm, the other pointing toward the brothers, fingers splayed. My eyes started to itch. Ringed in by too many demons, the brothers didn't see this. I screamed at Jared in my head, hoping that by some miracle he might hear me.

A flash of light arced straight down to the boy's arm then out the other one straight at the combatants. The impact this time shook the house and the bunker, driving me to my knees and pitching Jensen forward. The screens and the room went dark and didn't come back on. A faint cracking sound filled the ensuing numb silence.

Scrambling blind, panic nipping at me, I reached out to where I thought Jensen might be. I felt the fabric of his jeans and continued until I found his arm. "We need to get up there!"

"What?"

I couldn't tell if he was questioning my choice or just hadn't been able to hear me. His response sounded as if it came from a deep well. That's when I realized the cracking I'd heard before could be a lot worse than my senses were telling me. So instead of fighting to be understood, I tugged on his arm and pulled him in what I hoped was the direction of the stairs.

I stumbled into them more than I found them. They didn't feel quite right as if out of alignment or slightly twisted. Trepidation slapped me. What if the damage had jammed the door? We could be buried in here.

Trying not to think about it, I let my hands search frantically for the release. I should have paid more attention. "Jensen, I can't find it! How do we open this thing?"

I felt him scrunch in beside me and then a barely audible click. "Push, Tamara!"

I did as I was told.

The door fought us. We turned around, putting our backs to it and lifting with our legs, sweat breaking out all over me from fear and exertion.

"Open, dammit!"

As if it'd heard me, it gave way suddenly, and we were free.

CHAPTER FIFTY-NINE

Until that moment, everything that went on before had been like watching a movie. Something not entirely connected to me, possibly not even genuine. But up here, with the smell of burnt wood and the stench of cooked flesh, and sulfur, it brought it all home. This was real. And I'd willingly walked into it.

The cabin lay in ruins, illuminated by the glaring headlights of the vans parked in front. Twisted pieces of metal were all that was left of the protective window panels. The energy hit with such force the walls splintered apart and turned to ash rather than burn. It coated everything, including the air. I coughed several times as it tried to get inside me. Fruitlessly I waved it away. Tears welled up in my eyes as the ash irritated them. "Jared! Ross!"

Toward what had once been the porch something moved. We stumbled in that direction.

As the ash continued to settle and we worked our way past charred oozing remains, light flared before us, a strange, wondrous light. Then the light stood up.

At its feet sat Jared, his clothes smoking tatters, his body covered in ash and burned demon blood. Then he rose to stand beside the shaft of brilliance, and I realized the light was Ross. His flesh and bone body were gone. His true self exposed for all to see. It was beautiful.

"NOW I WILL HAVE IT."

No, you shall not!

The light stepped past Jared putting itself between him

and the young boy in the circles. Ross suddenly wavered and flickered where he stood as if he would fall at any moment and disappear into nothingness.

The boy laughed, the clanging tones bashing in my head. He raised his arms and brought them forward. New, fresh demons surged to begin the battle again.

Jensen pulled me down off to the side to lay flat on the exposed and warped ceiling of the bunker even as he drew the gun Ross procured for us earlier. With a shaking hand, I brought out my own. With my free hand, I grabbed the cross Jensen gave me back on the day we first met. If there were ever a time for God to interfere in the affairs of men it was now.

Squeals, growls, grunts, all manner of noises and gagging smells issued from those surging to destroy the brothers.

"Save your shots. Use them on any who try to go behind them." Jensen's breath tickled my ear, his voice barely audible over the ensuing din.

The demons' attentions were totally focused on the brothers and paid us no heed. The swords of light returned, cutting the spawn left and right. With Ross's human shell gone, the fact the sword was a part of him was plain to see. The two fought hard, but it was clear even to my untrained eyes they weren't doing as well as before. The destructive force of whatever the boy had sent at them had definitely hurt them both.

Jensen fired his pistol at a short demon with stubby legs that somehow managed to get past the wall of death that was the brothers. The iron-hearted bullet dropped it where it stood. I spotted another and squeezed the trigger. Nothing happened. Its arm rose to slam a blow at Jared's head. After a panicked moment, I realized my safety was still on, and thumbing it off, tried for my target again, calling on every TV moment I'd ever seen to try to do it right. I miraculously hit it on the shoulder. It broke away.

The brothers should run. Escape and heal up, fight another day. They were slowly being worn down. Losing was only a matter of time. From what I'd seen before, I got the feeling the boy was in a hurry. I caught glimpses of his unhappy face as the death dance continued. He was probably afraid one of his superiors would catch wind of what he was up to and put a stop to it. But they hadn't caught on yet. If he took the time to call another one of those power blasts we'd all be done for. Yet the brothers were the only ones who knew where the ring was. Vaporizing them wouldn't leave much of anyone to ask.

So he'd have to do something else. Even as the thought occurred to me, that was precisely what he did.

The demons leaped or shuffled, weirdly giving me a clear view of the traitor and boss demon past their feet. I spotted the old man and his little box. He finally opened the thing and then threw the contents out in front of the boy outside his circle.

With a gesture, the boy caught them in mid-air then flung the small things right toward the brothers.

"Watch out!"

My warning was too late. Almost invisible from their speed, the projectiles cut through the demons keeping Jared and Ross pinned then hit the brothers.

Several hit Ross, a keened wail piercing my ears as he collapsed to the ground and dimmed to a mere ember. The majority hit Jared, his body jerking at each impact. Then he too fell to the ground.

The remaining demons surged to tear him apart.

"STOP. TO ME."

Every one of them ceased in midmotion and then

slowly, grudgingly stepped back, hate, love, disgust, and triumph shining coals in their eyes. It made my flesh crawl. Those who'd taken my body and made of me a puppet were in essence slaves and puppets themselves. They still didn't know what they'd been fighting and dying for and the boy planned to keep it that way.

He'd have to get his human ally to come find the prize.

That was his big mistake.

"Jensen!" I scrambled to my feet and lunged for Jared's form, shooting randomly in the direction of the demons and the boy. The ex-priest didn't hesitate and hurried to do the same.

Not looking at Jared, knowing if I did I'd lose all momentum, I grabbed him by his armpit and started dragging him back toward the opening to the bunker. Jensen reached out for the ember that was all that there was of Ross and swept it into one of his vest pockets then grabbed Jared's other arm.

"YOU WILL STOP!"

The boy's gaze locked with mine and it was as if a switch had been thrown. The floodgates were opened, and a paralyzing fear seized me, stealing my breath. This wasn't me, it was somehow being done *to* me, but it made no difference, I couldn't move, my heart threatening with every pulse to explode inside my chest.

"Tamara!" Jensen's worried plea sounded as if it were miles away. There was only the boy and me.

The smile that grew on the demon's face promised me endless pain and torment, atrocities beyond my most horrid nightmares, and eternal pleasures for himself. It also said it claimed me for his own. That he owned me.

The spark which never left me flared. Even as my eyes continued to be trapped by that endless gaze, the heat inside me built. I dropped the gun and used all the rage inside me to move my hand.

Jensen grabbed me and tried to drag Jared and me along, but I was rooted to the spot. He started a Latin chant, his voice unbelievably steady. From the corner of my trapped gaze, I saw the old man reaching inside the van for another box.

Perspiration gathered at my brow and back as I forced my hand up just a little higher, the foreign fear trying to drown everything out. Jensen's hold on my arm felt warm and seemed to grow warmer. It helped push the fear just a little further back.

It was all that I needed.

I swept my hand as hard as I could, and using the very skills demon kind had brought forth in me, I slapped the bastard with my mind.

CHAPTER SIXTY

The moment my telekinetic smack hit his face and turned it for a precious second, I was free as we broke eye contact. I buckled to my knees, head pounding, my body shaking with all the different input.

"Tamara, we have to move now!"

A groan escaped me as I tried to shake off the lingering fear and watery legs. I grabbed at Jared again and stumbled for the stairs to the bunker. Though demons or worse could have been nipping at our heels, I fought the temptation to take a look. If his mind grabbed me again, I wouldn't be able to escape a second time.

We half stumbled, half fell down into the darkness.

Jensen yanked the door closed, though we both knew it wouldn't hold. I heard him stumbling about, but for the life of me, I couldn't fathom what he was looking for. Until he found it. Light cut a swath across the room from a heavy duty flashlight.

I could now take a look at Jared and almost immediately wished I hadn't. Dozens of what looked like small, engraved arrowheads peeked from wherever they'd managed to embed themselves into his body. One stared up at me from where it jutted out from Jared's splattered right eye. Gagging, I looked away. I had no idea if he was alive or dead. But he could come back from that. I knew he could. I'd seen him do it before.

To help him, I knelt down beside him and started pulling out the arrowheads as fast as I could, staring at nothing but the small area around each injury.

The wounds bled for a moment then began sealing up. Jensen pitched in, thankfully taking the task of removing the one from Jared's eye for himself.

"GIVE ME WHAT I WANT OR YOU'LL BE MADE TO SUFFER."

A grin tried to pull at my face, even as his words made me shiver. Someone was getting desperate. He wouldn't be sending his minions after us as they might realize what the brothers' had, yet he wasn't going to do it himself, or he'd have avoided the whole asking part. From the movies, I knew pentagrams were used to summon demons but also to keep them trapped and stop them from hurting whoever summoned them. Yet in this instance, I had the sneaking suspicion it served another purpose entirely, one it seemed the head demon wasn't willing to give up on just yet.

But for how long?

Jared gasped, his one working eye opening as if he'd been turned on like a machine. I could see it trying to focus. "Le-Leja?"

My hand rested on his arm before I realized what it was doing. "No, sorry. Just Tamara."

A flash of pain and sadness flickered past then got buried, deep.

Jensen scooped out what remained of Ross and held it out toward him. "You and your brother need to disappear. Now. We won't be safe here for long."

A boom ricocheted above us cracking the ceiling and dribbling dirt and dust from above. "GIVE IT TO ME!"

As inappropriate as it might be, I felt the grin tugging at my lips again. Someone was having a tantrum at not getting his way. The shame.

"Can't. Need time. Reserves too depleted." Jared reached out toward the pulsing flicker that was his brother. A small bolt seemed to leap from his finger to the light. It grew a little brighter but not much. There was movement beneath his newly closed eyelid, his damaged eye healing beneath but slowly. All his wounds were healing a lot slower than I'd seen them do before.

"Can we give him energy like that? Can we give it to you?" Jensen asked.

I stared at White, the possibility never having occurred to me. His expression was earnest, his scar almost glowing. I didn't know if it was a trick of the light or just my imagination, but Jensen looked younger than his years right then. Focused, driven, faithful, a downright martyr—as if his life had been leading to just this moment.

Jared's astonishment and then dawning gratitude made him look beautiful despite the ash and dried blood covering his face. The gem piercing his nose seemed to glow with a light all its own. "If you will allow it, he can reside inside you for a time. It will make it easier for him to reenergize. You'll be a conduit of sorts."

Jensen nodded and without another word closed his other hand over the light, first cupping it between his palms then squishing them together. When he separated them Ross was gone. The ex-priest held a satisfied and awed look on his face.

"NOW!"

The whole bunker shook. A chunk of concrete smacked the floor about a foot from me, making me yelp. Looked like the boy's patience was coming to an end. Maybe picking through our bones was becoming a viable alternative. We had to do something.

"Jared, give it to me. Give me the ring. Let me use it."

He jerked away and stared at me as if I'd slapped him. "No!"

"We don't have time to argue this! Like it or not that thing is coming to take it from you. You won't be able to stop it! Do you want it to win? Because being stubborn right now is exactly what will make that happen. I'll give it back. Trust me. *Please!*"

The room shook again, throwing me off my feet despite the fact I was kneeling. The cracks on the walls and ceiling multiplied, throwing even more dust and ash around us. The bunker wouldn't stand much more. It might already be too late.

Jared's brown-eyed gaze swept across my face as if he dared not believe, dared not take that leap, despite all the information his inhuman senses told him. Had he been forced to make this choice before and it went badly? Was there something else about all this he hadn't said?

"I can do this, Azzael." I stared back, hiding nothing. I would do this for him. "Let me."

With those words, Jared's expression smoothed out. "Give me your knife."

That I'd not expected. But if I wanted him to trust me, I needed to show my trust for him as well. Miraculously, it was still in my back pocket. I handed it over.

The bunker shook again.

"Hurry!"

That's when he plunged the knife into his exposed stomach.

CHAPTER SIXTY-ONE

"*No!*" Horror swept through me as the blessed blade cut through his skin. I leaned forward to take it from him, but it was too late. My whole mind went numb. Even though he wasn't human, surely even he had limits. "Why?"

Jared pulled the blade out and let it fall to the side. Saying nothing, he drove two of his fingers into the opening. He grimaced in discomfort, blood pooling from inside, but he kept digging as I just stared.

A moment later he brought his fingers back out, a ring clutched between them.

I don't know what I'd been expecting the thing to look like, but it didn't 'look' like much. It was a simple ring in a reddish brown color, probably bronze, with an embedded piece of onyx with a five-sided star carved atop it. My eyes itched a little as I stared at it, verifying it must be the real deal. When I saw the ring repel Jared's blood from itself, I was left with no doubts at all.

With an open, vulnerable look on his face, Jared extended the ring toward me.

Taking a deep breath, suddenly nervous at the responsibility I was about to take on, I reached out to grab it. The sound of a gun ricocheted in the room. Jared's arm jerked as the special bullet connected with his flesh and the ring flicked off into the darkness.

"That's not for the like of *you.*"

A quick look over my shoulder showed a rifle barrel and a scope poking through one of the larger cracks where the concrete had fallen through. "Jensen, the light!"

I dove off to the right as the room was plunged into darkness, hoping the rest were doing something similar in other directions. A shot rang out again. Our only hope was that the rifle didn't have a night scope or the crack didn't give it too much leeway in movement, or we were all screwed. I'd forgotten all about the traitorous council member. I shouldn't have. As the one who'd possess the ring if things went according to plan, he had as much to lose if not more than the demon outside if things didn't go their way.

"Turn the light back on. Stop this nonsense. Give us what we want, and we'll let you live."

I didn't spare a moment to think about the offer, sure it was bogus. Only one thing would get us out of this mess. All I had to do was find it. But how? I couldn't see anything in this pitch black darkness. Exploring the place with only my hands would take forever. Sooner or later the old man or boy would come up with something else to try, like poison gas, or caving the whole place in on us, or who knew what. We only had minutes if not seconds.

"Relax…Look around."

I jerked at the voice so close to my ear yet I felt no one beside me. It'd been so soft, like a tickle, but I was pretty sure it'd been Jared's voice. He knew something I didn't. Maybe something that would get us out of this mess. So I sat still and deepened my breathing, trying to calm down, and stared out into the dark. It felt so weird. Unable to see yet working so hard to.

Making a circle from where I sat, I looked from my lap out toward the wall then back again. When my eye twitched as if bothered by something, I finally understood what Jared was having me do. I quickly crawled in that direction, trying to be as quiet about it as possible.

I almost collapsed in disappointment as I reached out and touched Jensen's protected trunk. Pulling it out and sitting on top of it so it wouldn't be in the way of my blind gaze, I tried again.

There.

I started crawling.

The old man must have realized we were up to something because he started shooting indiscriminately into the room. Since I couldn't see, that was a guess or more of a hope. Flinching every time I heard one of the shots ring out, I finally got to where I hoped the ring sat.

My fingers closed around something small and incredibly light. The shape was right. I put the ring on.

Nothing changed. I was still swallowed by darkness. Shots still rang out randomly in the room.

"Jared, I need a name." I didn't say this loudly, hoping he'd hear me anyway. I had one name but didn't want to use it. Not yet. I had other plans for him.

"Staxxis."

The whispered voice made me jump. It hadn't been Jared's. It could have been Jensen's, but there was something off about it.

I fiddled with the ring on my finger, only then noticing how it seemed to fit me perfectly. Ignoring the goosebumps this sent racing down my arms, I realized I didn't have the faintest idea how to use the thing. I'd have to wing it. "Staxxis, to me."

The air stirred somewhere close to me. The ring grew warm on my finger for a moment. A hissing sound filled the air. "I ammm hereeee."

Fear gripped me for a second. Any one of the demons could have done this at any time? It felt strange feeling grateful for the boy's iron-fisted grip on his minions.

"Protect the four of us who are inside the bunker." I didn't understand why I was so specific. Yet something inside me insisted I do so. Was it too many movies of people not being careful with their wishes? Or was there something to the ring being partially responsible for Solomon's wisdom?

Another shot rang out. A presence shifted in front of me. I heard a dulled sound of something hitting meat. It was hard to breathe. The bullet didn't touch me. But if I hadn't called for the demon, it would have. We could all lose our lives at any moment if this didn't get resolved and soon.

"Staxxis, open the door from the bunker." The dead certainty I needed to be extremely specific in anything I asked from the demon kept resonating inside me. "Then incapacitate the old man, but don't kill him."

As if to prove the point, the bunker door exploded outwards with a whoomph. I heard a cry of pain right after that. With what Staxxis had done to the door, I didn't really want to think about what it had made of the incapacitate command. Yes, I'd need to be *very* specific.

Jensen turned on the flashlight again, and I rushed for the stairs. I was gambling the boy would feel he still needed the old man enough not to blast the general area and take us with it.

CHAPTER SIXTY-TWO

This was the second time I'd walked out into a disaster zone. I didn't think it would shock me as much as the first, but I was wrong. In the few minutes we'd been gone, the area around the bunker had been turned into a weird alien landscape.

All remnants of the cabin were gone as if it'd never existed. The ground was scorched, parts of it melting, yet there was no heat. The body parts which had littered the area of the porch had disappeared, completely obliterated.

The old man stood out like a sore, his body limp, his eyes closed. His dirtied robe rose and dropped at his chest, the only evidence he was alive at the moment. The rifle he'd been using stuck up from the ground, still trapped in the crack he'd wedged it into trying to get at us.

I turned my attention to the evil out in the yard.

It was eerie. Every one of the demons stood, crouched or sat absolutely still. Even the ones that could fly were on the ground. Staring. At me. As if in anticipation or dread.

I couldn't see the boy behind them. It was probably better that way.

Time to get a little crazy.

"Listen to me, demons! Hear and obey. Go back to

where you came from. Go back to your own plane. You are forever banished from this realm. Now go!"

My eyes itched like crazy. I could hear my voice echoing through the zone much louder than I'd yelled it. I felt an unexpected surge of pride, even power, as for once I wasn't the helpless one. I was the one who could act.

The demons continued to stare at me, shaking, almost flickering where they stood, but not disappearing as I'd hoped. I felt Jared step up beside me, so I half turned toward him. "Did I do it wrong?"

"No. But they can't leave. You've forgotten about the gate. It wasn't their own power that brought them here." He shook his head slowly, staring with pity at our foes. "They will do their utmost to do as you've commanded, but your commands do not supersede what they can or cannot do. They're trapped here until they kill themselves trying to do your bidding or the gate is opened."

Cries rose up amongst some of them, their efforts to do as I'd ordered hurting them as they got no results.

Whatever I'd been feeling before soured and turned toward disgust. I'd forced my will on these vile things and in so doing made them hurt themselves to carry it out. I had no doubt any one of them would laugh as they tore me limb from limb if given the opportunity, showing no pity or remorse, but I wasn't one of them.

"Stop. Arrange yourselves over there until the gate can be opened and you can return safely home." I pointed to the left of me near the line of trees. "Do not touch the humans."

It chilled me to watch most of them fall on the ground, exhausted and wounded from their efforts. Then almost immediately begin walking, hopping, some crawling to follow my commands. I'd done this. I'd hurt them. Inadvertently or not.

With the way clear, I could see the boy. I tried not to make direct eye contact, not wanting more of the blood chilling dose of fear he'd poured into me before. He stood in his circle, eyes burning, a petulant pout on his face. He appeared totally unaffected by Solomon's Ring. The circles were protecting him from its influence just as he'd planned.

He suddenly smiled. "WELL PLAYED, HUMAN. BUT NOT GOOD ENOUGH." His smile grew fangs. "I DO NOT NEED THIS RABBLE TO DESTROY YOU. GIVE THE MONK THE RING, AND I WILL CONSIDER SPARING YOUR INSIGNIFICANT EXISTENCE."

"You will not harm her. We will not allow it." Jared placed a hand on my shoulder as he spoke.

To my surprise, Jensen stepped up and placed his hand on the other. Staxxis put itself before the three of us in the form of a shimmering veil. My first command looked to be superseding the others, that or it found the thought of his superior getting its hands on the ring as distasteful as the rest of us. That was an amusing thought.

"You're running out of time, and we all know it." The words, astoundingly, were my own. I could feel my thoughts speeding along making connections faster than ever before. Wisdom was a strange thing. "Those above you will be wondering where you've gone off to by now. With the veil so thin, it'll be easy for them to send messengers to search for you here. How do you think they'll react when they find out what you're actually up to?"

"SILENCE!" His roar shook the very trees, sending what few brave birds and small animals that had stuck around the area scuttling off elsewhere. The sky lightened behind him, the black going to purple and then a mixture of gray and pink.

Looks like I'd hit a nerve. Now how to exploit it without getting us all killed? The fact his human tool was with us would only hold him back from blasting the area for so long.

"Go home, demon. Go home. Aside from the loss of a few lackeys and time, you're no worse off than before." I gave him a self-deprecating smile. "I'm only human. I will die. The cycle will run its course and return. The veil grow weak once more. You can always try again."

I raised the hand with the ring. "None of your fellows will get a chance to try for it either. Not while I'm wearing the ring and have protection."

I was giving hope and an out to an evil, corrupt, immoral thing. Yet for all its power there were those above it with their thumb poised over his fate, dictating his actions, robbing him of freedom. There'd been fear in his last shout—even if he didn't realize it. To be part of Hell was to be a slave for all eternity. Hope was cheap, but sometimes tough to gain and even tougher to keep.

The boy stared at me long and hard—as if rifling through my mind or taking apart my aura. Then he smiled. Unlike all the times before, this was a genuine smile, full of actual happiness. "THIS HAS BEEN QUITE UNEXPECTED AND INTERESTING. VERY WELL PLAYED."

Then he clapped his hands together.

Next thing I knew I was on my back, blinking as dark stars swam before my eyes, my ears ringing.

Struggling up on my elbows I saw I wasn't the only one knocked down. Where the boy had stood, the space was empty, the circle broken by cracks on the darkened ground.

He was gone.

CHAPTER SIXTY-THREE

I stared at the spot where the demon had stood, not quite daring to believe it. "He didn't turn himself invisible or something, did he?"

"No. He's definitely gone." Jared helped me up to my feet then let go. I wouldn't have minded if he'd held onto me a little longer.

Jensen rose as well. "You saved us, Tamara. Possibly even the world. Or should I say, two worlds." The look of pride and awe changed to a grin, one that had never belonged to Jensen.

"I happen to agree. Good job." His voice had changed slightly.

For a moment I'd forgotten Ross was in there. They appeared to be sharing the one body. I don't know that I could have been that accommodating. It was one thing for you to piggyback to heal, quite another to occasionally exert control.

I looked away so they wouldn't see how much it bothered me. "We're not done yet." I waved in the general direction of Hell's teeming horde.

"I'll go open the gate so they can leave." Jared barely spoke before he was speeding down the road. I noticed it wasn't quite as fast as I'd seen it done before.

The shimmer that was Staxxis slowly solidified into a thing with bat wings and shiny multicolored scales. One large eye sat where a chin should be, two mismatched others higher in the face. Two mouths with flickering tongues were attached on the sides of its round head.

"Though I know you didn't help us of your own volition, I want to thank you for it anyway. You can go home with the rest."

The three shimmering eyes stared at me. Reptilian, alien, inhuman. After a moment Staxxis bowed its head as if accepting my words and floated off towards its brothers.

"Since they're still here, I can give them one last order before they go." It probably wasn't the 'good' thing to do, and definitely not something I would like to have someone force me to comply with, but it was the right thing.

"What do you have in mind?" The puzzlement showing on Jensen's face looked two-fold.

"You'll see." With a grin, I turned towards the demons and held out my ringed hand. "Listen to me, I have one final order before you leave here.

"Before you banish yourselves back to your plane forever, I want you to find one of your brethren out there in the world and give them an order in the name of your master. Tell them that they're to return to Hell instantly or suffer mightily. Whether they do what you say or not is not your concern, just deliver the message and go home. That is all."

One by one they headed off toward the open gate or disappeared where they stood. I'd let them off easy, and I knew it, but any other orders would have probably had nasty consequences. Demons didn't seem to understand the notion of not causing collateral damage.

When the last one left, I finally allowed myself a sigh of relief. Next thing I knew my knees gave out and Jensen barely caught me before I hit the ground.

"Are you all right?"

An embarrassed giggle escaped me, which

embarrassed me even more. Guess all this posturing took a lot out of a person. "Yeah, just tired. Long night. I'll be okay in a second."

Jared was suddenly there helping me back to my feet again. It was nice to have him close.

"The demons have gone. The immediate danger is past. Return the ring to me... Please."

Eyeing him and his whispered request I realized I wasn't quite finished. Whether he liked it or not.

A moan from the old monk behind us prodded me along. "I'm not quite done with it. Not yet." I tried to give him a reassuring smile even as he frowned at me.

I was sure he considered trying to make me, except we both knew he couldn't.

Jensen glanced between the two of us. "Is this wise?"

I gave him a full blast, wicked girl grin. "Probably not." But I was doing it. I held up the ring and shouted out into the air. "Rosier, to me!"

Blue smoke bubbled in mid-air and then there he was. Strangely, he was stunning. Androgynous, with red eyes and a long mane of hair so black it looked purple. Tiny scales decorated him from head to foot as if he'd been born one thing and later made into another. The annoyed look on his face turned into a pleased heady one. A look I'd seen many times looking at me from my mirror while I was locked away inside my own flesh. This was my tormentor. The bastard who'd ruined my life.

"Bow before me, *worm*." My hate rushed up hot and searing. I shook as I tried to hold myself in check even as every fiber in my being screamed for me to string his entrails from one side of the clearing to the other as payback for what he'd done. I would not forgive him, not ever.

The demon gracefully got down on one knee. He even

dared give me a lustful look while he was at it. My hands clenched into fists, my nails cutting into my palm.

"How may I serve you, master? I know all your inner desires and am eager to please."

"Quiet! You will not speak unless I tell you to. You will not look at me unless I tell you to. On your belly, worm."

Rosier looked away, a slight pout on his face, then moved to comply. He wasn't afraid of me. Though I held his very essence in my hands, he didn't seem to care. I didn't like that.

"Tamara, this won't solve anything. What's done is done." Jensen's voice was low, for my ears alone, but I doubted I was the only one who heard it. Not with the company we were keeping, not with the fallen angel inside him.

My anger flared, irritated by just about everything. "Sorry, but I'll have to be the one to judge that."

A hint of movement from the corner of my eye made me half turn before a body plowed into me and took me down.

CHAPTER SIXTY-FOUR

My jaw smacked up, jarring my teeth and also making me bite my lip. Groping hands went for my hand. I didn't know who it was and didn't care. I swept my arm and sent them away from me, the unexpected interruption of my revenge and the fury that brought with it fueling me.

The body landed ten or more feet away with a definite thud. Rosier was still on the ground, and Jared and Jensen stood nearby with identical looks of disbelief on their faces. The old monk struggled to get back up from where I'd thrown him.

"Give it to me. It belongs to *me*! You're just some woman. You've no idea of the power you hold. You've not the wisdom or knowledge to wield it properly. When the Order learns of your sacrilege, you will be hunted down and killed." The venom in his voice would have stripped flesh if I'd cared about anything he had to say.

"The Order will learn of your betrayal, *sir*." Jensen got between us.

The old man swayed on his feet, his robes dirty and ripped in several places. His thin hair stood in clumps like a madman's. The expression on his face was one of pure hate. "As if they'd believe one such as you over me. If any of those I brought with me are still alive, they will condemn you, just as *I* will condemn you."

I'd heard more than enough. "Rosier, possess him. Show him what it's like."

I felt a twinge at the glee which shone on the demon's face a moment before it turned incorporeal. There was a greasiness to the air in front of me that moved of its own volition. This is what it was like when I was taken. There was a reason why I had no memory of what went on. I wouldn't have realized something was there until much too late.

"Stay back, demon spawn!" The old monk moved to reach for something in his robes, but the demon was so much faster.

The man's whole body shook as the oily air infiltrated every orifice—his mouth, his ears, his nose—and disappeared inside him. I knew it was done when that hated smirk appeared on the old man's face.

"Quite comfy in here, if I do say so myself." He preened for a moment. "Though nowhere as wonderful as you were, master."

"Shut it!" The bastard had a death wish. If he didn't watch it, I might just oblige him.

"Tamara, this is wrong." Jensen's expression was cold. "No one deserves this, and you know it."

"So you're okay with the fact he wanted to kill us?" I couldn't be hearing him right. This man deserved so much worse than just a little taste of possession. "You're okay with him wanting to grab Solomon's ring and start a reign of terror here and in Hell the likes of which had never been seen before?"

His expression softened. "It is not for us to judge or punish. He will be found out. If not here a higher judgment will lay in wait for him when his time comes. And it isn't him I'm worried about anyway. It's you."

I blinked, not having expected this turn. "What are you talking about?"

He stared me straight in the eye. "I think you know."

I blinked again confused. But I did know what he meant, didn't I? The ring did its work, and I saw all the different things it could be, discarding each one before I even realized what they were, heading inexorably to the one and only answer—the state of my soul.

The same worry I'd carried all through high school and part of college as I wrestled with my anger at the unfairness of the world and God's lack of interference, struggling not to let it consume me, rule me, drag me down a path of actions I'd be unable to undo.

Yet here I was again. This time not even thinking of the consequences to myself, only of venting my rage, getting revenge, actions that would fix nothing yet taint me like I'd never been before. Consequences be dammed.

Jensen wasn't the only one aware of it. Jared's guarded expression told me much, a thick sadness and regret coming through no matter how hard he tried to suppress it. Even Rosier, though commanded to silence, his expression spoke volumes—his stolen eyes full of eagerness, his own possible death a small price to pay to corrupt a personage with such power in the finger of her hand.

I stood on a precipice of my own making, and it was a long way down. I had a choice to make.

"Rosier, you're never to possess anyone ever again. Also, you are forever banished from this plane. Now go back home to Hell and those that *own* you."

Shocked anger flashed on the old monk's face before it went blank and the man staggered as the demon left him. This would have to do for my revenge. I doubted the bastard would forget me anytime soon.

Good.

"Someone should probably rip up the old geezer's robe and tie him up. Make sure to gag him."

I wasn't sure, but it looked to me like Jared enjoyed following my suggestion just a little too much. Moving faster than the old man could counter, he was trussed up like a turkey pretty darn quick. He still looked dazed from his encounter with Rosier, but I couldn't take the chance he hadn't learned his lesson. Selfish bastards hardly ever did.

"We could go wake up the woman who showed up here first. Let her know what was really going on before he gets his chance. Maybe she can call someone who can use their 'gift' to tell if he's lying. Unless you just want to port out of here?" I wasn't sure which was best or even if it was my call.

Jensen traded one of Ross's looks with Jared. I wondered what that was like. For the moment I was the odd one out.

There was one more thing I wanted to do, but couldn't until I knew what we were doing about things here.

Jensen nodded. "I'll stay. They know who I am and they might listen to me long enough to give them doubts, at least enough to call someone to verify my claims. If we were who they were told, they'd be dead or possessed, not just put down for a nap." The smile was definitely Ross's. Someone wanted to have some fun.

Jensen might have gotten more than he bargained for, housing a fallen angel inside him.

"The two of you should run somewhere safe, and Ross and I will come find you once we're finished here."

"Sounds good." I was tired, worn down, it'd be nice not to have to deal with all the forthcoming drama.

It didn't escape me that neither one of them asked me to take off the ring again. I wasn't quite sure what to make of that.

CHAPTER SIXTY-FIVE

Like he'd done once before, Jared scooped me up and ran. I had to half turn my face into his chest so I could breathe, the air pummeling me and moving much too fast for my lungs to grab it when faced head-on.

I'd no idea where he was taking me, and I didn't really care. I was just glad he was with me. That I wasn't alone. I felt numb, drained, so much had happened in such a short span of hours. Though I hardly knew him, we'd been through so much together. There was a connection there, even if I wasn't willing to look at it too closely. I supposed deep down I trusted him because before we reached wherever he was taking me, I fell asleep.

When I awoke, I found him sitting close, staring at me with his dark brown eyes, staring as if I held some secret he couldn't figure out. Or maybe that was just me. "Hey."

"Hey." I sat up slowly, not entirely feeling awake. The scent of evergreen was thick. It was only then I realized I'd been lying on the ground beneath a giant tree, a thick blanket wrapped around me. Down a small incline, sunshine shone off the ocean as its waters encroached on a short beach.

It was beautiful. I didn't have the foggiest idea where we were.

"Hungry?"

As if summoned by the question, a ravenous appetite gnawed at my gut. "We have food?"

Jared brought around a basket full of cut cheeses and bits of fruit and nuts. That's when I noticed his clothes weren't torn up anymore. He even had a new black leather jacket. Someone had gone shopping. But that wasn't important right then, so I spent the next several minutes making my stomach happy instead. I felt Jared's gaze stuck on me throughout. It started making me feel a bit self-conscious. Did he suspect what I planned to do?

"Ross and Jensen?"

"Still busy. It seems the Order has several layers of management they must navigate through before they acknowledge the truth as a whole." He smiled, and I could tell from it he was just as happy not to be involved in that circus as I was.

"What about the cycle? Is the way still open?" While we'd held back the boy and all those he commanded, if the veil was still thin, all manner of chaos could have happened while I'd been asleep.

"Thankfully this was one of the short ones. Your gambit to have the demons profess to others they'd been ordered back home paid off. It didn't stop all of them but did minimize the damage done."

That was good to hear. "Thanks for watching over me."

He shrugged and looked away. Not exactly the reaction I'd expected. Then those weird lines of wisdom went whispering through my mind again.

"You weren't exactly watching just me, were you?"

"I believe you know the answer to that."

At least he had the decency not to blast me with the truth directly. Still...

"I release you, Jared and Ross, Azzael and Azza. By the power of Solomon's Ring, I release you both from your bondage to protect it." I'd not been sure until that moment when or how I would do it, but I'd planned to in some way all along. Freedom was precious, and after a millennium or two of being enslaved to it, I was sure no one deserved it more.

Jared twisted around, mouth open and eyes wide. "Wha-What have you done?"

"I used the power of the ring. To do something which needed doing for a long time now." I stared down at the hollow thing on my finger wondering how many demons and spirits it could house within it and knowing I would never find out. "To give you freedom. To give you a choice."

Looking up at him, I watched the conflicting emotions flipping one after another across his face. If the Big Guy in the sky didn't like what I'd done, He could come on down here and tell me so—but this was my choice. I took hold of the Key of Solomon and slipped it from my finger. I possessed power of my own, and it was more than enough, I didn't need to become a slave to it by gaining more. Placing it on my palm, I held the ring out to him. "Now you can decide for yourself if you want to guard this thing or just chuck it into the ocean. It will be what *you* want for a change. To live with the repercussions either way, like the rest of us monkeys."

He stared at the ring, brows furrowing, smoothing, and furrowing again, the light sparkling off the rudy stud at his nose. "Such a choice is not for one such as I." His voice was small. It rang of uncertainty, and weirdly enough, fear.

Was it because the one real choice he'd ever made turned out so badly in the end? Did he regret having known Leja, of loving her and her people? But as someone who'd had her world turned upside down, I knew too that it was hard leaving what you've always known for something you don't. "Sure it is. Welcome to the ugly wonder that is being human."

Jared's expression cleared. "The decision is not mine alone."

"Oh no, you don't! Ross can make his own choice. The two of you don't have to pick the same." Would they know how to live without each other though? That was something they'd have to work out amongst themselves.

It didn't stop me from feeling bad for him as a look of panic crossed his face at the thought. Then I did the thing I'd wanted to do for a while. I leaned in close and kissed him.

A small kiss. Nothing fancy. Something that lasted but a moment, his small gasp echoing in my ears. Even though I was the one with the ring, I still felt that little jolt as flesh touched flesh. The salty flavor of his lips couldn't have been sweeter. I then pulled back to look into his face.

"I, I need to think." He stood up half turning away from me.

"Of course. It's a big decision. And there's no hurry." I slipped the ring into my pocket. "Just make sure the decision is yours. Not His, not your brother's. Not even mine. What do *you* want to do?"

He nodded and moved away, shoulders hunched as if under a massive weight. If there was ever a place for heavy thinking though, this was it—the shade from the trees, the wind from the water, the soft lapping sound of the waves striking the beach below. Yes, a great place for thinking. I realized I needed to do some of my own. But something occurred to me first. Though it might have repercussions to do with me, I went on with it anyway.

"Jared!"

He glanced back at me over his shoulder, a wary expression on his face as if afraid of what else I would dump on him. He knew me too well.

"Don't forget. You just finished saving this plane from terrible evil and chaos. There's bound to be some clout in that, even if you were bound to the ring. Maybe it's time to see if someone up there would let you back into your family."

He frowned at me. "I didn't save anything. You did. And those above me do not forgive easily. As far as they're concerned no time has passed at all. Still..." He turned away again and skidded down to the beach below.

CHAPTER SIXTY-SIX

Hours passed. I stared out at the water thinking deep thoughts, while at the same time worrying about Jared, Ross, and Jensen. We'd been through battle together. Oddly, I felt closer to them than anyone ever before. It felt awkward yet at the same time right and wonderful.

The sun was reaching for the horizon, putting on a gorgeous display of reds and oranges over the gray water. Then Jared appeared beside me.

"They're here."

For a startled moment I thought he meant demons or angry monks, but then realized it was neither as a solitary form approached us from the dense forest. Jensen and Ross had finally come back to us. A knot of tension I hadn't even realized I was carrying slipped away. "How did it go?"

"Slowly." Jensen's voice sounded raw as if he'd had to do a lot of talking, even yelling. "But eventually they got hold of several people with gifts that could confirm what we were telling them. Olivia has a good head on her shoulders."

Olivia was it? Looks liked I'd missed out on a few things by not sticking around.

"Yes, but those gifts revealed a little too much for my taste." The change in timber announced Ross as the speaker. It was so weird. "We had to 'sneak' away." He snorted. "Let's just say some people were getting a little too curious about certain things."

I could imagine. "How long before you can leave

Jensen's body and survive on your own?"

"Now. But not good enough yet to get my body back."

My brows drew together.

"No worries! I have his consent. He's well aware of my status. Aren't you, White?"

Little bits of Jensen's face changed as the two switched places. This was more than weird, it was creepy.

"Yes. I'm quite aware. And he remains with my permission. So don't worry. He's a much better tenant than my previous one. All is well."

I supposed I had no choice but to take his word for it. I saw him slip a glance in Jared's direction. I got the feeling Jensen and his body mate had been talking. "Whatever you decide, no one will hold it against you. Either of you. You've earned it."

Jared raised a brow, seemingly unimpressed his brother had spilled his secret. "Be that as it may, I've reached a decision." He held out his hands towards me. "I choose to continue."

I wasn't entirely surprised. Secretly, it made me happy. The responsibility for keeping the thing was rather steep, and I wasn't sure I was up for it. Especially as I would have to find someone else to carry the burden when I grew old. Plus temptation would be a constant companion.

Fishing the ring out of my pocket, I bid it a silent farewell as I handed it over. My eyes itched for a moment, the ring converting back to its larger original size, almost as if saying goodbye.

Jared took it reverently then opened his button up gray shirt. Prepared, having assumed he'd be doing this sooner or later even before I set him free. He pushed the ring against his exposed chest. It slowly sank into his flesh. I guess it was one way to make sure you didn't lose the thing.

He sighed for a moment, as if welcoming back an old friend, then rebuttoned his shirt.

"Just remember you can quit anytime you want. Having the choice, even when you don't take it, makes all the difference." I grinned at him. Surprisingly, he smiled back. Looked like he might be getting the hang of this choice thing after all. Maybe I'd get a shot as well.

Jared turned toward his brother. "Ross? You can choose not to. I won't have you feeling obligated to make the same choice I have."

Jensen's body shrugged. "I'm not quite tired of you yet, brother. So for now, I'll hang around. But if you don't do something about that glowering disposition…" he threw a half glance in my direction. "Well…" A wicked gleam glinted in his eyes.

Jared looked away, from embarrassment or sappy happiness, it was hard to say. I was just glad my color hid the heat that glance had brought up to my cheeks.

"Fair enough."

I wallowed in the good feelings for a moment, then told them of my own choice. "I don't know what I'll do with myself after all this, but now that it's over, I have to go home. I need to confront my parents and explain what happened, what really happened, even if they don't believe me. As their child and the sacrifices they made for me, I owe them at least that much. What they decide to do after that will be up to them."

I tensed, not sure if the brothers or Jensen would argue against my plans, preferring for me not to reveal secrets better left untold. It also meant I might not be able to follow up that small kiss with anything else if they decided against me.

"I'll go with you."

Jensen's words shocked me.

"It'll make it more difficult for them not to believe you if I am there backing up what you say."

"You would do that for me?" Didn't he realize that most likely they'd just think both of us insane rather than believe?

He smiled at me. "Of course. It's the least I could do."

It felt good not to have to go at this alone. I hadn't dared hope.

"I'll come as well."

If I thought I was shocked before, I'd been mistaken. Jared's words floored me and elated me all at once.

"It will become even harder for them not to believe you with three of us. If worse comes to worst, I can prove certain things to them, both of you cannot." The small smile on his lips and the glint in his eyes, very much like his brother's for once, implied he was actually looking forward to it.

Gratitude welled up inside me so much it hurt. Warm tracks coursed down my cheeks before I could stop them. "Th-thank you. Truly, thank you."

"If I've healed enough by then, count me in as well," Ross added. "With four of us, they'll have no choice but to believe."

And for the first time since this madness started, I felt a spark of hopeful optimism and perhaps more.

THE END

ABOUT THE AUTHOR

Gloria Oliver lives in Texas making sure to stay away from rolling tumbleweeds while bowing to the never-ending wishes of her feline and canine masters. She works full time shoveling numbers around for an oil & gas company and squeezes in some writing time when she can.

Due for release in 2019 is "Alien Redemption." This is Gloria's first science fiction novel. This is also her eighth book to see publication. Her previous works have been fantasy, urban fantasy, and young adult fantasy novels. Several contain romantic and mystery elements. Her short stories of speculative fiction can be found in all manner of anthologies, covering things from the fantastic and strange to a Bubba Apocalypse.

Gloria is a member in good standing of BroadUniverse though she has yet to make the list for Cat Slaves R Us.

For some free reads, novel related short stories, sample chapters, appearance schedules and more information on her and her works, please drop by and visit her at www.gloriaoliver.com

The Price of Mercy

CHAPTER 1

I am a fool.

Jarrin sat in his rented coach, waiting in line to enter the gate. The emperor's ballroom glowed softly in the night. Behind it, much farther off, was the palace proper. Nestled in the center of the city, the emperor's domain was like a small kingdom itself. The ballroom was at the farthest edge, a mere drop of all that was there.

More than three-fourths of the funds the baroness gave him were already spent–his reward for services rendered before he was summarily dismissed. Between the coach and his elaborate costume, he was about to make his life very difficult if he didn't succeed tonight.

The baroness's second gift had been an invitation to the ball and, if he dared use it, the possibility of gaining other employment. The problem was, he wasn't even sure he wanted to succeed but hadn't been able to think of another course that didn't involve shame, poverty, or starvation.

The coach crawled through the gate.

Jarrin could just make out some of the guests as they exited their vehicles at the ballroom's entrance. Ladies and gentlemen wearing costumes of all colors, tall wigs and hats, tiaras, necklaces, rings but, most of all, masks to hide their identities, weaving an air of mystery and daring.

When his turn came, he forced himself to wait until the coachman got down and opened the door for him before getting out. With feigned calm, he presented his invitation to the guards then sedately ascended the stairs to the entrance.

On this night, no introductions would be made,

everyone seemingly oblivious to the identities of everyone else. A simple veneer, easy to see through in some cases, yet all would pretend to their fullest not to recognize anyone else. And somehow, here, he would have to make himself an opportunity.

A few couples swayed to the music in the cleared middle of the extensive room while others loitered about the heavily laden tables set up against two of the four walls. The steaming food and colorful drinks set out as delicious temptations but a few steps away of those attending.

The light fragrance of roses filled the air from hundreds of scented candles held aloft by a dozen giant chandeliers. Too soon, though, it would be joined by the cloying aromas of heavy perfumes and perspiration.

Jarrin caught a glimpse of himself in one of the tall standing mirrors as he slowly made his way to the floor. Scarlet floor-length cloak, a black embroidered skirted coat with heavy cuffs and matching vest, black knee breeches, tall leather boots, blood-red shirt and cravat, black gloves, and a wide black hat with red feathers-the well-known rendition of the Crimson Lover. His dark hair was tied with a large ribbon and reached a little past his shoulders in back. His dark-blue eyes seemed to leap from the black mask around them. He was sure there would be a few others posing as the Lover tonight, but none would be as dependent on the message the persona conveyed as he would.

As if he possessed all the time in the world, he strolled the periphery of the room. In truth, now that he was here, he had no idea how to go about his purpose. How did you woo yourself a patron? How did you even choose one? He should have come dressed as a buffoon.

He spotted two of those in short order, although they

were the most expensively dressed fools he'd ever seen. Emperor Drusnian, the reunifier of the empire after the Age of Blight, had several representatives as well-his double chins and flaming red hair made him unmistakable. There were several other famous personages portrayed among the partygoers, as well as heroes and villains from pieces of literature-Dullain, Marquis Sablet, the Crooked Man.

The room filled quickly, the noise level rising over the music being woven by a group of twenty men and women on a slightly raised dais in a corner.

At one point, he paused at the sight of a new arrival. His old patron, the baroness, had finally arrived. Her stooped form and calculating eyes gave her identity away easily, especially to one who'd known her so intimately for so long. Still, it was the person at her side who drew most of his attention. It could be none other than his replacement-the baroness's latest protege.

With a hard swallow, Jarrin realized he knew the popinjay. A year younger than him, Rillian was already a coveted performer, an exceptional violinist. They'd seen him perform less than two months ago at a lavish birthday party.

He'd lost track of the baroness during the festivities for a few moments when asked to render a reading. Now he wondered if that was when the wheels began to turn against him. Did Rillian approach her or she him?

He forced himself to turn away as they merged with the crowd. He had other business to attend to.

He'd circled the ballroom twice, the musicians starting in on the fifth or sixth long piece of the evening when he spotted her. She stood by the end of one of the buffet tables, her back against the corner it made with the wall as if to assure herself she couldn't be approached without her knowledge—or perhaps to shield her back. She was short and plump, dressed in layers of lace and silk of the lightest pinks and whites. Her stance was stiff as if she were nervous or excited, and she was looking about as if searching for something. Perhaps that something was him.

Jarrin rubbed his suddenly sweaty palms on his cloak, realizing his moment was here. Proceeding at a calculated leisurely pace, he grabbed a glass of wine from a passing waiter as he approached his possible salvation.

She wore a half-mask made of feathers that curled around her face and matched those pinned to her curled brown hair. Surrounded by white, her dark-brown eyes stood out, and he saw them widen as she noticed his approach and his costume. He didn't let this deter him, knowing he had no choice.

"You seem thirsty, madam, would you care for a glass of wine?" He presented the glass to her with a flourish, as he'd seen the men do in the operettas the baroness liked so much. What he could see of her round face blushed, paled, then blushed again.

"Th-thank you."

She reached to take the glass, and although she tried to avoid it, Jarrin made sure their fingers touched. The lady jerked the glass back, almost spilling the wine. Had he read her wrong after all? He felt uncertainty nibble at him, as it had the last several days, but pressed on. He tried to give her his brightest smile.

She blushed again, shielding her face with the glass as she took a large swallow. As she did, he noticed her finely cut earrings, bracelets, and necklace, half-hidden in feathers. From the baroness, he'd learned something of such things in the last year. Although not overtly large or showy, the cut of the stones and the settings spoke of extreme wealth.

"Is this your first ball?" He couldn't tell her age but thought it might be close to his own. She could have already been married for years and was here looking for fresher entertainment, or even just companionship.

"No…I have attended before."

Jarrin thought he saw her eyes sparkle, as if at a hidden joke. They were large and expressive and made him curious about the face beneath the mask. If all went miraculously well, perhaps he'd get a chance to see it.

"Is it yours?" Her gaze lighted on him, keenly intent.

"I attended last year…as a companion to one of the baronesses." There, he'd said it. With any luck, she would understand the message beneath the words and things might prove easier. From the way she glanced at his costume and at his face, then blushed again and drank more of her wine, he was sure she understood quite clearly.

Much to his chagrin, however, he found his own face heating up as well. He hoped his mask hid from view most of the embarrassment he felt at being what he was.

"I see…" Her voice was tight. She drank the rest of her wine in one gulp but made no move to run off. He hoped it was a good sign.

She grabbed another glass when a waiter waltzed by and drank part of it down. Perhaps she was as nervous as he was. Unlike her, though, he couldn't afford to imbibe, no matter how tempting or helpful he thought it might be. It was amazing how he could feel so totally alone in a room so filled with people.

"Would the lady care to dance?" He half-bowed and held out his hand.

She had opened her mouth to reply when trumpets sounded from across the room. Everyone grew abruptly silent, their attention turning to the golden doors on the far side. While all others could disguise themselves and perhaps for a time forget who they were beneath a thin veneer of anonymity, there would always be the one none would be allowed to forget.

"All hail the mighty Emperor Tremere the Fourth!"

The golden doors opened, and the emperor and his entourage swept into the room, a small dais and grand chair carried by servants behind them. Tremere was a short, stocky man dressed in tastefully cut rags of purple, gold, and silver. Jarrin was pretty sure his costume was meant to be that of the Wandering Beggar. Resteel had been a mighty monarch brought low, bereft of everything he held dear through his own foolishness. It was said he then wandered the world, seeking to atone for his unbecoming deeds and regain favor with Melak, the Crafter of All, by crying the virtues of the True Way to any who would listen. A rather interesting choice for a man in the emperor's position. Especially since he was himself the living avatar of Melak.

The empire had seen better days in ages past but was still prosperous at this time, at peace. He caught a glimpse of the heir apparent, who wore a much more colorful and less reserved costume than his father's. He also spotted the prince's much younger brother and two sisters. He thought there was supposed to be a third daughter but couldn't remember if she was currently at court or not, having been married off several years ago. One of those two, then, would be the one betrothed to Crevail, a duke in the far provinces. From the gossip around the baroness, the emperor heartily approved of the unusual match.

"Welcome, friends and patriots! Please indulge yourselves this evening. Leave all your cares behind. We of the imperial house will carry your burdens for you." The emperor made a rolling gesture with his hand, and the musicians began playing again, the waiters once more making their rounds.

Jarrin turned to his prospective employer and found her staring intently at the emperor, her lips pressed into a thin line.

"Madam?"

The young woman blinked and looked away, then brought the glass of wine to her lips and drank it all. When she turned to him, her gaze was veiled, and a not so very convincing smile was plastered on her lips.

"You offered me a dance. I would very much like to accept, but not here. It is getting uncomfortably warm, don't you think?" She took his hand in a strong grip, her chest rising and falling rapidly. "It will be much cooler and more private in the gardens."

She turned away, and not wanting to offend her, he had no choice but to follow as she set her empty glass on the table and hurried along the wall. She led him outside through the first of the open glass doors, out into the imperial gardens that surrounded the ballroom.

It was, indeed, cooler there, the night breeze caressing them as the darkness swallowed them whole. Jarrin worried about colliding with trees or bushes in their continued haste, but the lady led him without mishap. Finally, out of sight of the open doors, she slowed to a stop.

Melak's Eye floated above them, giving a semblance of light as Jarrin's gaze adjusted. She'd brought them to a small open area with a cozy gazebo in the middle. Still holding his hand a little too tightly, she drew him into the dark interior. The heavy scent of roses and violets perfumed the air, a whisper of the music being played indoors teasing their ears.

He stood quietly as the young woman turned around to face him, waiting to take his cue from her. He felt his nervousness rising, knowing his testing was almost upon him and still wishing there were some other way.

"We can dance here."

Her voice was low, guarded as if she expected an objection. Instead, Jarrin raised the hand she already held and slipped his other around her waist, leading her into a slow waltz.

She was stiff in his arms at first, but as they rocked gently to the barely heard music and he asked for nothing else, he felt her gradually begin to relax. After a time, she sighed, as if letting the rest of her tension go. A moment later, she stepped in closer and hesitantly placed her head against his shoulder.

He found he liked the sensation of her leaning against him, the smell of her scented hair close to his face. The baroness never danced, feeling it was something only for the young.

They stayed that way through several pieces as if neither one were eager to go further. Jarrin felt a little puzzled at this but wouldn't look at his own reasons for holding back. As for her, he knew naught of her and so possessed nothing on which to base her reluctance. Perhaps something as simple as being held was normally denied her. It might be something he would learn about with time.

Eventually, they migrated to one of the benches of the gazebo. He took off his hat as he sat and waited patiently. She wouldn't look at him, but when he took her hand in his, she didn't resist. He caressed her fingers softly then worked his way up her arm, enjoying the feel of her skin. She shivered at his touch, but still she did or said nothing.

Although it shamed him, he was enjoying himself. For once, he was the instigator, not just reacting to a command, even if he possessed no more choice in the matter now than then. It was still different.

When he kissed her shoulder, tasting her, she gave a little gasp, yet she didn't resist when he gently turned her face toward him. Hesitating only a moment, he leaned forward and touched her warm lips with his own. A moment later, he felt them soften as she surrendered to him. It seemed the baroness had taught him well after all.

Read Chapters 2 and 3 at: www.gloriaoliver.com/price